PROPS FOR A MURDER

There was a scorpion on Lisette's soft smiling lip.

Involuntarily Nick froze, his hands on the shoulders of her coat in the Dean's front closet. Lisette's photograph was pinned to the lining of her coat, and the grisly little creature glued to it was arched for attack in all the glossy realism of an expensive novelty shop item. Party laughs. Pretending to fumble for his own topcoat, Nick unpinned the photo, folded it, and slipped it and its unpleasant cargo into his own inner pocket. Then he put on his social smile and turned back to the other guests. It was beginning to look like college life could turn deadly after all.

Other Avon Books Coming Soon by
P. M. Carlson

MURDER IS ACADEMIC

Audition for Murder

P. M. CARLSON

AVON
PUBLISHERS OF BARD, CAMELOT, DISCUS AND FLARE BOOKS

AUDITION FOR MURDER is an original publication of Avon Books. This work has never before appeared in book form. This work is a novel. Any similarity to actual persons or events is purely coincidental.

AVON BOOKS
A division of
The Hearst Corporation
1790 Broadway
New York, New York 10019

Published by arrangement with the author
Library of Congress Catalog Card Number: 84-091234
ISBN: 0-380-89538-2

First Avon Printing, May 1985

Printed in the U. S. A.

WFH 10 9 8 7 6 5 4 3 2 1

For Marvin

I say, we will have no more marriages. Those that are married already—all but one—shall live; the rest shall keep as they are. To a nunnery, go.

—*Hamlet,* Act III, Scene I

I

Nick O'Connor put down the telephone, his broad, muscular body sagging a little. So she hadn't been merely tired. Hell. He changed to worn jeans and his old leather jacket, and made a mean face at the mirror. Nick the hustler tonight. Man of a thousand faces, said his agent, and every one of them homely. A regular one-man Dickens novel. Nick headed out for the West Forties.

The snow was not sticking much. It made the sidewalks shine darkly, splashed with gold and rose and white reflections from bars and street lamps, and pasted down scraps of paper that otherwise would be scuttling across the streets in the bitter wind. His way led past whores, pushers, tired old men huddled over warm grates. Without a hurt, the heart is hollow. No hollow hearts on this street.

Franklin's place was halfway down the block. A worn brass door handle, chipped paint. Nick wiped a few snowflakes from his thinning hair and pushed through the crowd to the end of the bar. In a moment the bartender, black, with a trim mustache, had worked his way down to him.

"Hey, man, where ya been?"

"Is she here, Franklin?"

"Been here for hours."

"Yeah, I was working tonight. I just heard."

"She said she got fired."

"Hey, we can't all be self-employed minority success stories."

Franklin chuckled. "You watch your honky mouth." He went off to break up a loud argument about whether or not the Vietcong were winning, served a whiskey, and returned to Nick. "Room 6B," he said.

"Okay. What's she had?"

"Well, man, first she practically cleaned me out of bourbon." Franklin jerked his head to indicate the stock on the back wall. "Then she said she wanted something stronger. So I pretended to be out of horse, gave her charley instead."

"Thanks." Nick paid him and started for the door at the rear of the long room. A short, serious Oriental man barred his way suddenly. Franklin playing games again, Nick thought tiredly. There was still a white line across his left rib cage from an earlier game. He located the knife with the corner of his eye and raised his right hand as though to push the Oriental away, then came up hard with his left, smashing into the man's wrist with a numbing blow. The knife dropped. He stepped on the blade while he jerked the numbed wrist back and up between the man's shoulders. Many eyes were staring at them. Nick pulled him around again to face Franklin, who was beaming.

"Hey, Franklin," he said mildly, "you ought to pay me extra to be in the floor show."

Franklin laughed. "Hey, man," he said to the Oriental, "leave be. We got a understanding, see?"

"Yes, sir," said the Oriental.

Nick nodded, unsmiling, playing John Wayne for Franklin's benefit, and went through the door and up the creaking stairs. Cocaine. Well, Franklin was right, it was a hell of a lot better than the alternative.

He checked the numbers in the smelly upstairs hall and knocked. A scrawny black man looked out at him, then moved back to let him enter. Ah, the glamour of life in show biz. Peeling paint, a high grimy window, a metal bed with a torn Army blanket, dented chairs. On the bed, in a soft rosy dress, lay a woman of heart-stopping beauty.

She had been humming to herself, but now she broke off. A silken toss of honey-brown hair, lily skin, a slender body wrapped in the flowery fabric. Her warm eyes smiled into Nick's.

"Nicky!" she said in muddled delight. "I'm so glad you came!"

Nick looked at her helplessly. Her white teeth caught at the soft lower lip. She became serious.

"Is it time to go?"

"Yes, Lisette."

"Okay." She sat up gracefully and blinked at her slim bare legs and feet. "I prob'ly have some shoes."

"She had boots," volunteered the black man. "Under the bed."

Nick fished out the boots and a warm scarf. Thank God, she was still high, she was playing by the rules. He was in time. The U.S. Cavalry personified. Ta ra. He helped her pull on the boots, slid the long zippers up carefully, and helped her gently to her feet.

"Thanks," he said to the black man. "Franklin pay you?"

"He said you'd pay."

Probably true. Nick nodded and gave him his last twenty, then opened the door and steered his wife carefully down the stairs and out into the bleak night.

The cold air revived her a little. She sucked in her breath sharply and stood a little straighter at his side. "C'mon, Blossom," he said. "We'd better walk it."

It was a long walk, and she stumbled sometimes. She said little, just looked at him occasionally with those wide eyes, or smiled hesitantly. Beauty too rich for use, for earth too dear. He smiled back, and she walked on. Once she stopped.

"I gotta pee."

"Okay. We'll go in there." He indicated a hamburger place nearby. Nick the nanny. While he waited he bought an order of French fries. Then they went on, eating the fries, soft and gritty with salt, from the little paper packet.

"Are you hungry?" he asked as he unlocked the apartment.

"I'm all right." She still smelled of bourbon. He got her into a nightgown and was hanging up her dress when she said, "I got to thinking," apologetically.

"Yes, I know, Lisette." He closed the closet door and turned to look at her. She was sitting up on their bed, her slim arms around her knees, frowning groggily.

"It won't go away," she said.

"You'll learn how to manage," said Nick. "Today is over. We'll talk about it tomorrow."

"Nicky. Love me?" She held out her arms.

Nick went to her and held her close to him, this familiar stranger, so like and so unlike the woman he had married seven years ago. Because he loved her, and because she would feel a failure if he didn't, he made love to her; but it was not very satisfying, because she was so drowsy and even the coke did not keep her from dozing off after a few minutes. The rape polite, thought Nick bitterly. He lay beside her afterward, stroking the silky hair for a long time before he slept.

Near dawn there was a muffled rattle, a little distant clink, and Nick's subconscious raked him awake in terror. He hurled himself across the room, wrenched open the bathroom door, squinted against the glaring light. She held a glass of water in one hand, a heap of little pills in the other. He seized her fist, shook the pills into the toilet, tipped back her head, and poured water into her mouth. Then, one hard arm immobilizing her, he ran the fingers of his other hand back into her throat so that she gagged, heaved, vomited all over his arm, all over the floor. He made her drink again, vomit again, until at last she was shuddering with dry retches, so weak that she sagged weeping across his arm. He carried her to the bed and held her while he picked up the telephone.

"No," she whispered painfully. "It's okay."

He started dialing the ambulance. "What do you mean?"

"Nicky, I'd only swallowed three."

Their eyes met. She was telling the truth. "Okay," he said.

He bathed her, changed the bed, scrubbed himself and the bathroom. She said little; it hurt her to talk. When finally he lay down next to her again he was silent too. Arms barely touching, isolated yet linked, they grieved their separate ways to morning.

She was still miserably hung over. Nick canceled his morning dance workout, but had to leave her in bed, dozing, while he went to a TV audition their agent had set up. She was still in bed when he returned before dinner, although she had apparently managed to get out and find a bottle of bourbon in the interim. She had not drunk much. A medicinal dose. He kissed her and went to the little kitchen to start dinner. Belting a daffodil-colored housecoat, she joined him while he was turning the fish.

"Have we got a lemon?" she asked. Her voice was still hoarse.

"Yes, in that bag." Looking up over his shoulder as he squatted to dribble butter onto the fish, he decided to ask. "How are you?"

A slim shoulder shrugged. "I never knew so young a body with so old a head."

"Dear Portia." He grinned at her. Quoting was a good sign.

The honey-colored eyes, circled with pain, looked down at him. "I'm going to go get dried out tomorrow."

"Okay." He didn't let too much enthusiasm into his voice. She had to do it for herself, not him.

"And then I want to get out of the city."

"Get out?" He straightened, looked at her. This was new.

"Yes. I need a vacation or something. We've only been away once in four years, to Compton to see Mom."

"That's true." His warm brown eyes smiled at her. "The celebrated O'Connor treadmill. Athletes marvel! Tourists gawk!"

She smiled, rearranged the lemon slices. "Well, I think the change might help."

"Will you want me to go with you?"

"Yes. Oh, yes!" Her glance was frightened.

"But you know I can't get away for a while."

"Well, I wouldn't be ready either, for a while."

It was awkward. His role in this musical was the best he'd had yet. He wouldn't get reviewed, of course, this late in the run, but people in the business would hear about it. And it was obviously going to keep on running for quite a while, with a small but steady income. Money. Just like being a real person. Most importantly, of course, it was stage work. Nick did TV spots eagerly for the money—hell, he waited tables for the money—but TV had very little to do with his reasons for being an actor. Every night now, though, as he stepped through the little curtain made of streamers and began the opening song, he felt that intense communion with the audience, a sense almost of priesthood, as his voice and body communicated the fleeting yet eternal emotions of the play. Nick the witch doctor. Quitting when he had this fulfillment was unthinkable.

But Lisette knew all that. She would not ask him to give it up lightly.

"I had sort of an idea," she said.

"Oh?"

"Because you have such a good part now." She did understand. "It would be bad to just quit."

"Yes."

"God, my head hurts."

They sat down on their mismatched flea-market chairs and she ate a bite or two, the fine skin between her brows furrowed. Nick squeezed lemon juice onto his fish and waited.

"It's something George was talking about yesterday," she said. "There's this college upstate. They're doing some sort of special *Hamlet* and they're hiring professional leads." The long-lashed eyes looked at him anxiously. "They'll pay scale. We're supposed to help with the acting classes too."

"You'd be a delicious Ophelia."

Lisette smiled a little. "Yes. In fact, it's funny, George said someone called him and asked if I'd consider a job upstate. Anyway, I thought it would be a change."

"When is it?"

"Starts in January or February, I think, for their whole spring term. Auditions week after next."

"You want to be back in a college?" The question was ugly. But it had to be asked. The little line reappeared between her brows before she nodded.

"I never really quite finished, emotionally. I thought it might help me work things out."

Nick buttered his roll doubtfully. "Are you sure?"

"Hell, no! But Nicky, what else can I do? It's been four years. Almost five. And it never interfered with my work before! Time isn't helping. The shrink didn't. Our friends don't. Maybe nothing will ever help." He put his big hand over hers and she blinked a little. "Well, you've helped."

"I know what you mean. In the end it's just you, all alone."

"So, who knows if this is right? I thought it might be worth a try." She looked up. "I know you'll have to give up a hell of a lot."

"If they even want me."

"Oh, they will! You could do any of the big parts. Hamlet, Claudius, even Polonius. Though I always think of him as skinny."

Nick grinned. "We two know I could do it," he said, "but I suspect Claudius is what they'll think. If anything." Hamlet, Thick Balding Prince of Denmark. Dear loyal Lisette.

"That's not as good as what you have now, is it?" The dark-circled eyes were sad.

"No," he said honestly. "But it's Shakespeare. God, I'd love to do Shakespeare again. In my heart I'm Sir Laurence O'Connor."

She looked hopeful. "Yes, well, I thought it might work."

He picked up her fragile hand and said diffidently, "Um, Arnie Hutton told me you were drunk at rehearsal."

Her fingers stirred in his, and then were quiet. She said, "Yeah. Three times this week."

Damn. He'd suspected it. But she'd said she was just tired, and he'd wanted to believe her. This time she'd been sober five months. He asked, "Did anything special happen to set it off?"

"Well, they were rewriting my character. She was supposed to stab someone."

He frowned, concerned. "Ophelia's father is killed. She goes mad."

"But Nicky," she explained earnestly, "it's different. Ophelia gets to die." His mouth tightened, and she glanced down at her plate and murmured apologetically, "Well, it makes it easier. And anyway, I have to get at that part of me sometime, or I'll never get beyond diet-cola commercials."

Nick nodded. It was true. An actor's instrument, infinitely more complex than a musician's, was his own body and voice, mind and emotions. With talent and training, he could find the complex sequence of emotional and bodily memories that combined best with the words of a particular part, then coax his bones and muscles into living another life. But secret horrors and buried memories could not be sealed off and forgotten. They were his sources, his raw materials. If Lisette was right about what had broken her in these last rehearsals, she was crippled as surely as if she had lost a leg. Ophelia might be the key to finding what she had lost. Close, but not too close.

"You're a gambler, kiddo," he said.

"I'm sick of how things are. I'm sick of playing things shallow so I won't freak out. I'm sick of Franklin's and making you play these idiot games."

"Okay. Let's try it. And if these fellows won't have us, we'll find someone who will. Stratford, maybe? The Royal Shakespeare Company? The Pumpkinville Junior Thespians? But right now I must go."

"Hey, Nicky." She smiled up at him.

"Yeah?"

"We'll be okay."

He kissed her hair. Today she smelled of violets. Also of fish. He smiled too. "We are okay. We'll be even better."

Nick was one of the last to audition because of his schedule. They had agreed to wait for him so that he could get there from his matinee. Lisette had read the day before, although she had come back a little concerned.

"They made me read Gertrude too, Nicky. Isn't that odd?"

"Yes. How did you do?"

"Okay with Ophelia. I did part of the mad scene, of course. For Gertrude they wanted part of the scene with Hamlet. 'Alas, how is it with you,/That you do bend your eye on vacancy?' But they couldn't seriously want me to be some big hulk's mother, could they?"

He grinned. "They'll have trouble finding a young enough hulk. Maybe they're really going to stress the Oedipal angle."

"Oh, God."

"Well, we'll see. Did they seem okay otherwise?"

"One fellow, Brian—I guess he's the director—seemed very bright and helpful. The other one was creepy. Just sat in the corner watching me. Looked like a cowboy."

So it was when Nick arrived. Two young men wearing storm coats were sitting on rickety folding chairs. The loft's long radiators were all ice-cold.

"Mr. O'Connor?" One of the men jumped up immediately, muscular, decisive, blue-eyed.

"Yes." Nick handed him his photo-résumé.

"Brian Wright." He shook Nick's hand. "I'll be directing this project. This is my colleague, Cheyenne Brown." He indicated the other man, who was rocking back in his folding chair, wearing a sheepskin jacket and cowboy boots. He had a thin mustache. "Cheyenne's our designer. He's worked here in the city professionally too; you might know his stuff. Anyway, this project is his idea as much as mine."

"Glad to meet you both."

"I—well, before we get into anything, I'd like to hear you read Claudius," said Brian.

"Fine."

"The scene in Act Four after you've explained to Laertes that Hamlet killed his father. I'll read Laertes for you."

"Okay." Nick glanced at the scene in his book. He had reread the play that weekend with Lisette, back from the detoxification center.

Brian took a young man's stance, one hand toying with the hilt of a nonexistent sword. "Go ahead."

Nick's body, even in corduroys, became regal. The weight of ermine replaced the storm coat on his shoulders. Only the pleasant, flexible voice revealed the strain and urgency that Claudius felt in appealing to Laertes. They read through the scene, Brian a skeptical Laertes slowly won over by Nick's coaxing King. "Fine, fine!" said Brian at last, breaking out of his role. He seemed pleased. "Let's do the prayer scene."

Nick paused a moment to shift his mind and body from royal persuasiveness to royal shame. He dropped to his knees to read the scene, searching for the misery of a soul that cannot repent. "O, my offense is rank, it smells to heaven!" When he had finished, Brian glanced at his designer. Cheyenne nodded, the thin mustache drooping at the sides of his mouth.

"That's the one," he said.

"Okay," said Brian. "That's all."

"No interview?" asked Nick.

"We're frozen! We've got to get out of here. But we do have some questions for you. Can you come have a cup of coffee with us?"

"Sure."

In stark contrast to the chilled loft, the coffeehouse was overheated. Their booth was badly lit by a hanging light with a tinseled Christmas decoration attached. Steam filmed the window next to them so that the colored lights outside, refracted by a thousand tiny droplets, shimmered gaily through the pane. Cheyenne, in the corner, leaned back into the shadows. "Three coffees," said Brian to the waiter.

"Yes, sir." The waiter snapped his notebook closed, disappointed that they weren't having dinner. Nick had been a waiter often enough to sympathize. Brian picked up the saltshaker and inspected it, then the quick blue eyes shifted to Nick a little uncertainly.

"You said you had some questions," Nick prompted.

"Yes, well . . ." He hesitated.

"Why the hell are you auditioning for our show?" Cheyenne's voice spoke brusquely from the shadows.

Nick's eyebrows lifted a fraction. "Is it really so remarkable?"

"Frankly, yes." Brian had found his tongue again. "We've had a couple million try out for Hamlet, of course. It's the best part in the world, and there are plenty of young actors who'd love to get paid for doing it. And at the other end we have a lot of old-timers—tons of experience but getting senile or alcoholic—reading for Claudius or Polonius. And every one of them is between jobs. Or soon will be."

"You're suspicious of me because I'm working."

"Look. You could be exactly the Claudius I need. Shrewd, mature, virile, tormented. Head and shoulders above anyone else who tried out. Okay? But a couple of nights ago Cheyenne suggested that we ought to go see *The Fantasticks* again."

Nick's brown eyes danced. "Spies."

"Exactly. Because I wanted to know what I'm getting. And now, well, I don't want to have you turn me down. But you claim to be willing to throw away one of the best parts in New York, and take a cut in pay besides, to come to Hargate for fifteen weeks and act with a bunch of students."

"Yeah, my agent thinks I've gone berserk too," Nick admitted. "Seriously, I'm not playing games with you. But there is a catch."

"Okay, good. Cards on the table, okay?"

"Okay. You see, my wife auditioned too."

"Ah! I see." Brian frowned a little. "What's her name?"

"O'Connor, believe it or not. Lisette O'Connor."

Brian began flipping through his folder and pulled up Lisette's picture as the coffee arrived. "Mmm," he said, with a rather surprised glance at Nick's balding homeliness. "Yes, I remember. I remember her quite well."

"She read both Ophelia and Gertrude."

"I remember. But you see, we weren't really reading for Ophelia."

"You weren't?"

"Yeah, let me explain. What we're doing is a centenary production. It turns out that a hundred years ago, the very first play done at Hargate was *Hamlet.* Now we've got a full-fledged theatre department and some grad students in acting, but we're more modest, I guess. We don't feel equipped to do *Hamlet* or *Lear* or any of the real toughies."

"You've learned a lot in a hundred years."

"Yep. Well, this spring we're having a big birthday celebration. And we went to Dean Wagner and said, hey, let's do *Hamlet* again, and he said fine. And Cheyenne said, let's get professional actors, and showed him the Equity book. Well, Dean Wagner got excited and said, okay, how much? Turns out he has a special fund. But it's limited. He found enough money to hire four of you."

"Claudius, Polonius, Hamlet. And Gertrude," said Nick. So much for Lisette's plan. "Well, you're right. Those are the parts that really need age or experience."

Brian was watching him closely. "You seem disappointed."

"Yeah." Nick shrugged. "We really wanted to go. For various reasons."

Brian took a sip of his coffee, then asked, "Is it out of the question for you to come alone? Or, I mean, she could come along, of course."

"Not without a job. She's professional too. We'll just have to find something else."

"Love me, love my dog," said Cheyenne from his corner.

Nick glanced at him and said mildly, "Exactly."

"Shut up, Cheyenne," said Brian irritably. He looked down at his notes again. "She's very good," he added. "My note says, 'delightful Ophelia! But out of the question for Gertrude.' "

"We really didn't get excited about any of the Gertrudes," came the voice from the corner.

"Well, no." Brian frowned at the designer. "But a dozen of them would be more appropriate."

Nick, suddenly tired and anxious to get out, swallowed the last of his coffee. "Well, thanks for letting us read, anyway. I understand your problem. Hope you have a successful production."

Brian ignored him. He was still looking at Cheyenne. "You meant something by that," he said accusingly. Nick realized suddenly that, whatever their official ranks might be, the dominant person in this pair was the taciturn designer. The professional.

Cheyenne leaned forward, the intense dark eyes and the thin droopy mustache becoming sharp in the brighter light. "I meant, we've got a couple of good Hamlets."

"Right."

"And a couple of Poloniuses, if you can decide which one is least senile."

"Right."

"But this guy"—Cheyenne pointed at Nick as though he were an object on auction—"this guy is the only one who makes you say, yes! perfect!"

"Well . . ."

"And his wife makes you say, delightful!"

Brian whistled. He leaned back in the seat and stared up at the tinseled lamp above them. "Oh, God, Cheyenne," he said. "Think of the repercussions!"

Cheyenne shrugged. "Amateurs think of repercussions. Professionals think of the show."

Nick, interested, watched Brian wrestle with the problem. Cheyenne had leaned back into his corner. No one said anything for a moment.

"Even if I could fend off the raging female acting students," said Brian, "who the hell could play Gertrude?"

"Grace," said Cheyenne.

Brian whistled again. "Oh, God," he said. He looked down at Lisette's photo-résumé again. "Your wife has a B.A. in theatre, and other courses since."

"She could teach, if that's what you mean."

"I know, damn it. She impressed me. I couldn't bring myself to tell her we weren't reading for Ophelia." He raised a miserable gaze to Nick. "I haven't read your résumé yet. You've got some academic background too, I suppose."

"M.A. in theatre. I taught in a college for two years before the Army, and came to New York afterward."

"God. The perfect pair." Brian was silent a moment, then said, "Actually, Grace could be damn good."

We're in, thought Nick, silently blessing the unknown Grace.

"I'd better warn you," said Brian. "Your wife will probably encounter an incredible wave of hostility from all our Ophelia hopefuls. Will she still be interested under those conditions?"

"I'll ask her." Nick grinned wryly. "New York actors are not always paragons of good sportsmanship, you know. We've worked under hostile conditions before. We can probably cope with your local Furies."

"They'll get over it soon, I hope. When can you let us know?"

Nick checked his watch. "I'll give her a call before my show tonight so she can think about it. We can probably let you know by tomorrow morning. Our agent will get in touch."

"That'll be fine."

Nick tapped the copy of *Hamlet* on the table. "I noticed in your reading of Laertes that he responded to Claudius's political arguments, not to the personal ones."

"Yeah, we'll be playing it that way," said Brian eagerly. "I'm really going to be working with the state of Denmark concept, the wider implications of Hamlet's problems. That's why Claudius, the statesman, is so important. For example—"

"Ahem," said Cheyenne.

"Oh, right. Sorry, that can wait. What else can I tell you?"

Nick pulled out his notebook. "Dates. Duties."

"Okay. First rehearsal, two p.m., January 18. Classes start the next week. *Hamlet* opens at the end of April, five nights a week for two weeks. We'll want you to stay a week after it closes, to finish up your classes."

"I see. And the classes?"

"Your official title will be artist-in-residence. You'll each have two sections of basic acting. But . . ." He weighed something for a moment, then blurted, "Look, if you decide to come, it would be criminal not to give the grad students a chance at you."

Nick grinned. "Invitation to a lynching, from what you say." He felt good. "Let me ring Lisette right now, in case she has any questions," he added.

"Fine."

The phone booth was new and plastic, but already smelled of the breath of many users. Lisette answered almost immediately.

"Hi, Blossom," said Nick. "I think we've got the parts if we want them, but there's a hitch." He explained.

She said, "So the problem is that the acting students will be resentful. Well, I would have been too."

"It'll be fifteen weeks. We'll be teaching these people and working with them every day," he warned.

"Well, hell, Nicky." There was a bit of spirit back in her voice. "The first thing they'd better learn about this business is that they'll be turned down for ninety-nine percent of the parts they want."

"True."

"I want to go. Nothing in this life is easy."

"Okay, Blossom. You don't want to think it over longer?"

"I'm sure. I really want this."

Months later, looking back in sorrow, he remembered her enthusiasm. But the choice she made led to her salvation too.

Brian was counting out the tip when he got back to the booth. "She says yes," announced Nick.

Brian glanced up, surprised. "Already?"

"I told her she'd be cordially hated at first. She said not getting roles should be Lesson One in every acting class."

"Terrific!" Brian bounced up and embraced Nick, then stepped back, abashed. "I'm not very sophisticated about this process yet."

"You're doing fine," said Nick, returning his thump on the back. Cheyenne was looking at them sardonically from his corner. "It'll make up for your enraged students."

Brian shook his head glumly. "We're in for a rocky end of the term, all right." Then, enthusiasm returning, he clapped Nick on the shoulder again. "But, God, it's going to be a terrific *Hamlet!*"

II

The third week of January brought two snowstorms, back to back. Ellen Winfield was exhausted by the drive from Pennsylvania, on slick two-lane country highways. She went immediately to bed when she reached the dorm and slept late the next morning. Her roommate had apparently come and gone. There was a half-unpacked suitcase on the other bed, under the Comédie Française poster, and a note. "Dear Rip Van W.—See you at the theatre, M."

Ellen grinned and stretched. Time to go foraging. She pulled on jeans and a heavy sweater and frowned at herself in the long mirror. Winter was not her season. Her roommate, taller and bonier, looked fine in thick furry things. But all that wool made Ellen's more average frame look like two hundred pounds. Should have gone to UCLA. She brushed her straight brown hair back from her face. A reasonable face, only a little tired-looking from the drive. Hazel eyes, a straight nose maybe a touch too long. Jim liked her nose. The hell with Jim. She pulled on her parka, adding yet another hundred pounds to her looks, and went out into the snow.

Hargate was spread over the top of a hill in the approved collegiate fashion. Today it was beautiful and quiet; only a few figures, bundled up like herself, moving across the snow. Most of the buildings were nineteenth-century, crowned by the Victorian extravagance of the original library at the end of the quad. Below her, the town of Jefferson spilled down the hillside like crumbled steps to the flat floor of the glacial valley and the lake.

A familiar figure was standing at the newsstand in the lobby of the student union when she entered. "Hey, Paul!" she called.

He turned, beaming. "Hi, Ellen! How was vacation?" A nice crooked smile, dark eyes, sturdy build. Paul Rigo was the staff of life around the theatre, putting in long hours building sets, hanging lights, hunting down props.

"Fine. Even Dad took a couple of days off. How're you doing?"

The smile left his face. "Not so good. Failed chem again." Paul's hours in the theatre were notoriously detrimental to his grades.

"Hey," said Ellen, trying to look on the bright side, "you can take it again."

He shook his head sombrely. "Nope. Twice is all I'm allowed. Now I'll have to take physics instead. That's even harder."

"Oh, dear."

"The real problem is, if I mess up anything at all this term, I'm out."

"Christ, Paul. There's *Hamlet!*"

"Yeah. There's also the draft."

Vietnam. The unspoken, ominous presence. The interminable war that threatened to suck in everyone she knew as it grew, inexorably, each year.

"Hell, Paul." Ellen looked down and knocked the toe of her boot on the floor to get rid of some snow. What could she say? "Maybe you'd better ease off around the theatre."

He laughed. "Fat chance. With Cheyenne around?"

"Won't he let you off a little? Under the circumstances?"

"Well, you remember what he told us that time. He had to miss his sister's funeral because he was building a show. I mean, he's a real professional. I don't think there's anything in the world he'll accept as an excuse." Paul seemed to think this was admirable in Cheyenne.

"Well, run when you see him," Ellen advised.

"I'll have to."

"Listen, I'm starving. They're not feeding us yet in the dorms. Is the cafeteria here open?"

"Yeah, just came from there."

"Thank God. See you this afternoon!"

She had some coffee, scrambled eggs, and, guiltily, an English muffin with lots of butter, and felt much better. As she started out of the cafeteria, a voice hailed her.

"Ellen!"

She turned back. "Oh, hi, Judy! Hi, David."

Slender, regal, with dark hair and aristocratic cheekbones, Judy Allison was one of the graduate acting students. She was to be Brian's assistant director on *Hamlet.* A consolation prize. The earnest velvet-eyed young man beside her was David Wagner, an undergraduate theatre major. He would be playing Laertes. He was also Dean Wagner's son. With them was a stranger, a tall, blue-eyed blond man, who, for no obvious reason, was magnetically attractive. Judy beckoned him from the cafeteria line.

"Rob, this is Ellen Winfield. Pre-law. She's our stage manager."

"Hi, Ellen." His smile sparkled. Ellen became conscious of her thick boots and bulky parka.

"Rob Jenner?" she asked stupidly.

"Right," said Judy. "Hamlet."

"Well," Ellen said, her voice small and tight. "Hi."

His hands were thrust into his jeans pockets, pushing back his unzipped parka to reveal a knit shirt on a torso as lean and muscular as Jim's. "Judy and David have been showing me around," he said. "But so far, all we've seen is snow."

Ellen pulled herself together. "That's our specialty," she said, ignoring his disturbing gaze. "Fifty-seven varieties of it. I collapsed after driving in through last night's variety."

"So did I." He smiled that shattering smile again. "I hope everyone else gets here all right."

Ellen asked, "Have the others arrived yet?"

"You mean the New York actors?" said Judy. "I haven't seen them. Have you, David?" The dean's son shook his head.

"Brian told me you've got the O'Connors," said Rob.

"Yes. Do you know them?"

"A little. About two years ago I did a ghastly TV show with Nick. We had dinner a few times and so forth. But you lose touch."

"What is she like?" asked Judy, too quickly. Rob's shrewd blue eyes regarded her thoughtfully. An uneasy lump gathered in Ellen's middle.

"Lisette?" He frowned. "How shall I put it? Like Vivien Leigh, maybe, if only Vivien Leigh had been truly beautiful."

"Oh," said Judy, the disappointment too thinly disguised in her voice. "Can she act too?"

"I'm afraid so." Damn it, he'd figured out what was going on. "She's a little erratic, maybe, but who isn't? I take it you're a would-be Ophelia?"

The phrase hit Judy to the quick. Warmly, Ellen said, "She would have been a damn good Ophelia!"

Too warmly. His eyes, bright as blue flames, shifted to her. "I'm sure she would have been," he said mildly.

"Not for this show. It's Brian's decision, and he should know." Judy recited the official position, her desperate manner telling Ellen to shut up. David's soft gaze was uneasy.

"Nick is really good too," said Rob, shifting ground smoothly. Unreasonably, Ellen felt grateful. "He's done some amazing things."

"A few of us went into the city before Christmas and caught his show," said Judy, scrambling to recover her aplomb.

"He was terrific," added David enthusiastically.

"I didn't see it," said Rob. "But I was impressed with what he did with the stupid lines they gave us in that soap opera. He was the only one of us who came out looking human."

"A bad show is a tough test," said Judy. "But we're supposed to be getting Rob breakfast. Can you join us, Ellen?"

"Thanks, I just finished."

"Well, we'll see you at two."

They went back to the cafeteria line. Ellen stood watching him a moment. So that was Hamlet the Dane. His quick eyes flashed back once and caught her still rooted in the same spot, gaping. She jerked around abruptly and pushed out through the door. Time to buy some books.

Lunchtime. Her errands finished, Ellen returned to the cafeteria for a salad and found an empty table next to the wall. A moment later, Jim appeared. Damn. He saw her at the same instant, hesitated, and then approached with his tray.

"Hi." His thin tanned face was questioning.

"Hi, Jim," she said calmly. "Join me?"

"Sure." He was wearing his Irish sweater, a blue shirt under it. And under that, Ellen knew, the tan skin, the lean powerful chest and arms. Damn him. She concentrated on spearing a cherry tomato.

Jim indicated her clipboard. "I see you're ready to start."

"Mm-hmm. Tabula rasa."

"Brian said he'd give us the cuts today."

"I'd hate to have that job. Can you imagine deciding that a line in *Hamlet* isn't worth giving?" She risked a glance at him.

Jim grinned around his sandwich. "Just try it uncut, and see how much of the audience sticks with you until two a.m."

"I know. I still wouldn't like to have the job."

"You legal types idolize the written word too much."

"Well, it should be performed. Better half a loaf than none."

"In this case, better half a loaf than a whole."

Ellen stabbed at a chunk of lettuce. He was so easy to talk to. Surely they could be friends. "You're probably right," she said. "Have you met Hamlet?"

"You mean Jenner? Not yet. Have you seen him?"

"In glorious person."

"Really." His eyebrows lifted. "It's like that, is it?"

"This campus is about to receive a visitation from Apollo himself."

"He sounds difficult."

"Well . . ." Ellen decided she was being unfair. "Look, I only saw him about two minutes. In that time he ran Judy and me all the way from slavish devotion to blind fury and back again. I don't like that."

"I know," said Jim.

Ellen ignored him. "I don't know anything about his work."

"Brian said he had good small parts behind him, and a star-studded career in North Carolina rep before he hit New York."

"I suppose we'll survive him. But it's a double-threat cast. According to him, the female O'Connor will be doing to you males what he'll be doing to us." She picked up her coffee mug.

"What a term this promises to be." He was watching her, she knew, but she kept her hazel eyes obstinately on the mug. After a moment he said, resigned, "What do you hear about *Blithe Spirit?*"

She relaxed a little. "The staging people were all going out of their minds before Christmas. Cheyenne got a bunch of them to come back last week, though, so they're in good shape now."

"The actors were optimistic when I saw them last."

"They're always optimistic before tech, poor ninnies." She grinned at him. He smiled back, appreciative and warm, and then the plea flickered again in his dark eyes. Warnings clanged in Ellen's mind. She pulled her gaze away and stood up abruptly.

"I've got to get over there early," she said.

"Okay. I'm done too. I'll go with you."

"Fine." But she didn't look at him again.

The first meeting would be on the stage itself. Brian wanted to give the newcomers a tour of the backstage areas after his initial pep talk. Then they would settle into the more comfortable auditorium seats to record the lines that would be cut. They couldn't rehearse on the stage until after *Blithe Spirit* closed.

Jim and Ellen went down the half flight of stairs from the stage door to the greenroom and on through to the stage itself. Some rehearsal benches and a few chairs were scattered about among the tall, half-painted units of the *Blithe Spirit* set. Stage lights were on, for some reason, instead of work lights, and there was a large brilliant pool in the middle of the stage. Ellen looked up into the cavernous fly area above the stage, but could see nothing but blackness behind the glare of the big Lekos. She dumped her parka and clipboard in a corner and, with Jim, began to arrange the seats in a rough circle. The lobby door banged, and she turned to see a frail man walking down the aisle.

"Hello," she said as he mounted the temporary steps from auditorium to stage. "Are you Mr. Morgan?"

"Chester Morgan," he said, beaming. He stepped instinctively into the lighted circle and placed an artistic hand on his heart. "At your service. Polonius and Gravedigger."

"Hi. I'm Ellen Winfield. Stage manager. And this is Jim Greer. He'll be Horatio."

"Glad to meet you," said Chester. "I'm delighted to have

an opportunity to do *Hamlet.* I've been on the stage now forty-five years, and never did it. Can you imagine?"

"Well, we're pleased to be working on it too."

Cheyenne and Laura Eisner entered, carrying folding chairs. "This ought to be enough," Cheyenne said to Ellen without greeting her. He looked at her arrangement. "Cozy circle, eh?"

"Yeah. Figured Brian would prefer that."

"Probably will," said Laura, a touch resentfully. She was a graduate actress too, an intense, tawny brunette; her consolation prize was heading the costume crew.

"Hello, Cheyenne!" called Chester.

Cheyenne nodded curtly and walked into the dim shadows in the wings to inspect the fly ropes.

Judy Allison came through the shop door with David Wagner and some other acting students. "Lost your escort, Judy?" asked Ellen, smiling.

"He stopped off to talk to Brian. They'll be along."

"Have you met Mr. Morgan?"

"Yes, briefly," said Judy. "Hi again."

Other people trickled in. Grace Halliday, the speech professor who would be playing Gertrude, strode over to talk to Judy and Laura. Paul Rigo gave Ellen his crooked smile in passing but joined Cheyenne immediately. Various members of the costume and properties crews sauntered in, and actors with minor parts. Many carried soft drinks or coffee mugs. They clustered together, catching up on the post-vacation news.

Ellen was writing a note on her clipboard about announcing the theatre rules when she became aware of a hush spreading through the groups of chattering people. She looked up and saw a man and woman, both in jeans, approaching from the shop door. The man was big, balding, with friendly, interested brown eyes. The woman, tall and slim in a buttercup-yellow ski sweater, was devastatingly lovely. Honey-colored hair, clear smooth skin, soft rosy mouth as gentle as a child's. She stepped into the lighted circle and paused. The man stopped just behind her, hands in pockets, his warm mild gaze traveling around the group.

No one said anything.

Ellen realized suddenly that they didn't know anyone here, except for Cheyenne, who had never been known to introduce anyone. Judy and Laura, she saw with a sidelong glance, were still stunned by the injustice of this slender beauty. So it was up to Ellen. Ellen, who had spent most of the day already feeling like a three-hundred-pound dwarf. She mustered what dignity she could and clumped over to them sturdily, footsteps echoing through the silence, to present her unlovely self.

"Hi, I'm Ellen Winfield. Stage manager. You must be the O'Connors."

"Right." The man's brown eyes, intensely friendly, thanked her. It was hard for them too, Ellen realized, and suddenly felt less clumsy. He said, "I'm Nick, and this is Lisette."

"Hi, Ellen." Lisette's smile was friendly too, and her voice. "Glad to meet you."

"Come meet the others," said Ellen. People were beginning to pick up their conversations again. The bad moment was over. "Brian isn't here yet, but his assistant director is. Judy?"

Judy had prepared herself by now. She joined them with a regal smile and said the proper things when introduced, then led them to Chester Morgan to talk. Ellen gazed after them.

"Once more unto the breach," said Jim's voice softly in her ear.

"Well, someone had to do it," she said crossly.

"Granted. You just beat the rest of us cowardly oafs."

Ellen, startled, looked into his comprehending eyes an instant, then clutched her clipboard to her chest like a shield and marched to the ring of seats to sit down on the end of a bench. Jim, undaunted, took the folding chair next to her. It was a sort of signal; other people, glancing at their watches and finding it a couple of minutes after two, sat down also. The three New York actors sat near Ellen—Lisette at the far end of Ellen's bench, then Nick and Chester and Judy on folding chairs. Ellen noted wryly that no one took the wide space on the bench between her and Lisette. Laura had pointedly crossed to the other side of the circle. But Lisette seemed unoffended.

Ellen heard Brian a moment later, approaching from the dimness of the greenroom door. Then Rob Jenner's voice exclaimed, "Hey!" and rapid steps rang through the vast dusky space. Laura, alone on the bench across from

Ellen, looked up in alarm as Rob hurdled her bench and landed in the center of the brightly lit, startled circle.

"Nick! Zetty!" he cried, delight in every line of his body. "It's great to see you!" He lifted Lisette from her place on the bench and whirled her around exuberantly. The light glanced off the spinning pair, the two beautiful smiles, the two shining heads, one the color of sunshine and one the color of honey. Then he replaced her, gently, beside her husband and seized Nick's burly forearm. "Hey, Nick! How've you been?" He sat on the bench next to Lisette, leaning toward them eagerly.

"Fine. Good to see you, Rob." Nick seemed amused rather than impressed. Ellen decided she liked Nick O'Connor.

Brian, following, stepped over Laura's bench in his turn and into the circle. "Looks like everyone's here," he said, glancing around. "Most of you have probably figured it out, but just for the record, our four guest actors for this production are Rob Jenner, Hamlet; Lisette O'Connor, Ophelia; Nicholas O'Connor, Claudius; and Chester Morgan, who will do both Polonius and the Gravedigger." The four newcomers nodded affably at the circle. Brian faced them apologetically. "Now the big job; introducing us to you. You've all met Cheyenne." In the dim light by the pin rail, Cheyenne saluted them as they turned to peer at him. "You've met Judy too, I see. How about Ellen Winfield, our stage manager?"

"Yes," said Nick, smiling at her.

"Okay. This is Grace Halliday, our Gertrude. Also our speech coach."

"Hello," said Grace. She was an attractive woman in her thirties, fit and sturdily built, with sun-streaked brown hair.

Brian introduced Jim, David Wagner, and the other actors with major roles, then started on the crew heads—properties, makeup, publicity. Hands waved as Brian identified them. "Hope you're remembering a little of this," he said to the four newcomers apologetically. "Let's see. There's Paul Rigo, staging." He indicated Paul back near the ropes, with his pleased crooked grin. "Laura Eisner here, costumes." Laura inclined her head, but didn't smile. Brian squinted around the circle. "Okay, now. Did I miss anyone?"

"Lights," said a clear feminine voice from the vast blackness above their heads.

Oh, God, thought Ellen. She peered up into the dark beyond the glaring lights.

"Oh, yes," said Brian. "Come on down, Maggie, we can't see you."

"The paradox of our profession," said the voice philosophically. A pair of sneakers appeared out of the darkness above, followed by a gangly pair of jean-clad legs. "We are invisible that others may be visible." She bounced lightly onto the bench beside Laura. There were lively blue eyes, a tumble of unkempt black curls, and a rangy athletic figure in a scruffy sweatshirt. Clown, thought Ellen.

But Brian was amused. "Maggie Ryan, lights," he announced.

She bowed to the newcomers with a balletic flourish, then skipped back over the bench, out of the light, away from Ellen's exasperated glare. Rob Jenner grinned and leaned toward Nick O'Connor. Ellen, cringing inwardly, was near enough to hear him whisper, "Knows how to make an entrance."

"Topped yours," observed Nick, to Ellen's relief. Rob chuckled. Brian started talking, but Ellen listened shamelessly instead to the whispered conversation beside her.

"Do you suppose she tries to act, too?" Rob went on.

"Maybe."

"Not bad-looking, really," added Rob judiciously, "but too bony and tall for an ingenue."

"Oh, much too gawky for that," came a new whisper. "More of a soubrette, I always thought." Maggie Ryan had come up behind them. Ellen's embarrassment gave way to guilty pleasure at the instant of discomfiture in Rob's eyes before his brows arched indignantly at Maggie.

"Do you always intrude into other people's private conversations?" he demanded, as severely as he could in a whisper.

"Only when I know more about the subject than they do," she replied with equanimity, stepping over the bench and sitting between him and Ellen. "Now, let's listen to Brian," she added soothingly. They stopped talking, but

Ellen was aware of the amused glances that Rob occasionally gave the lanky young woman beside him.

Brian finished explaining the plan—the quick tour of the backstage areas, followed by a meeting in the auditorium to get the cuts—and then looked at Ellen.

"That's all for me," he said. "Do you have any words of advice, Ellen?"

"Only the usual," she said. "Check the call-board every day. Don't smoke anywhere except in the greenroom. And don't spit on the stairs."

Everyone laughed and started to get up to show the New York actors around. Ellen, turning in their direction as she gathered up her things, noticed Rob leaning forward, preparing to say something to Maggie. But, as Ellen half expected, Maggie's dark curly head turned away, ignoring him to look at Ellen instead.

"Goddamn showoff," Ellen muttered to her.

Maggie laughed. "Delighted to see you too, roomie!"

III

Stifling a yawn, Ellen caught Nick O'Connor's amused eye on her. She gave him a guilty grin. The greatest tragedy ever written, it turned out, was exceedingly dreary when read for cuts.

Even Brian sounded bored. "Okay. Same speech—522 will be the last line, cut 523 to 526," he said at last.

"Okay."

"And that's it. We'll play straight to the end of Act Two."

"Thank God!" Ellen heard Rob say. "I thought I was going to lose 'Oh what a rogue and peasant slave am I!' "

"He probably knows you'll drop so many lines, he won't have to cut it," said Lisette impudently.

"Nick, how do you live with this vicious creature?"

"Cotton in my ears," said Nick. "Look, must be break time."

At the front of the auditorium, Brian was standing and stretching. "Be back in ten minutes, okay, gang?" he said. "Say, has anyone seen Cheyenne?" When no one answered, he wandered off. Rob and Nick followed him out.

Lisette appeared at Ellen's elbow. "Excuse me, Ellen. Where's the rest room?"

Maggie was standing beside Ellen, one long leg propped on the seat in front of her. "I'll show you the one backstage," she said.

"Thanks." They moved toward the stage, two tall slender figures, one dark and athletic, the other golden and delicate. Ellen was left alone, Miss Three-Hundred-Pound Dwarf of 1967. She glanced around. Most people, including

Jim, had left the auditorium. After a few minutes, Rob and Nick returned, discussing something as they strolled up the aisle. A few student actors followed them bashfully—David Wagner; Maggie's tall admirer, Jason, who would play the Ghost; and several others, including Jim. Ellen joined the group.

"Doesn't anyone have an umbrella?" Rob was asking plaintively. "Well, okay, let's use pencils." He reached into the pocket of his parka, which was draped over a seat, and pulled out two, tossing the blue one to Nick. "Okay. The yellow Eberhard Faber here is poisoned. Back, everyone, out of the aisle. *En garde!*" Brandishing the ridiculous colored sticks, he and Nick assumed classical fencing posture in the middle of the aisle. "Now, what we did—I'm Laertes and he's Hamlet, folks—we fenced for a while, snickety snick." The pencils clicked together for a moment. "Now Hamlet jabs me one." Nick obligingly thrust at Rob. Nick was a lot more agile than he looked at first, thought Ellen. " 'A hit, a very palpable hit,' et cetera," continued Rob. "Now the King drinks and Hamlet hits again. Then there's the business with the Queen drinking the poison. We play again and Laertes thinks he hits Hamlet, but Osric says 'Nothing neither way.' They hadn't invented grammar teachers yet."

He paused, finger raised for emphasis. "Now that makes Laertes mad. When Hamlet turns away to wipe his weary brow"—Nick followed directions—"Laertes lunges from behind." Rob jabbed Nick in the arm. Nick, hurt astonishment on his face, whirled, and for an instant Ellen thought it was a real fight as the two grappled, rolling down the aisle. But a second later they were on their feet again, crouched elegantly to fence, pencils at the ready, and Rob was saying calmly, "Notice now that I have the blue Woolworth's pencil, and Nick, clever thing that he is, has come up with the poisoned one from Eberhard Faber. Now all he has to do is jab me again and I'm done for." Nick poked at him. "Now we both die."

"Our specialty," said Nick. The brown eyes, twinkling, met Rob's, and suddenly they both began groaning hilariously, reeling about, and eventually subsided, twitching, in the aisle. Ellen, gasping with laughter like everyone else, collapsed into a seat. Rob, lying picturesquely dead with his head down the slope of the aisle, pale hair light as flame against the dark red carpet, opened his bright blue eyes and looked up to see Brian, who had come back in and was standing at his head.

"Well, what do you think?" asked Rob innocently, without moving. "Shall we do it that way?"

Brian's mouth twitched. "I had hoped that by hiring professionals we'd get someone with more ability than my six-year-old," he said dryly. Rob laughed and rolled neatly to a sitting position. Nick was already standing up again, smiling. Brian went on, "If you're talking about the motivation, we may go that way. I agree that it's probably better to have Laertes do the deed in a fit of anger. Hamlet too, for that matter." Rob nodded. "But nothing is really set, of course, until we work it through. Our Laertes will have a lot to say about it."

David, excited and earnest, said, "I think I can work with that. He has a hot-headed side."

Nick said, "Some of the hot-headedness may be a calculated effect. More political than real."

"True." Brian glanced at him appreciatively. "Please, let's not make any decisions on motivation until we've had a chance to go through it together. It's a complicated play."

"Sorry, boss." Rob stood up, grinning unrepentantly, and dusted himself off. "It's just that we growing boys need our exercise."

"Yeah, I hate these cut rehearsals too," agreed Brian.

"Sacré merde de Dieu!"

The urgent exclamation rang into the auditorium as the shadows on the stage swayed slightly. Recognizing her roommate's voice, Ellen sprang down the aisle, followed by Nick and Jim. As they ran up the steps to the forestage, the voice continued, still shaken, "Cheyenne! What kind of mental defectives do you have in this outfit? Is Cheyenne there?"

"Yeah," he said from the wings. He walked out onstage, squinting up at the flies.

"Would you tell those idiot amateurs on the *Blithe Spirit* crew that even sandbags should not be flown without counterweights?"

Ellen shaded her eyes, but still could not see Maggie. Cheyenne too seemed puzzled. "What's the problem?"

"Well, maybe if someone would give me a hand, I could talk about it more calmly."

Nick gave an exclamation and leaped for the ladder that led up to the flies. Ellen saw her then, too. She was dangling upside down off the edge of a catwalk, knees wrapped around the horizontal pipe that supported some of the lighting instruments, the baggy sweatshirt rucked around her shoulders. She clutched a big sandbag to her chest.

"God!" said Rob, and started for the ladder too.

Ellen, not quite as worried as the others, watched Nick throw himself flat on the narrow catwalk with amazing precision. He reached down.

"Here, give me the damn sandbag first. Can you hold on another second?"

"Sure. Here you go." Maggie transferred the heavy bag to him carefully, and he maneuvered it onto the catwalk. He reached back, ready to help her up, but she had already pulled herself up to perch on the edge of the catwalk. Rob arrived behind Nick. Maggie brushed aside a curl that had fallen across her eyes and regarded them with mock awe. "Goodness! What a stellar rescue committee! Aren't you breaking Equity rules? To say nothing of the stagehands' union."

Nick glanced down at Lisette below, then, briefly, at Maggie. "So we are," he said good-naturedly, and added to Rob, "I think the wench is telling us to leave."

"Too late again," said Rob sadly. He squeezed aside to let Nick by, then, poised even on a catwalk, held out a courtly hand to Maggie. "If you won't let me rescue you, dear lady, may I at least escort you down?"

"Kind sir, you are confusing me with the ingenue again." The two pairs of blue eyes, equally mocking, equally speculative, locked for a moment. Then Maggie smiled, stood up gracefully on the narrow walk, and extended her hand.

Ellen, who suddenly felt as though she were intruding, went to join Nick and Lisette in the wings. Shakily, Lisette was saying, "I just about cashed it in, Nicky. That thing was right over my head."

He frowned. "Over your head?"

"We came in from the scene shop door back there. And suddenly Maggie said, 'Wait a minute' and went up that ladder." She pointed to the rear ladder that led up past two levels of catwalks to the grid at the ceiling. "Well, I thought I'd go on back to my seat, but I was looking up to see what she was doing. And suddenly right over my head that sandbag started to fall."

"You mean she knocked it off?"

"No. She wasn't close. It just started to fall. I was looking up, so maybe I would have ducked in time."

"She wasn't close? Then how did she catch it?"

"I don't know. She just swooped out of nowhere and grabbed it. For a second I thought she'd fall on me too. But she didn't."

Nick still looked puzzled. Ellen explained, "She's a gymnast. Loves the bars."

He smiled. "Perfect training for lighting personnel."

"Yeah. We ought to make it a prerequisite."

"Good idea." He frowned up at the catwalk again. "But that was pretty careless of someone, all the same. This is the main path from the scene shop. Everyone has to walk right under it. Someone could have been hurt."

"Right," said Ellen.

"Was that a flying harness it was fastened to?"

"Yes. They're using the harness for the spirit entrances in *Blithe Spirit.*"

"Sounds like fun."

"Yeah, I've always wanted to try it. A childish whim. Anyway, when they finish with the harness they hook on the sandbag and pull it up out of the way until the next actress needs it."

Lisette shuddered. "God! What if she'd put it on without the counterweight?"

Ellen didn't much want to think about that. She said, "Well, I'm sure it won't happen again." She nodded to the pin rail, where Rob and Maggie stood inspecting the ropes and talking to Cheyenne. The designer's sharp eyes peered up toward the catwalk, then he began fastening the missing counterweight to one of the ropes. "Cheyenne doesn't say much," Ellen explained, "but when the oracle does speak, the earth shakes."

"I know," said Nick quietly. He turned back to Lisette. "Come on, Blossom. Let's go sit down."

Ellen accompanied them. As they descended the steps into the auditorium, a glimmer of chrome caught her attention in the shadows next to the stair. She reached down. It was a briefcase with a shiny catch.

"That's strange!" said Lisette. "How did it get there?"

"Is it yours?"

"I thought I left mine on the seat." Lisette opened the case and looked through it. "Yes, there's my script, and all those forms to fill out for the Hargate personnel department."

Then she frowned, and Nick asked, "Something missing?"

"My résumé pictures. I usually have about a dozen in here. They're all gone."

"Strange," said Nick. "You must have a fan club already. Is anything else missing?"

"No. Nothing. Thanks for finding it, Ellen!" They went back to their seats.

Ellen plunked herself down in her own place. Jim came into the row behind her and sat, leaning forward, elbows on the back of the seat next to her. She could feel his warmth on her cheek.

"Is Maggie all right?" he asked.

"Never better." Ellen shifted away from him a little. "She's soaring into battle. Ready to take on Apollo himself." She jerked her head toward Rob, who was striding energetically up the aisle.

"I rather like Apollo, actually. The others too."

"Yeah, it's not as bad as I thought. Looks like we're all going to be boys together."

He grinned, and for an instant she was afraid he would ruffle her hair, the way he used to, but he didn't. Instead he said, "We'll learn a lot this term."

"I don't even want to think about it!" Which was true. If the cut rehearsal, that acme of boredom, could be this lively, she hated to contemplate the real ones.

Brian banged on the brass rail that held the curtain

around the orchestra pit. "Quiet, gang! An important announcement before we start. Next Saturday afternoon, five o'clock, the entire cast and crew is invited to Dean Wagner's for a welcoming reception. We really do appreciate everything the dean has done to make this show a reality, so I hope you'll all come thank him. In your Sunday best." The undergraduates groaned, and he added sternly, "The apparel oft proclaims the man! Oh, one other thing. Claudius, Polonius, Ghost-Fortinbras, and First Player are all scheduled to wear beards. Grow your own if you want. But please, please don't start until after the dean's party." Everyone laughed. "Okay, gang. Back to work. Act Three, Scene One."

The tedium began again.

Late that night, back at the dorm, Maggie poured milk into two mugs of instant coffee and handed one to Ellen. "There you are," she said grandly. "*Café au lait maison du jour.*"

"Oo-la-la. How fancy." Ellen was sitting cross-legged on her bed in a checked nightgown, long brown hair combed over one shoulder. She cradled the mug in her hands, appreciating the warmth. It had been a full day, concluding with an evening of unpacking and making lists of things to do on upcoming, equally busy days. She watched her roommate deploy her angular frame across the other bed and asked, "What exactly is a soubrette, Maggie? I thought it was usually a maid."

"Yes." Maggie smiled. "But not just any maid. She's the clever, flirtatious maid, the one who thinks up schemes and keeps the plot moving."

Ellen nodded knowingly. "Ah, I see. The one who arranges to have a pool of stage light instead of work lights, so she can make a big entrance."

"That's the one." Maggie's grin widened. "Maggie *ex machina.* Actually, a couple of the work lights were burnt out and I was just using the others temporarily while I changed them. But then you and Jim started arranging chairs in a circle, and Chester Morgan came in and headed right for the light, and I thought, why not? Let's see what professionals do with this setup. Lights and audience, what else does an actor need? And they all used it."

"Except Nick."

"Oh, he was part of Lisette's entrance. His job was to make her seem protected, but not threatening to anybody's private life. Which he did."

"But that's probably the truth," protested Ellen. "She's not here to rock the boat. She's here to do a job."

"Of course it's the truth! Who says a big entrance has to be a lie? I'd say all of our entrances told the truth."

"Theatre people." Ellen shook her head. "Overgrown children, all of you."

"This overgrown child is in math, not theatre. Anyway, you love it too. I saw you looking at Jim."

"Oh, God, Maggie. What am I going to do?"

"What do you want to do?"

"I want to be friends. Period."

"In an ideal world? If you could arrange things any way you wanted?"

"The world is not ideal!" said Ellen vehemently.

Maggie drew her knees up to her chin. "Yeah. Can't argue with that." She was looking at the bookends on her desk, little copies of Notre Dame Cathedral.

"Alain?" asked Ellen sympathetically. "But that was years ago."

"Over, but not forgotten."

"I thought it tore you apart."

"Yeah, you don't know the half of it. But you can't choose what to forget. Anyway, I'd do it again."

"I sure wouldn't. I'm keeping away from trouble."

Maggie inspected Ellen kindly. "That's what makes you a good stage manager. You avoid fluster at all costs."

"Oh, quit patronizing me. I'm not the juvenile in this room."

"Yeah, you're positively stuffy," agreed Maggie cheerfully. "So why are you still hanging around the theatre?"

There was no good answer. Jim? No, she had become fascinated by backstage work long before he had joined the graduate program. And it had to be admitted, the work in the theatre was the source of most of the fluster in her life.

"Stupidity, I guess," she said. "Maybe the feeling that the whole project would vaporize without me."

"It might at that. Poor Lisette almost got vaporized."

"That was strange."

"It was. It really was." Maggie frowned. "I still don't understand it. I saw that the harness was hanging too low, and went up to look. And it was okay, just low, until the very instant she got under it. Weird."

"You must have bumped it somehow." Ellen got up and took Maggie's empty mug and her own to the sink in the corner.

"Maybe. I didn't think so. Anyway, the real problem was with the dummy who removed that counterweight. Paul said it was probably the *Blithe Spirit* crew. They've been rigging things."

"Yeah. This place is crawling with dummies. Some of them make big entrances from the catwalks. Hey, did I tell you someone stole Lisette's photos?"

"Her photos?"

"Took her briefcase, stole about a dozen résumé pictures, and dumped the case by the steps."

"Poor O'Connors. Probably thought they were coming to a low-crime district." Maggie frowned. "That's sort of disturbing."

"Oh, not necessarily. She's so gorgeous, it's probably just some smitten sophomore. There are a lot more disturbing things than that around."

"What do you mean?"

Ellen plunked the clean mugs onto the desk and crawled into bed. "All those new personalities. Especially Rob. Don't you find Rob a bit disturbing?"

"Rob?" Maggie was surprised. "Why?"

"Well, I told you how he ran over Judy's feelings today."

"Yeah. But he won't do it again." Maggie stretched out on her bed and pulled up the cover.

"What do you mean? Why wouldn't he if he felt like it?"

"Too easy a mark. I think he was just testing. He's not

out to hurt anybody. He just wants to have a few mental wrestling matches with people. Unlike you, he enjoys a little fluster. And he's probably a little lonely."

"You think you're a mind reader? How do you know all that?" Yawning, Ellen pulled the chain on the desk lamp and the room went black.

"Because I'm like that too."

Ellen jerked the light back on and sat straight up to look at her roommate with alarm. "Oh, Maggie, watch out. Watch out," she said earnestly.

Maggie, stretched out on the bed, didn't move. "Simmer down," she said. "There's nothing to worry about. I'm too bony, he said so himself. Anyway, he'll have a sweetie or two waiting in New York. All we have to do here is keep him from getting bored for a few weeks. And that," she said firmly, "should be fun."

IV

There was a scorpion on Lisette's soft smiling lip.

Involuntarily, Nick checked an instant, his hands on the shoulders of her coat in the dean's front closet. Her photograph was pinned to the lining of her coat, and the grisly little creature glued to it was arched for attack in all the glossy realism of the expensive novelty shop. Party laffs. Pretending to fumble for his own topcoat, Nick unpinned the photo, folded it, and slipped it and its unpleasant cargo into his own inner pocket. Then he put on his social smile and turned back to the others.

Dean Wagner had followed them into the front hall and now stood smiling at Lisette. Clearly she had made another conquest. David Wagner had welcomed them to the reception with shy enthusiasm, but it was his father who had appropriated Lisette almost immediately, clucking at her insistence on ginger ale at the bar but then escorting her proudly from one departmental chairman to another like a trophy. In fact, all of them had had their little triumphs. Rob had charmed Mrs. Wagner and her friends, then had fascinated the drama students with accounts of the earlier production of *Hamlet* he had been in. Old Chester Morgan had joined a small circle of older faculty to trade stories about theatre in the Depression. Even Nick had dusted off his academic skills for a pleasurable discussion of Victorian theatre with the head of the English department. Nick the egghead. It had been fun.

Yes, he thought with surprise, Hargate was fun. It had been a long time since he'd thought of himself as having fun. Life in New York was busy, filled with joys and disappointments, the tension of auditions and sporadic poverty, the glorious highs of performance and the grinding dullness of temporary jobs, the alternating worry and hope about Lisette. He had learned to enjoy the good parts and cope with the bad. He knew he wouldn't trade with anyone else. But it wasn't exactly fun.

And, as the scorpion demonstrated, life here at Hargate was not free of tension. Laura Eisner and Judy Allison were still determinedly cool. In his movement class for graduates, most of the students quizzed him eagerly about the daily details of life as a working actor. O'Connor's Guide for Actors: Squalor Made Easy. Judy and Laura, though, sat pointedly on the sidelines until the classwork began.

Fortunately, Lisette seemed happy. She was intrigued with Ophelia—a bright and capable young woman, she had decided, overwhelmed at last by forces beyond her control. She enjoyed teaching her freshman acting classes, too. But Nick had to admit that he was still concerned about her. Important challenges still lay ahead, far more important than coping with the joke scorpion he would show her when they got home. No, Lisette's enthusiasm alone was not the source of this sense of fun.

Rob, perhaps? On the TV show two years ago, Nick had enjoyed working with him, although at that time Rob had been in the midst of an unpleasant divorce and suffered from sporadic depressions. Now he seemed full of life again, a good colleague, serious about the show and irreverent about everything else. And he did make a striking first impression. Singling them out as special friends had helped take Lisette out of the category of usurper and into the category of glamorous professional. Nick grinned, remembering the two of them spinning in the lighted circle, an enchanted pair. Quite an entrance. Score one for the pros. And then Hargate had evened the score with their remarkable lights girl. Maybe that was the moment, thought Nick, when things began to be fun, when that young creature had dropped in lightly from above, challenge and laughter in her sunlit grin, and he had realized that he was in the midst of youngsters. Lively, buoyant, eager youngsters. Full of worries, of course, or even anger, like Laura and Judy, but still resilient, ready to try something new, flexing their muscles and minds. Playing games not quite so grim as city games. Most of his New York friends were a little tired. It must be the kids, then.

He was enjoying them in classes and rehearsals, enjoying their questions and admiration, enjoying the sensation of this brief stint as a superior being. A clumsy-looking, balding superior being. And it was fun.

But now it was time to go. "Thanks again, Dean Wagner," he said. "We appreciated the chance to meet everyone."

"Well, we've all been looking forward to meeting you." The star-struck dean was basking in the success of his reception.

"And thanks for making this whole project possible," Rob added. "Brian tells me you had to work a small miracle to get this production going."

The dean looked pleased. "Well, it did take some doing," he admitted. "We have a centenary fund that our alumni set up, but there was a little bit of foot-dragging about this project. You have to understand, the alumni are very jittery right now. The campuses keep challenging their values. And the worst is this damn war. Demonstrations and marches and draft card burnings and boys running off to Canada. It's a terrible time to try to raise money."

"It was a terrific selling job," said Rob. "Thanks for everything." They shook hands and stepped out onto the snow-dusted gravel of the sweeping driveway.

A knot of people stood there talking seriously—Grace Halliday and her husband Jon, Cheyenne and Paul, Ellen and Maggie, several graduate actors, and even David Wagner, looking chilly without his topcoat. Rob strode over to throw his arm around Maggie's shoulders, white and furry in a French rabbit coat. "Maggie, you're all so solemn, I'm sure you're in the midst of an important discussion of Spinoza or Buxtehude. But please, take pity on a stranger and tell me where to get dinner."

"Dinner! A great idea!" She smiled back. "I knew something was missing from my life!"

"I'm hungry too," admitted Jim.

"Let's go to a restaurant," suggested Nick. "All of us."

In the general enthusiastic chorus, only David looked hesitant.

"Come on, David," urged Rob. "You can't tell me your parents are ogres now that I've met them. They'll let you come. Go get your coat." Pleased, David ran back in.

Rob turned back to Maggie. "You still haven't told us where."

"Somewhere good. We're all so elegant," said Nick. Everyone looked good tonight. Rob, of course, and Lisette; Ellen the stage manager, attractive in a soft brown dress; tall Jason the Ghost, almost debonair in his charcoal suit; and Maggie in French boots and a vivid slash of a cardinal-red dress that transformed her lankiness to elegance. Even Cheyenne had on a necktie. The undergraduates, Nick knew, went to this much trouble maybe twice a year. He added, "If you're penniless students, Lisette and I can subsidize you at five dollars a head. Okay, Lisette?"

"Fine. We just got paid."

"Great! I can throw something into the pot too," said Rob. "Where's the best food in town?"

"Chez Pierre?" suggested Grace.

"Whoopee!" said Jason. And so it was decided.

Nick and Lisette had come with Rob; their own old car did not like cold weather. Now, as they waited for him to bring it up the driveway, Nick found himself standing next to Maggie. Because he was curious, he asked, "Maggie, with all due regard to Buxtehude, what do you people really talk about here?"

For an instant, the deep blue eyes that met his were serious. "Vietnam, of course," she said.

Chez Pierre turned out to be on the lake road beyond Hargate Heights, a tall old farmhouse converted into a restaurant. "Is this place really French?" Nick asked dubiously.

"The chef is French," said Maggie, letting Jason take her white coat into the coatroom. "But the others are only pretending."

Rob said, "I always wonder what they'd do in a place like this if some real Frenchman walked in."

"Squirm, I imagine," said Nick. Maggie's delighted glance flicked from him to Rob, then she stepped forward, graceful in the dark red dress, as the maître d' entered through an archway.

"Bonsoir, messieurs, mesdames," he said intimidatingly, silencing everyone. "Reservations?"

"No," admitted Nick, finding himself with Maggie at the front.

"How many, please?"

Maggie turned to Nick with a helpless bewilderment that was so uncharacteristic that he hesitated in confusion. Then, in sudden pleased comprehension, she exclaimed, *"Ah, oui! Nous sommes quatorze personnes!"* The merry smile challenged Nick.

"Zat's right," he said, responding instinctively with a heavy French accent. "We are fourteen person."

"Fourteen. *Oui.* Yes," said the maître d'. He picked up a handful of menus, looked at them nervously, and led the way through the archway.

"Mon Dieu," said Jon Halliday, diverted.

Rob, anticipation in his pleasant features, surveyed the others. *"Allons, mes amis, pour la gloire!"*

"Oh, Christ," muttered Ellen in disgust.

"Mais non, ma belle Hélène!" Rob's lean, navy-clad arm slipped around her shoulders, and Rob's finger touched her surprised lips in gentle admonition. *"Soyez gentille."*

Ellen subsided, and they all followed the maître d' and Maggie. Halfway across the room, Maggie stopped abruptly. Lisette, nudging Nick, put on her best French pout, and he realized that Maggie too had shifted nationality subtly. *"Mais non,"* she was objecting, looking back unhappily at Nick. Her accent was flawless to his inexpert ear. *"Je préfere m'asseoir un peu plus près de la fenêtre."*

She had chosen the most public spot in the restaurant; two rooms full of well-dressed people looked up surreptitiously, intrigued, then looked away politely. Nick was tickled; the maître d', turning at Maggie's voice, was obviously at a loss. Beaming, Nick sprang to his rescue. "Mademoiselle Marguerite, she say we sit zere, by zee—how say you, *la fenêtre?*"

"Zee weendow," contributed Jason, and received an approving grin from Rob.

"Oh. Yes. Of course." The maître d', looking around frantically and seeing the sharpened attention and politely averted gaze of the other diners, gave in.

The tables Maggie had chosen were set apart in a little windowed alcove, and once they were seated, the waiters did not seem eager to hover nearby. Rob said quietly, eyes sparkling, "Okay, ground rules. When the waiters are around, speak French if you can, English only with an accent. And let Mademoiselle Marguerite take the lead."

"Cheyenne and I don't speak French at all," said Paul, worried.

"The rest of the time English is okay. Paul, you're in the middle there, that's the best position for a lookout. Just give a cough whenever anyone is approaching."

Grace Halliday said nervously, "Aren't we going to tell them it's a joke?"

"At this point," said Ellen, with an exasperated glance at Maggie, "it's kinder not to tell them."

They discussed the menu, then Paul Rigo coughed, and the waiter arrived for their order. Nick, projecting his voice professionally, ordered for them in expertly mauled English. The waiter accepted it humbly. Everyone kept a straight face until he left, and Rob, his cigarette drooping Gallic-style from the corner of his mouth, said, "How zee mighty are fallen!"

"We should sell this idea to *Candid Camera,*" suggested Jason.

Lisette, sitting across from Nick, was looking down the table at Maggie. "Are you a French major?" she asked with interest.

"No. I have a double major. English and math."

"Our Mag can do anything." Jason patted her possessively on the back.

Judy was watching Paul hand the breadbasket to Cheyenne next to him. "Our Superwoman," she said, not completely kindly.

Rob pinned Judy in his bright blue gaze. "Excellence is often unwelcome and difficult to forgive," he said. There was a flicker of anger in Judy's face. Cheyenne, who had passed bread on to Lisette, stopped buttering his roll and looked thoughtfully at Rob.

"Yes," he said, the brusque voice unexpected, as it always was. "Especially when we are excellent ourselves."

There was an odd silence, somehow centered now on Lisette instead of Maggie. Lisette herself broke it, saying gently, "Here, Grace. Have some bread," as she passed on the basket.

"It's lucky that theatre people are all aiming at the same goal, or we might hurt each other," said Rob generally, looking around the table. "But I've never known any professionals who couldn't subordinate their own feelings for the good of the show." His gaze stopped again at Judy, who reddened, and he didn't see the slight tightening around Lisette's mouth. Nick decided it was time to lighten the atmosphere.

"Remember Harmon, Rob?" he asked. "The guy who played your father in that soap?"

Rob abandoned his lesson in theatre ethics and acquiesced with remembered delight. "Oh, God! Old Harmon! Talk about subordinating his own feelings!"

Paul Rigo coughed.

"Le pauvre Monsieur Harmon," continued Rob smoothly. *"Ah! Voici la bonne soupe!"*

Maggie chattered gaily to the stammering waiters as the soup was served, supported occasionally by Rob and Nick and the others who'd studied French. Even Ellen, at Maggie's end of the table, was joining in, encouraged by her roommate's amusement. But when the waiter left it was Grace who said eagerly, *"Et le pauvre Monsieur Harmon?"*

"He was a miser," explained Rob. "And Nick and I were always out of quarters for the soft-drink machines."

"Especially when we discovered his weak point," added Nick.

"And what was that?"

"We'll illustrate. Rob, you play Rob, and I'll play Harmon." Nick's friendly face aged before them, jowls puffing, chin receding. Grace and Ellen laughed in delight. He coughed self-importantly.

"Harmon, old friend," said Rob, eager, wide-eyed, "do you have four quarters for a dollar? I'm all out." He held out a dollar bill hopefully.

"Certainly, my boy." Nick fished carefully into his coin purse and counted out four quarters. He took the bill from Rob and then, methodically, counted the four quarters into Rob's hand. "There you are, son."

"Thanks, Harmon." Rob's hand closed on the quarters and then opened again as, in afterthought, he held them out in plain view to check. "Thanks a *lot!*"

Everyone laughed. There were now five quarters. The old man stared, amazed and horrified.

Rob said, "The only trouble was that our sleight-of-hand was too good; he quit making change for us. We had to go thirsty."

The conversation continued in friendly reminiscence

about shows and people they had known, broken occasionally by French interludes when courses were cleared and brought. The food was much better than Nick had expected to find this far from the city. A college town had its points. Its well-traveled population could appreciate and support a few decent restaurants, while it retained many of the pleasures of the country. And all underlaid by the singing spirit of youth trying out its wings.

And Vietnam, of course, Maggie had said. He looked around the table, at David Wagner next to him, listening attentively to Rob; at Paul Rigo; at quiet, sensitive Jim Greer; at Jason, whose long finger was lazily tracing the drape of Maggie's red sleeve. He wished them well with all his heart. Maggie and Ellen, Judy and Laura too, whose affections were bound up with their classmates and who, he knew from experience, might well suffer even more in the end.

Grace, across the table, was regarding him solemnly, and Nick realized he had not been masking his thoughts. He smiled at her guiltily, and she turned hastily away to talk to Lisette, her hands playing distractedly with Lisette's dessert plate. Rob leaned back in his end seat, eyeing Nick lazily.

"More wine, Uncle?" he asked, smiling.

Nick pushed his glass toward the offered bottle. "Uncle?"

"Uncle Claudius. Also, you were looking very avuncular."

"Felt that way, I guess. I was thinking about the war."

Rob refilled his own glass with a reproachful look at Nick. "That doesn't bear thinking about." Unasked, he refilled David's glass and Grace's, and glanced briefly at Lisette's, full and untouched.

"You know someone over there?" Nick asked sympathetically.

"Drafted last month," said Rob. "Just a kid with a bit part in my last show. It seems so unfair."

"It's really changed life at the university," said Jon Halliday.

"Yes, I'm sure. All the protests."

"There's also the problem of grades," said Grace. "You can't really fail anyone anymore, for fear that your mark is the one that will send him to Vietnam."

"Is there any way to find out?" asked Rob. "I mean, suppose there's some lazy, terrible actor in my class. How do I know if he's on the verge of flunking out, or if he's actually brilliant in everything else and it won't make any difference?"

"Well, that's the problem, you see," said Grace. "You're supposed to stay objective."

"But it's also bad to encourage people who shouldn't be acting," said Nick. "It's a poor enough life when you know you belong. Still, I agree with Rob. I don't want to be the one who sends someone to the front lines."

"At least you don't have to have qualms about flunking women," said Laura bitterly. Nick's mild gaze turned to her.

"Not the same kind. Not qualms about having her sent to war. But there are always other worries with something as amorphous as acting. Are my methods helping or hurting people? I'm a good teacher, but maybe not for every single actor."

"I've been curious about that," said Jon Halliday. Grace's husband was square-shouldered, athletic, with a streak of gray at his temples. "How can you teach acting? I can understand Grace's part of it, because speech comes in units. You can analyze it and describe it. But acting isn't like that, is it?"

"No. It's a tough problem." Nick drank some wine.

"It's a serious question," insisted Jon. "Where do you start?"

"I start with myself. I'm an actor. Well, okay, the Queen of England hasn't knighted me or anything."

"Yet," said Grace. Lisette smiled at her.

"But it's not all self-delusion," Nick continued. "People pay me to do it. This very institution has made me an artist-in-residence. So it's official, we'll assume I'm an actor. Next question: how did I become one?"

"Right," said Jon.

"And I'm afraid the answer is guesswork. We can list the basic equipment. A voice. Two legs, two arms, a head. Hair, as you can see, is not necessary." Rob and Lisette were listening, amused. "What have I done with this equipment? Lots of vocal exercises. Lots of hard physical training. Learning where every little muscle is, what it does, how to control it. Narcissistic hours in front of a mirror. Constant analysis of how I feel, what makes me feel that way, what I do when I feel that way."

"So it is analytical."

"Except that you can't equate an isolated emotion with an isolated set of movements, of course, because feelings don't come isolated, and movements are parts of whole people. But it helps to store up the pieces. And I add in lots of reading, all the plays I can get, and novels and poetry too. Paintings, sculpture, music, dance. Real people, businessmen and lifeguards and old men on park benches. Saving up images, sights and sounds and smells and tastes."

"I see," said Jon.

"All of that is just step one. Piano tuning. Getting the instrument properly adjusted. Making myself into an acting machine."

"And what's step two?"

Nick shrugged. "I don't know. All I can teach is step one."

Rob and Lisette were nodding in agreement. Jon said, "So step two is inspiration, creativity, and so forth. The important things, but you can't teach them."

"Do you know anyone who teaches them, in any field?"

Jon grinned suddenly. "You're right. No one can."

"But I disagree that step one is unimportant. Even Glenn Gould can't do much with an untuned piano. I can help people get the instrument in shape, make sure they know how to play scales, and then if there's art lurking somewhere inside, maybe it'll get out."

"So even our artist-in-residence doesn't know what makes an artist."

"No. But I'm a hell of a good teacher for piano tuners."

Jon nodded, amused. The academician, a bit frightened of the unruliness of artistic creation, rightly suspicious of anyone who claimed to have it under control. Nick had apparently passed his test. "Well, I admire you for trying," Jon said.

Suddenly, Paul Rigo began coughing and sputtering. Ellen, next to him, with admirable coolness patted him on the back. A look of apprehension flashed across Maggie's face before her squared chin rose a fraction and the light of battle filled her eyes. Nick, turning to follow her gaze, found himself face to face with the French chef.

"Bonsoir, messieurs-dames," he said, much too fluently. *"J'espère que vous avez bien dîné."*

"Très, très bien," said Maggie with delight. Was that a kind of relief in her voice? *"Vous avez une vraie table française."*

"Merci, mademoiselle." Why was he flattered? The man was beaming.

"Et vous êtes canadien, n'est-ce pas?" she asked.

So that was it.

"Oui, mademoiselle. Et vous êtes parisienne?"

French Canadian, then; and Maggie able to pass for the real article, though not, to judge from her momentary anxiety, in front of Parisians. What a busy child she was. Nick, amused, drank his wine and beamed at the chef, who returned to his kitchen, basking in Maggie's warm compliments. When he had finally gone she rolled her eyes up.

"Whew!"

Nick grinned at her. "What if he'd been from Paris?"

"Then I'd have been from French Guinea or some such place."

"Well, you've made his day. Did everything but promise him a listing in the *Guide Michelin.*"

"A happier joke than the one we played on poor old Harmon," said Rob; and he and Maggie, a table length apart, exchanged a glance of pleased understanding.

After the first cup of coffee Jon Halliday suggested to Grace that they leave their share of the bill and depart. "Could I get a ride back to campus with you?" asked Laura. In the end the Hallidays took her, David Wagner, and Paul Rigo, who was worried about his physics homework.

The waiter refilled the coffeepot and left it with them, and Maggie poured seconds for everyone remaining. Cheyenne gulped his down, and at Lisette's request passed her cup up for a third refill. Then he stood. "*Blithe Spirit* tech tomorrow," he said. "I'm going. My money is on the tray with the others'."

"We'd better go too," said Ellen sternly to her roommate.

"The evening is still young," protested Rob. "And we have half a bottle of this good wine to finish."

Cheyenne and Ellen were determined, though; and since they had the only cars besides Rob's, it was clear that the party was breaking up. Rob leaned forward from his end of the table, earnestly. "Please," he said. "Take anyone else you want, but leave us Mademoiselle Marguerite, in case that frightening chef returns."

Ellen and Maggie exchanged a glance, and Jason, throwing a fond arm around the cardinal-red shoulders, protested. "How can you desert me, Maggie, when I offer you both my soul and my peerless body?"

"You've been drinking, Jase," said Maggie gently, disengaging the arm and standing up. She smiled at Ellen and said, "Goodbye, eldest oyster." With a despairing shrug, Ellen went out with the others. Maggie brought the coffeepot and her cup to the other end of the table, where she sat in David's vacated place between Rob and Nick.

Rob gave her a slow, appreciative smile and murmured, "A fair hot wench in flame-colored taffeta."

She blinked, then replied coolly, "Merely trying to be of service to the unlettered."

"Tell us, little soubrette, where did all this linguistic skill come from?"

"France, of course."

"At an impressionable age," said Nick.

Her expression did not change. "Yes."

"And do your thoughts and wishes bend again toward France?" asked Rob.

"Often. You've been there too. Don't yours?"

"Occasionally. But when I was there I was too old to be impressionable."

"Silly Rob," said Lisette, yawning. "You're always impressionable. Could I have some more coffee?"

Nick and Rob finished the wine and smoked cigarettes while Maggie had a leisurely cup of coffee and Lisette, apologetically, her fifth. "I don't know why I'm so sleepy," she said. "I guess it was a harder week than I thought."

"There's been some strain," said Nick, thinking of the scorpion. "Well, Rob, ready to go?"

They decided to use the Jenner credit card because O'Connor was too Irish. Rob pocketed the pile of money that the others had left and settled the bill in broken English. Maggie and Lisette went to the rest room while Rob and Nick waited next to the coatroom. Rob held Maggie's coat over his arm, one elegant hand smoothing the soft white fur. He looked very tired.

"Exhausting to be French, isn't it?" said Nick.

"Mmm." Rob didn't raise his eyes. He said, "They're so young."

"Yeah. I was just thinking that today too. It's fun. I haven't felt this alive in years. But they are exhausting, especially Mademoiselle Marguerite."

"Yes. Amusing kid." There was a pause, then Rob said, almost to himself, "I'm thirty-two, Nick."

"Yeah, me too. Age with his stealing steps hath clawed us in his clutch."

Rob didn't smile. The lean hand stroked the fur quietly for a moment. Then he said, "Zetty was an undergraduate when you found her."

Nick was suddenly uneasy. "Yes," he said, then, not sure if it was the right thing to say, he added, "But we'd have fewer problems now if we'd waited a bit."

"You didn't wait then. Would you have waited if you'd been thirty-two?" The blue eyes, burnt with exhaustion and loneliness, suddenly leveled with Nick's.

Nick said forcefully, "Rob, you've been here one week. Fourteen to go. And you've got the whole damn show riding on you. Plus the future of Brian's department."

Suddenly restless, Rob straightened and turned his back to look out the window, the white fur tossed over the shoulder of the camel topcoat, soft blond hair against it. He said, "Nick, I'm a professional too. You know the damn show will be all right. Whatever it takes."

V

Lisette stumbled on the way to the car, and Nick caught her elbow to steady her. Rob had unlocked the back door, and Nick helped her in while Rob let Maggie into the front passenger seat and then went around to the driver's side. There were a few snowflakes blowing in the wind, and his pale hair licked about his forehead like little flames. He sat down, closed the door, and stared at the wheel a minute.

"God," he said. "I'm stoned. A little."

"Do you want someone else to drive?" asked Maggie.

"No. I'll be fine." He raised a dramatic finger and declaimed, "Good wine is a good familiar creature if it be well used."

"Every inordinate cup is unblessed," countered Nick, who had maybe had a drop too much himself.

"I'll be extremely careful," Rob promised. He turned the key and started out of the lot. Lisette lurched against Nick as they rounded the corner onto the highway.

"Are you okay?" he asked.

"Very tired," she said.

Nick tipped her chin up and studied her a minute in the headlights of the car behind them. "You look bad," he said, concerned. He could see her honey-brown eyes in the wavering light. The pupils were tiny. "Do you feel sick?"

"M'all right," she said. The eyes closed. Nick leaned forward.

"Rob, she looks bad. Could we get her to a hospital, do you think?" Maggie turned to look at Lisette.

"She says she's all right," objected Rob. "Are you sick, Lisette?"

She made an effort. "Just tired. Bed."

"I'll just take you home," said Rob soothingly.

"Home," murmured Lisette. Her cheek was cold and damp. Nick felt panic rising.

"Rob, please!" he said.

"Come on, Nick," said Rob. He had stopped at a stoplight, and turned to look back at them, the red glow making his hair shine like embers. "The hospital is miles away, and she says she's just tired. I believe her. I'm tired too."

"Nick's right," said Maggie suddenly. "She's not just tired."

"Jus' tired," repeated Lisette.

"See?" said Rob. "You two alarmists are interfering with her rest."

Maggie leaned across Rob, switched off the ignition with one hand, and opened his door with the other. "Out, Rob," she said.

"What?"

"Out. Get out. Now."

"You're crazy!" He stared at her unbelievingly. The light blinked to green.

"Sorry, kid," she said, leaning back against her door and placing an elegant French boot, still muddy, against his thigh.

"My God! My coat!" Shocked, he flinched away from the boot. She shoved, and he suddenly found himself outside, arms flailing for balance. Maggie slid smoothly into the driver's seat and turned the ignition. The car moved forward and left Rob on the pavement, staggering. When they were clear of him Maggie pulled the door closed and made a rapid U-turn, then pressed the accelerator. The car vaulted up the hill toward the hospital.

By the time they had run their third red light, a patrol car was chasing them. Lisette was slumped against Nick, and he braced himself to keep them both from ricocheting around the back seat as Maggie traced a complex, competent line through the other traffic. He was dimly aware of the flashing lights from behind intersecting the rapid flow of the light from street lamps. She did not slow, and the sirens and lights behind them got other traffic out of the way. When she turned into the hospital driveway the patrol car seemed to relax a little. She skidded to a halt in front of the emergency room and was out opening Nick's door instantly.

"Need help?"

"She's not heavy," he said. Lisette was unconscious.

"I'll follow when I've talked to the officers." She made sure the emergency door was open and then walked toward the patrol car. Nick carried the limp body into the emergency room. She was so pale, almost silvery in the bluish fluorescent lights. Instantly, a nurse and an intern were helping him.

"What is it?"

"Some sort of drug, I think."

"Burning sensations?"

"She didn't mention any. Just passed out."

"You don't know what it was?"

"No idea."

The intern turned to the nurse. "Oxygen. Cyanosis."

They hurried her away. Nick gave his insurance card to the woman at the reception desk and filled out forms. When he had finished he stood, suddenly extraneous, in the glare of the fluorescent bulbs, their artificial cheeriness ghastly in the night.

After a minute or two the cold air swirled through the door and Maggie came in, the white fur fluttering in the gust of wind. A constellation of snowflakes rested a moment in the black curls, then faded in the warmth. The two of them found chairs near the reception desk.

"Some kind of poison? An attack?" she asked.

"Did she take something in the rest room?" Nick felt very tired.

Maggie thought. "No. I'm sure. Maybe food poisoning?"

"The food. Maybe. I didn't think of that."

"You thought she did this herself? On purpose?"

She was very young and quite lovely. "Oh, Christ. It's all so squalid," said Nick. He rubbed his face. Whatever chance Lisette had now, she owed to this youngster. He ought to explain a little. "This is about the umpteenth time Lisette has had an overdose of something. On purpose, yes, most of the time. Not a truly dangerous dose, most of the time. She'll start with bourbon, go on to barbiturates or anything else that's handy. She wants to be rescued. But usually she's depressed, or there's some kind of clue beforehand. That's what I don't understand. She's been happy here, damn it! I was so sure!"

"She seems happy to me," said Maggie. She studied him a moment. "But I don't know her well."

"It's true," he said. "She hasn't been this happy since the first year we were married. I thought maybe, finally, she was finding her way out."

Blue eyes, serious and friendly. Not a child's eyes. "At first she seemed a little tense," she said. "Not at ease with herself, except when she was working."

"Work has always kept her going," he explained. "She's very professional. Until the last show before we came here."

"You mean she was worse then?"

"Started drinking again. But she got herself dried out and decided to get out of New York."

"So coming here has been a sort of therapy?"

"In a way. It was supposed to get her away from the pressures of the city. And we were both happy for a while in college. We were married there, you know. A while ago. 1960."

"You were undergraduates?"

"She was. I was an instructor, a two-year job I had while I was writing my master's thesis. It was a little place, Wilson College. We were the big frogs in a tiny pond. She was a freshman, but very good. We played a lot of leads. Eliza and Higgins. Antigone and Creon. It wasn't a very big department."

"Also you're damn good."

"That too." He grinned at her. He was beginning to feel a little hopeful about Lisette again. She really was happier now, he was sure. This must have been some sort of accident. "Anyway, I think she's enjoying it here. Enjoying her work and the whole atmosphere. I know I am."

"It's a good place," said Maggie. "In touch, but sheltered from the most horrible things, most of the time. Ivory tower. Like a lot of colleges."

"Yes. But still vital. I love it, I'd forgotten how much. And I think Lisette does too, even though she ended up having a rotten time in college."

"How do you mean?"

"My bright idea," he said bitterly. "Assuming that at twenty or so we were adult and unchangeable, and could casually take a couple of years out of our lives without altering anything. I finished my master's degree, you see. We'd been married ten months but she still had two years to go. We'd been very happy that year." Merrily, merrily shall I live now, under the blossom that hangs on the bough.

"Mm-hmm."

"And then I got the bright idea that everything would come out even if I got my military service out of the way while she finished school. Then we'd both go to New York and become rich and famous." He felt again the familiar twist of anger at that stupid blind youth, himself, who had ruined Lisette's life and his own.

"You enlisted?"

Nick caught the shadow of reproach in her voice. "I owed them for my education," he explained. "Anyway, this was before Vietnam. We were still the good guys. Kennedy was president. Since I knew some German, they sent me to Berlin. They had just built the Wall."

"I see."

"I grew up a lot. That one night . . ." He rubbed his eyes. He hadn't spoken of it for years. That stupid blind kid had paid for his sins in many ways. "There was an East German boy. Must have been in his teens. We were sitting there at the checkpoint, drinking coffee. I was off-duty actually, just saying good night to a buddy. Then there was shouting and we looked out and the kid was scrambling across the no-man's land toward us. And they spotlighted him and they machine-gunned him. Halfway across. And we stood there with our big guns and did nothing. Nothing. We were forbidden to shoot. Defenders of freedom. The kid lay there and bled to death and we couldn't do a thing."

"Christ."

"Except I got sick. A useful contribution to the cause of freedom." He rubbed his hand through his thin hair. With rainy eyes, write sorrow on the bosom of the earth. He looked at her sideways. "Ich bin ein Berliner," he said mockingly.

She shook her head. The young wise eyes were sad.

"I'm babbling," Nick observed. "Sorry to be so tiresome."

"Oh, lump that," she said tartly. "You're a pro, you know when your audience is hanging on every word."

"Okay." He smiled. "I'll admit that my shameful life is fascinating. Like a toad. No more false modesty. I promise."

"Done!" She extended a lean young hand and they shook solemnly. He noted the firm clasp and the thickened skin of the palms. A gymnast. He smiled again.

"What's so funny?"

"I don't know. You make me dredge up one of the worst experiences of my life, and I feel better."

"The talking cure."

"Dear old Freud."

"We can leave him out of it. But I would like to hear about Lisette."

Serious again, he tilted back his little chair. "Okay. Well, eventually I came home, the Army having made a man of me and all that. And after a week or so it gradually dawned on me that all hell had broken loose in Lisette's life too. And I think she tried to hide it. I know at least that there weren't any hints in her letters, because I reread them later."

"What happened?"

"What didn't? Alcohol. Drugs. Her senior year she was even dealing in a small way. I came back expecting to be comforted and coddled. All-American G.I. returning to his all-American wife. And here was Lisette with a police record, for possession only, thank God. She was a psychological wreck. She hadn't done any acting for a year and was on the verge of flunking out of college."

"God! What had happened to her?"

He spoke from the shadows of the past. "It was a wrench for her when I left. Her own dad had run off, and she felt echoes. From being the college queen, she suddenly found herself without much in common with the other students. There she was, a junior, and an old married lady who didn't date or do much of anything, in a college that had very few married students. Apparently there was some resentment among the theatre students because she had been getting so many leads. The directors explained to her that they wouldn't be casting her so often, because others needed a chance too." He shrugged. "But I think they were worried already about her drinking. Didn't want to expose the other undergraduates to a hard-drinking experienced married woman. It was rough. God, she was just a junior."

He caught the twinkle of amusement in the blue eyes and said defensively, "This was the early sixties, Maggie, when juniors were still juniors instead of hardbitten citizens of the world."

"Flatterer. Anyway, some of us were born hardbitten."

"Not back then."

"Maybe not." She became serious again. "She's not drinking or doing drugs now."

"No. But it's been up and down for years. And I still haven't told you the worst of it."

"There's more?"

"Apparently it happened late in her senior year, just before I got back, when she was starting to deal. Just in the dorms. She'd actually been cast in a play, and one of the smaller parts had gone to a freshman girl. Jennifer. I don't know exactly how it happened, but Lisette apparently gave her a small sample one night, heroin, and the next day Jennifer was found dead in her dorm room. OD. Quite a dose—she must have had other sources. Lisette was questioned and cleared, along with a lot of others. But somehow she convinced herself that her little sample was what killed Jennifer. The police said the kid had been shooting up for months. But it completely shattered Lisette. She's never forgiven herself. In the first shock of it she managed to quit dealing, at least, and got a job in a bar, because she still had to support her own habit." He swallowed, ashamed. "She didn't want me to know about it."

He remembered the night, a week or so after he had come home. Waking, he'd found her side of the bed empty, and soft noises coming from the living room. Puzzled and helpless, he had found her on the sofa, crumpled like a trampled flower. At the hospital they'd said it was an overdose. He couldn't understand at first; he just sat by her bed, bewildered. Big muscles, big brain—so what? He was helpless to protect her from the horror inside. Canst thou not minister to a mind diseased, pluck from the memory a rooted sorrow. Finally he had understood a word that she repeated in her delirium: Jennifer. Later, he had asked, "Who's Jennifer?" Lisette had been reluctant, but bits of the story had slowly come out.

"So there you have it, Nicky," she had said sadly. "A junkie and a murderer. Welcome home."

A light hand touched his shoulder. "It must have been bad," said Maggie's voice softly.

"Yeah." He opened his eyes again to the glare of the fluorescent light. "Yeah, it was." He looked down at his boots, the leather splashed with little runnels of cindered mud. "You see, somehow it was like that kid from East Berlin." He was explaining to himself as much as to her. "I just stood by and didn't help when she needed it most. If only I had been there."

"You've been there ever since."

"Yes, and it helps her, I think. I worried for a while that maybe it was bad for me to hang around, reminding her of things. But the worst happened when I wasn't there, and I think a lot of times I've been able to help pull her back. Maybe. She's trying to make a new start."

"She's a lucky woman."

He looked at her, astonished. "What do you mean?"

"A lot of people don't even get a second chance. You've given her a third, and a fourth . . ."

"But it has to be her decision. Oh, I tried the other way at the beginning. Don't worry, dear, big strong hubby will do all your thinking and feeling for you. A counselor finally straightened me out after her third suicide attempt. She's doing better on her own."

"Still, you're there when she needs you. She's lucky."

"I guess what I want you to understand is that for me it's not martyrdom or anything. Of course I'd rather have her healthy, but even at her worst somehow, the sordidness doesn't touch her." He shook his head. "I'm not making myself very clear."

But apparently he was, because after a moment she quoted, "Thought and affliction, passion, hell itself, she turns to favour and to prettiness."

He gave her a quick grateful glance and nodded. Then, like a blow, the anxiety returned, and he looked across at the desk and at the door where Lisette had disappeared.

"Maybe you should ask," she suggested.

He went over to the desk, but the nurse there had not heard anything. Nick returned to his chair. He looked down at Maggie, a little surprised at himself.

"That was all in confidence," he said. None of their friends knew, only the counselors. Lisette never mentioned it now. He felt faintly traitorous. Nick the blabbermouth.

"I know. I'm not that callow. I can keep a secret."

He nodded, convinced that he could trust her, and changed the subject. "Rob and I were wondering if you acted."

She laughed. "I clown around. I can't honestly say I've ever acted. Watching you people work has been a revelation."

"Of what?"

"Of the amount of work and commitment it takes to be an artist. Even if you have the basic talent."

"You must have known that before."

"Well, I was beyond the stage of exclaiming, 'Oh, my, I wonder how they remember all those lines!' " Nick laughed. "But you see, I'd never seen professionals work. Cheyenne is the only professional we have here, I realize now. Even Brian is forced to work in an amateur way because he's dealing with students."

"He does pretty well."

"Yes, I think he manages to give us a glimmering of the real thing. But in the end, our first duty is to stay in school, and he checks on us. Won't cast people in academic trouble. It's the only thing he and Cheyenne disagree about. He hates to—"

"Mr. O'Connor?" The nurse broke in crisply.

"Yes?" He jumped up.

"Doctor wants to see you. Through here."

He hurried after her, anxious again. She led him into a big room partitioned into curtained cubicles. In one of them Lisette lay drowsy but awake. Sick with relief, he seized her frail hand and kissed it, bending over her. Her tired eyes smiled at him.

"Mr. O'Connor."

"Yes?" He straightened and turned to face an intern.

"She should be all right now. We've performed a gastric lavage and given her oxygen and a little Metrazol. If she takes it easy she'll be bouncing around again in a day or two. May still have some headache or dizziness tomorrow. I'd like to observe her another hour here just in case, and I think we should make sure she doesn't go to sleep for a while, but you can take her home soon. Give her lots of coffee. It's lucky she'd already had so much."

"That's great, Doctor."

"Mrs. O'Connor wasn't able to tell me how she came to ingest the barbiturates. Do you have any recollection?"

"No. We had dinner at Chez Pierre. As far as I know, none of the rest of us feel sick."

"It wasn't food poisoning. It was barbiturates. Although it could have been added to something she ate or drank."

"That's very strange."

"Would there be a practical joker among your party?"

Nick remembered the scorpion. And in fact, the whole dinner had been a practical joke, hadn't it? But surely no one would knowingly endanger a life.

"I'll ask around," he said.

"I'll try to remember too." Lisette's voice was weak but clear now, and anxious. "I didn't take anything, Nicky."

He believed her. "I know," he said. "We'll figure out what happened. He says you'll be good as new before long."

She relaxed a little. "Okay. As long as you know."

"Doctor, can I stay with her here until she can go?"

"Yes, we'll want to make sure she stays awake."

"How about our friend who's waiting for us?"

"Only one of you back here at a time. It's the policy."

"Yes. I see. Lisette, look"—he turned back to her—"let me run out to tell Maggie what's happening. She may want to go home. I'll be right back."

"Okay, Nicky." She gave him a pallid smile. He squeezed her hand before hurrying out.

Rob was there. Maggie, standing next to him in the red dress and boots, was smiling a little. He looked contrite, the thick blond hair tumbling over his forehead, pale in the cold light. He turned to Nick eagerly. "Nick! God, how is she?"

"She'll manage now. They've pumped her out and given her some sort of stimulant. She may be able to leave in an hour."

"Thank God!"

"What was it?" asked Maggie.

"Barbiturates."

"Oh, God!" said Rob. "Did I ever blow it! Will you people ever forgive me?"

"Never," said Maggie cheerfully.

He looked at her in mock scorn. "Then we're even, because I'll never forgive you for trampling my best coat." She smiled.

"How did you get here?" asked Nick.

"Taxi. Standing in the middle of the traffic down there sobered me up a little. I thought I'd better come rescue my car from this mad maiden."

"Oh, you're welcome to it," said Maggie. "The suspension is going and the points need cleaning."

"Insult to injury. Nick, I'm really glad she's okay."

"Yes. She's looking a lot better." Nick saw that Maggie was carefully not asking, and added, "Apparently someone added them to her food. Maybe a practical joke. She knew nothing about it."

"A joke?" said Rob unbelievingly.

"We can't figure out how it happened," said Nick. "Look, I'm going back to stay with her till they let her go."

"Can we see her too?"

"No. They think it will get too crowded or something. But you two should go on home. We can get a taxi later."

"No, no," said Rob. "We'll get you back home." He looked at Maggie. "Unless you want to leave now?"

"No, I'll stick around."

"Okay, thanks," said Nick. As he went back through the double doors he heard Rob say something, and Maggie's answering murmur. He found his way back to Lisette's cubicle, where she was sitting up on the bed, trying to stay awake. She smiled and said hi, and he stroked her cool forehead and felt very alone.

When they took her home, Nick had to help her up the stairs, because she was still dizzy and exhausted. Maggie and Rob went ahead with the keys to open the door and turn on the lights. Nick was subletting the apartment from an anthropology professor, now in Kenya, who had decorated the walls with handsome African masks that leered at Nick as he settled Lisette on the sofa.

"How are you feeling?" Maggie asked her.

"Headachy, but a lot better. Except that about now I'm naturally sleepy too."

"We'll stay awake a little while longer, though," said Nick. He sat down on the arm of the sofa and put his hand on Lisette's thin shoulder. "Maggie, just saying thank you is completely inadequate. I wish I could repay you somehow."

"Same here," said Lisette, pale and sincere.

"As the obstacle which, overcome, helps make all this gratitude possible," intoned Rob grandly, "may I suggest that our Miss Ryan will be covered in glory for this exploit, and that we can all help her toward her goal of becoming a legend in our time?"

"How you tempt me!" Diverted, Maggie smiled at him, that wide flashing smile, and mimicked his pompous style. "A brilliant analysis of my character and motives. Why waste time studying math when instant fame is available by simply commandeering the visiting luminary's car?"

Lisette was smiling at Rob too. "That's the worst thing about the whole experience," she said lightly. "I was too zonked to see you get kicked out."

"Another great moment in the history of Hargate," said Maggie. "But actually I think we'd better say nothing at all."

"Come, Maggie," chided Rob. "Whatever your other virtues, you'll never convince me that modesty is among them."

But Nick had caught the seriousness behind her words. He didn't often need a cigarette, but now he was grateful for the one Rob offered him. "Because of that sandbag?" he asked.

She nodded. "Maybe that was an accident. Probably it was. But . . ." She paused. Nick had reached for his topcoat, pulled out the photograph.

"Sorry, Blossom," he said, unfolding it apologetically.

"Oh, God," said Lisette. She looked away.

"Christ! What kind of a sick mind are we dealing with?" flared Rob.

"Where was it?" demanded Maggie.

"It was pinned into her coat at the dean's party. A nasty joke. And anyone could have done it."

"I've been thinking about dinner, and anyone could

have done that too," said Rob. "We passed around bread, salad dressings."

"And coffee," said Maggie.

"Several times," said Lisette ruefully. "A lot of people handled my cup."

"But why?" said Rob. "Who would want to do these things?"

Nick's fingers played with Lisette's soft curls, mussed now. "Rob, did Brian tell you about the problem getting Lisette here?"

"No, not really. He just explained calmly that the original plan he outlined to me had been changed wh he found a good Ophelia. But the minute I arrived I started picking up the message from Judy Allison and Laura Eisner and a lot of others. The decision wasn't popular here."

"It was damn ugly," said Maggie. "Everyone felt betrayed. Even Grace almost refused to help do it. Cheyenne defused some of us technical people, saying that sacrifices always have to be made to get a good show. But the acting students are still upset. If Brian hadn't started out with so much good will, he would have had a walkout on his hands."

"You mean people would sympathize with these jokes, if they knew about them?" asked Nick.

"The scorpion, maybe. Not doping her food. Probably it was just to make her look drunk and silly, and people might sympathize with the feelings that inspired it, but it was dangerous. They'd be horrified. And everyone would be watching everyone else, and the most casual actions would begin to look suspicious."

"Yes, we have to think about the show," said Lisette. "I thought we'd built up a little trust this week."

"I think so too," said Nick. "Things are tense, but improving. And there's another thing. This little scorpion is nasty, but harmless. I can't reconcile it with an attempt to do real harm. The overdose must have been a slipup, an accident, really meant to get her embarrassingly woozy."

Rob asked, "What about the sandbag?"

"Yeah." Maggie looked unhappy. "I was thinking about that too. But Paul and Cheyenne are sure it was the *Blithe Spirit* people, just an accident. Another accident." She shrugged. "Lisette, you should decide. You're the one being threatened. If you think publicizing it is the way to make it stop, it's your choice."

"I'm not the only one," observed Lisette. "You've risked your life twice to help me out."

There was a brief pause. Then Rob said, "I think you're right. It's probably a string of ugly, thoughtless jokes. And the worst punishment we could inflict on the joker would be to pretend nothing happened."

"Worst for the joker, and best for the innocents," said Nick.

"Let's try it, then," said Lisette.

"Can you manage?" asked Maggie. "Because it looks as though you're under siege."

Lisette smiled. "A melodrama!" she exclaimed. "What dread affliction will strike our heroine next?"

Nick took her hand. "We'll watch your food and where you walk," he promised. He was angry at himself for taking the scorpion so lightly. Still, the danger to Lisette must have been a mistake; shock, unpleasantness, embarrassment had been the goals of the joker.

"Monday night we do the nunnery scene," said Lisette. "The headache should be better by then. I'll try to look normal."

"Okay. We're sworn to secrecy, then," said Nick. "But we four should keep our eyes open. I'd love to get my hands on whoever it is."

"I pity him if you do," said Rob, stubbing out his cigarette. "Well, O'Connors, we'd better go. I'm going to take our mute inglorious Maggie home to blush unseen. Then I'm going to New York."

"At this hour?" Lisette was startled. "That's three or four hours, Rob!"

"Well, there are some people I want to see tomorrow. I'll be back in time for Monday's classes."

"Okay, we'll make your excuses if anyone cares," said Nick, and then wished he hadn't. There was a flicker of pain before Rob's smile came.

"A poor, infirm, weak, and despised old man," he quoted in a quavery voice. "But the city will rejuvenate."

Nick gave him a friendly thump on the shoulder and watched them go down the stairs, two handsome people, blond hair, black curls, white fur. Then he closed the door and turned back to his own handsome pale person. "We'll find out who's behind this," he said with determination. "But now it's time for some more coffee. Come help me fix it."

VI

The rehearsal Monday was in two sections. At seven-thirty, Brian had scheduled some of the Ophelia scenes; at eight-thirty, the first rehearsal of the full-cast court scenes. Cheyenne had finished the model of the *Hamlet* set, and because the dress rehearsals of *Blithe Spirit* were running smoothly, he planned to take time out to demonstrate the model to the *Hamlet* cast.

Ellen, sitting next to Judy taking notes on the scenes, was not surprised that people came early. There was a lot of curiosity about the professional actors, and for many, this was the first excuse to see them working. By a few minutes after eight the majority of the cast, and many of the crew members, were crowded into the rehearsal room watching. The room was not much larger than the stage, and the dimensions of the set that Ellen had taped onto the wooden floor left only a few feet along the front and sides for spectators. Rob and Nick had been sitting behind Ellen; when Cheyenne came in with his bulky model, they stood up so that he could set it on their chairs, and the three leaned against the wall behind. The few seats had filled rapidly. People now stood along the wall or sat on the floor in front of the chairs. A couple of staging crew members, enthusiastic freshman girls, pushed up against Ellen's feet. Brian and the actors, professionally oblivious to the shuffling crowd, continued.

"Okay, let's do that again," said Brian. "David, clarity. This is Shakespeare. Okay, from the top."

Lisette, in jeans and sweater, hair braided into a no-nonsense plait down her back, joined David and one of the bit players in the imagined wings. Judy read out the cue:

"Foul deeds will rise,/Though all the earth o'erwhelm them, to men's eyes. Lights."

The bit player, struggling with imagined bundles, crossed the stage, David and Lisette following to center stage. "My necessaries are embarked. Farewell," read David, book in hand, and turned to Lisette. They looked like brother and sister, thought Ellen, his gentle good looks a lithe brown masculine version of her feminine perfection. He began to warn her not to take Hamlet's advances too seriously. David was working hard on pronunciation, and Ellen thought he sounded better than he had the first time through. What interested her, though, was Lisette; with only two lines, Lisette had to establish the character through her reactions to Laertes' long speech, and Ellen was fascinated to see an intelligent, ambitious young woman with a questing mind emerge from the unpromising interaction. At last Chester Morgan, a proud, pleasant father, came on and gave Laertes his too-lengthy parting advice, then suggested that Ophelia should test Hamlet by refusing further communication. Ellen was again impressed by the fresh, lively intellect of this Ophelia; her agreement was not submission, it was informed consent. The scene ended and Brian said, "Great! We're getting there. Chester, hit the part about honor a bit more. The fatherly love is fine. Good-looking family, don't you think, people?"

"Right," said Rob fervently, and others agreed.

"One thing, Chester. Remember that Ophelia's political value is in her reputation. You're really telling her the same thing you told Laertes. Telling her how to gain power and respect in the world."

"Okay," said Chester. "Am I concerned with her happiness?"

"Well, yes . . ." Brian frowned.

"Happiness would automatically come from honor, wouldn't it?" said Lisette. "Happiness and reputation wouldn't really be separate questions for him."

"That's right," said Brian. "Ophelia, you're projecting that. You like Hamlet's company and you encouraged him, believing in his honorable intentions. Now Laertes and your father give you second thoughts. You're going to run a little test now, to see if he really is as honorable as you thought."

"Yes," said Lisette. "On some level she probably wants very much to pop into bed with Hamlet, but at this point she simply wouldn't consider it."

"God, I would," muttered one of the staging crew girls at Ellen's feet. Ellen kicked her. The girl, turning to protest, saw how near Rob was behind her and turned away again, ears reddening.

"Any more questions on that scene?" asked Brian. "By the way, David, it's sounding much better, but we can't do much more until the language is automatic."

"I know. I'll work on it."

"Fine. On to the nunnery, people."

Rob and Nick joined Chester Morgan and Lisette in the taped stage area. Ellen stood up to stretch and look around. Maggie was leaning against the wall near the door now, and flapped an angular hand in greeting across the crowded room.

"Ellen," said Nick, puzzled, "I'm lost. Which line is the curtain we hide behind?"

Ellen stepped over the seated stagehands into the stage area. "Okay. In this scene you'll be behind the right curtain, just in front of the platform edge. This blue tape marks the edge." She indicated one of the lines in the maze of tape on the floor.

"Okey-doke," said Chester. He and Nick took their positions.

"Start with Ophelia's entrance," said Brian.

Ellen sat down again. Lisette waited upstage, behind the imagined back platform. Rob ran a hand through his blond hair and moved to a position downstage left. He looked tired today, thought Ellen. Maggie had said he had gone to New York Saturday night, after the French dinner. Actors' lives were hectic. She was well rid of Jim. She really was.

"To be or not to be, blah blah blah," said Rob. "With this regard their currents turn awry,/And lose the name of action." And, as Lisette came around the pretended barrier, "Soft you now! The fair Ophelia!—Nymph, in thy orisons /Be all my sins remembered."

"Good my lord,/How does your honor for this many a day?" She was cautious, testing. And Rob, love and doubt warring in his transparent face, took a hopeful step toward her.

"I humbly thank you; well, well, well."

Ophelia took courage; he was not the wild creature who had visited her in her sewing room. She said, "My lord, I have remembrances of yours /That I have longed long to redeliver./I pray you, now receive them."

"No, not I!" Hurt, unhappy, Hamlet turned his back to her. "I never gave you aught."

"My honored lord, you know right well you did," said Ophelia, delighted with the effect her little test was having. This must be love after all. "Take these again; for to the noble mind /Rich gifts wax poor when givers prove unkind." She thrust the rich gifts, played by Brian's car keys, at Hamlet's hand. Looking back at her sorrowfully over his shoulder, he saw Chester move behind the imagined curtain.

"Ha, ha!" he exclaimed, enlightened, letting the keys fall to the ground as he stepped toward the curtain, then, checking himself, back to Ophelia. "Are you honest?" he demanded.

And suddenly, the dynamic had changed. With Hamlet's discovery of the hidden listeners, Rob was now playing his speeches on two levels—the lover attempting to probe his beloved's true feelings, interpreting her words in the light of the eavesdroppers, and now also trying to fake madness for the hidden listeners. "I loved you not," he concluded.

"I was the more deceived." Dignified sorrow; she looked so beautiful. Hamlet responded, a quickly checked movement toward her, followed by frustration—if she loved him, why did she consent to this charade?

He shouted, "Get thee to a nunnery!" But his vehemence frightened her, and seeing it, he brought himself under control and continued gently, "I am myself indifferent honest, but yet I could accuse me of such things that it were better my mother had not borne me." It was a confession, skating near the edge of sane speech despite the listeners. Young, yearning, Hamlet was trying to communicate with the woman he loved, trying to reach her despite his knowledge that she was involved in this trick, trying to use words she would understand and the listeners would not. But she was upset; fright was stronger than love. She stepped back instinctively toward the two hiding behind the curtain. Despairing again, almost tearful, Hamlet made a last desperate appeal, glancing at the curtain and back to her. "We are arrant knaves all; believe none of us. Go thy ways to a nunnery. *Where's your father?*"

The question hung, electric, between them. Ophelia's last chance.

The coughs and shuffles in the room had stopped, and people waited, breathless, for her answer, as though they did not know it. Hamlet, immensely vulnerable, the yearning gaze more eloquent than the words he had had to edit so carefully, pulled her one way. The weight of her own upbringing and ambitions, and the knowledge of the two men hiding behind her, pulled her the other way. The slim body leaned fractionally toward Hamlet; then the eyes fell and the reluctant decision was taken. She faltered, unconvincingly, "At home, my lord," and backed away from him.

Defeated. He started away in despair, his free hand moving in reflex to his dagger. Already repentant, Ophelia clasped her hands. "O help him, you sweet heavens!"

And Hamlet, doubly betrayed at this demonstration of her real feeling for him, whirled, cursing her, and threw her to her knees. "I say, we will have no more marriages! Those that are married already—all but one—shall live; the rest shall keep as they are. To a nunnery, go!" He ran off.

"Oh, what a noble mind is here o'erthrown!" Mourning, on her knees still, Ophelia spoke her speech despondently; the intelligent, loving Ophelia, caught by forces she could not understand, knowing only that something of evil and great power had come between her and the love she knew Hamlet still felt.

The King and Polonius came out. "Love? His affections do not that way tend," said the King brusquely, and then explained his plan to send Hamlet to England. "Madness in great ones must not unwatched go," concluded Nick; and the scene was over.

There was spontaneous applause, and Ellen joined in. Laura, she saw, looked sullen, but Judy, tears sliding silently down her cheek, was applauding too. Ellen felt very sad for them. Lisette had won. There was no longer any doubt that Brian had judged correctly. Lisette was unquestionably the Ophelia for this production—the right sister for this Laertes, the right beloved for this Hamlet, the right young woman for this Court of Denmark. Even Cheyenne was gazing at her with an odd half-smile of cynical admiration.

"Fine. Really fine," enthused Brian. "A lot of rough spots, but the general direction is excellent."

"I have a problem," said Lisette, still kneeling in her place on the floor.

"Okay."

"Well, Rob is too sweet." She smiled at him across the stage. "I just think Ophelia would find him irresistible. She'd be ready to betray her father."

"I thought you would for a minute there too," said Brian. "But that's good. It's exciting."

"But I need a reason to change my mind."

Rob said, "Zetty, he's right. I thought you were going to holler 'Look out, Dad's behind the curtain!' and we'd live happily ever after." Brian chuckled, and Rob continued, "There was another place I didn't quite believe you, in your last speech. That stuff about my noble and most sovereign reason being jangled. Do you really think I'm mad?"

"No," said Lisette, reflecting. "I know you. I think I'm bright enough to realize that you're onto the eavesdroppers."

Brian said, "It would solve the immediate problem if you believed he was mad."

Lisette frowned. "But I don't think she would. Not completely. Hamlet's behavior upsets her, yes, but I think she senses that bigger things are going on. Outside the rules she knows."

"Right," said Brian. "I don't want to change your reading of 'Where's your father?' 'At home, my lord.' But if you could be uncertain, have a doubt cross your mind, it might help. Or what if we have Hamlet get impatient and get angry a little earlier?"

"But I'm not angry earlier, I'm devastated," objected Rob.

Lisette smiled. "I'll try the passing doubt. You can stay devastated."

"Many thanks," said Rob. "Something else. I also didn't believe Nick when he came out and told Polonius that Hamlet wasn't in love with Ophelia."

"Good," said Nick.

"Good?" asked Brian. "I mean, Rob's right. I believed

that you wanted to send him to England, but not that Hamlet had tricked you into thinking he didn't love Ophelia."

"Well, we haven't talked about this yet. But I think Claudius is perfectly aware of what went on. Any ninny could see that Hamlet loves her. Claudius also sees that Hamlet is only pretending to be mad, and that it's dangerous to his own skin."

"I see."

"So Claudius rejects Polonius's theory that the madness could be cured by marriage to Ophelia, because he needs an excuse to send Hamlet away."

"God," said Rob, "the O'Connors play such intelligent characters. This will be the highest-IQ *Hamlet* ever done."

"It's in the lines," said Nick.

"Yeah, but so are a lot of stupid Claudiuses. My poor little Hamlet won't have a chance."

"You were expecting to win this time?"

Brian laughed. "Okay. Any other problems?"

There was a brief silence, then Ellen said, "Excuse me for bringing up these mundane nonintellectual matters, but Hamlet and Ophelia dropped Hamlet's gifts downstage left, and nobody ever picked them up."

"Oh, hell." Brian glared at the offending car keys.

"I could pick them up on my way out," offered Chester. "Polonius would be interested in the gifts."

"Yes," said Brian, "but somehow I feel that Ophelia, as we're playing her here, ought to take them back. A concrete reminder that she was not imagining things."

"That's right," said Lisette. "She would do that."

Nick said, "How about the line in your last speech, about the 'honey of his music vows'?"

"Yes. If I were closer, I could pick them up then."

Brian frowned. "You're stage left then, but too far back."

"Why don't I just throw her further downstage?" suggested Rob. "While I'm cursing her."

"Hamlet, sadist of Denmark," said Lisette, smiling at him angelically. He gave her a sour look.

"Let's try that," said Brian. "We don't have time to run it again now, but next time we'll see if it works. It might even improve the picture at the end, with Ophelia on her knees mourning downstage left, and the two politicians plotting upstage right." He looked at his actors with satisfaction. "It's really coming along well, people. Keep it up."

Cheyenne had pulled a rehearsal table to the middle of the room and put the model of the set on it. Brian said, "Gather round, now. Here's how it works."

Cheyenne's design consisted of a permanent platform running across the back of the stage and some movable wagon platforms that could be pushed in at an angle from the sides. All three platforms were to be fitted with sets of rods so that curtains could be run either behind the platforms, allowing use of the platform level, or in front of the platforms, reducing the size of the playing area. The result was a wide visual variety. The most restricted scene, in the Queen's chamber, had both side wagons pushed in and the front curtains closed on all units, making a cozy tapestried room; the most open scene, a field, had only the bare arches of the back unit silhouetted against the great expanse of the sky cyclorama. The other scenes, including the ones they had just rehearsed, were made up of different arrangements of the platforms and curtains.

The only other unit was an immense castle wall on a wagon that rolled out across the front of the stage for the rampart scenes at the beginning. "How are we going to move that monster?" asked Ellen.

"Three or four guys can do it," said Cheyenne curtly. He seemed even less sociable than usual tonight.

"God, do I have to act up on that thing?" asked Jason, dismayed. "I'll freeze in terror and forget my lines."

"Ellen, here's your chance!" said Maggie. "Put on the flying harness and prompt him from up there." Ellen made a face at her.

"Anyway, you've got it easy," Rob informed Jason. "You just stalk around majestically. Jim and I have to come running and jumping after you up there."

"You won't be wearing armor," muttered Jason darkly. "Hey, Maggie!" He caught her hand. "You like heights. Want to be my stuntman? All you have to do is walk around in armor on rolling planks thousands of feet above terra firma."

"Jase, you have the soul of an insurance agent," said Maggie fondly.

He grinned at her. "Yeah. Well, wait and see the headlines. "Unfortunate Grad Tumbles to Death! Another First for Hargate! Ghost Played by Actual Ghost!' "

Brian, grinning too, said, "Shut up, Jase, or we'll fly you in like the *Blithe Spirit* ghosts. Ellen, could you and Paul run through the scenes so we'll have an idea of how it's going to look?"

They began, pushing the wagons in and out, and adding and subtracting the curtains and steps needed for each scene. Paul explained, "The curtains are plain in the model, just showing the basic color. The real ones will be painted to look like tapestries."

"Great!" said Rob approvingly.

Paul grinned. "That's easy for you to say. You won't have to paint them."

It was fascinating to see, in miniature, the changes in the space. Even Brian, who had spent hours with Cheyenne working out details, stared intently as the little scenes changed. Finally Ellen and Paul pushed the wagons into place for the final scene in the great hall, back curtains closed and front ones opened so that the platforms could be used as acting areas.

Nick said, "Question on this scene. The costume sketches show reds for Claudius and his men, blue for Fortinbras. But the curtains here are still red. Is there any way we could change that, or at least tone it down by the time Fortinbras comes?"

"Mmm," said Brian. "I see what you mean. The new order shouldn't look just like the old. The red curtains make a stronger statement than I envisioned. Could we dim the lights on them?"

"You've got the King and Queen both dying up on that level," said Maggie. "It'll be hard to light them adequately without some spill on the curtains. See, we have to throw from a front angle, or we get shadows from the arches."

"Yeah, we do need light for those death scenes."

"I could fade it down after they die. But, I don't know, I like the idea of light on Claudius all the way to the end."

"Nick won't object to that," said Rob.

Brian was using a pencil to estimate the direction of a beam of light from various positions. "How about from here?" he asked. "High on the side, in front?"

"That pipe is pretty crowded already," said Maggie. "Cheyenne, could we go any higher there?"

Cheyenne shook his head. "Fire detectors."

"Oh, right." Maggie explained, "We'll have to figure out something else, Brian. One of those big hot instruments could trigger the sprinkler system."

"Hey, terrific symbolism!" enthused Rob. "I stab the King, and the heavens open! Divine intervention!"

"Après moi, le déluge," declaimed Nick.

"Well, we'll think of something," said Brian, grinning. "But right now, let's get back to work. First court scene."

As usual, a few people lingered after rehearsal to talk to Brian. Rob waited until a couple of students in the Players' troupe finished their questions, then said, "Brian, I'd like to ask an important favor."

"Sure. What is it?" The two men faced each other in the middle of the imaginary stage.

"I'd like to switch the Saturday rehearsals to the morning."

"That's a real problem, Rob." Brian frowned, sympathetic but unwilling. "Some people have Saturday morning classes. And we've all planned our lives the other way."

"I know it's inconvenient. But the afternoon rehearsals turn out to be a major problem."

Ellen saw that Nick, halfway into his storm coat, had paused to listen to them.

"This is the way we outlined it to you to begin with," said Brian.

"I know that, Brian. But I still want to change."

"Damn it, Rob!" Brian couldn't understand his stubbornness. "Look at the whole picture! We can't rehearse in this room Saturday morning, there's a class in here at ten. It would really be difficult to change everything now. You knew what you were getting into. We spelled it all out."

"Things have come up," said Rob. He was calm, but coldly determined. Ellen's stomach knotted. Then Nick joined in.

"Brian, I know it'll be a big adjustment, but Rob is right," he said. "It would be a lot easier on Lisette and me too, and probably Chester, if we could shift the schedule just that little bit."

"It's not just a little bit, Nick," said Brian. "It's a major upheaval. We'll have to rework the whole rehearsal schedule because of people with Saturday classes. We'll have to locate a new room. We'll have to reorganize everything in a way I just don't have time for now."

"We have a real problem too, though," Nick said quietly. "I'm enjoying everything we're doing here. But we have to think ahead, keep up our New York City contacts. It's almost pointless to drive into the city Saturday night and spend just Sunday there. Part of Sunday."

"Nobody's even awake on Sundays," said Rob.

"Right," said Nick. "But if we can get there by dinnertime Saturday, we'll be able to catch most of the people we need to see. It's important, Brian."

"I see that, Nick." Brian, outnumbered, was not giving in. "But you did agree. And it's too damn inconvenient to change now."

Nick was sympathetic. "I know it is," he said. "And you're probably doing something important yourself on Saturday mornings."

Brian almost didn't answer, but Nick was friendly, and he finally gave a rather sheepish shrug. "It's my son," he said. "Gary. I take him skating. He's in school now, and with these rehearsals every night, it's the only time I see him all week."

"I'm sorry, Brian." Nick glanced quickly at Rob, who was looking unhappily at the floor, then went on. "I know that's important. But we have to worry about our contacts in the city."

"It's our careers," said Rob. "I'm not trying to hurt anyone's son."

"Oh, I understand that," said Brian. "But . . ."

"We probably won't all be gone every weekend," said Nick. "So we can switch back sometimes. But I still agree with Rob: it would be best for all of us if we could count on that time off." Brian was stubbornly silent, and Nick added, "You see, Brian, we're always job-hunting. We don't have tenure."

"Oh, hell!" Defeated, Brian shook his head. "I'll see what I can do. Damn it."

"Thanks, Brian. I appreciate it," said Rob warmly.

"It'll help us all," said Nick.

Brian nodded shortly and turned away to talk to Chester Morgan. Nick exchanged an unsmiling look with Rob before joining Lisette at the door. She said softly, "Nicky, it's for the best."

He shoved the door open with a heavy shoulder. "Yeah. For an encore, you want to see us drown a few kittens?" She took his arm affectionately and they went out.

The discussion that Chester and Brian were having looked like a long one, so Ellen picked up her books and took them into the little adjoining room to read. She found Maggie and Paul there already, heads bent together over a physics book.

"Okay, I see that," Paul was saying. "But I don't understand this step right here. Where does that number come from?"

"That's just algebra. You have to multiply both sides of the equation by the same number."

"Oh, right. Fine. All right, I've got that one. Now the next problem I had trouble with was this one."

Maggie looked up at Ellen. "We'll be a while," she said. "Want me to lock up for you?"

"Thanks," said Ellen. She tossed her the key and left.

Jim ambushed her in the hall, falling into step beside her as she started downstairs. "Great rehearsal," he said.

A safe topic. Ellen let her enthusiasm show. "That nunnery scene, Jim! I couldn't believe how exciting it was already!"

"They're professionals," he said, holding the door for her.

"Yes, but they weren't even off book yet. And Rob looked so tired before he started. But then it was so exciting. Like electricity between them."

"I'm glad you liked it too."

His voice was warm. Ellen fumbled for her car keys. There were snowflakes blowing in the bleak night. She said, "I'm going home, Jim. I have work to do."

"Can I ride along? I'll leave right away when we get there. I promise."

If he hadn't looked so cold, she might have said no. Damn him. But she unlocked the door for him and turned on the heater a moment before putting the car into gear and asking brusquely, "Okay, what is it?"

He was just a shadow sitting beside her in the moving car, a shadow that without touching her dragged at her like a magnet. "I love you," he said simply.

"Goddamn it, Jim! That's over!" No, no, Ellen, cool down, she told herself. Not worth a flap. She added calmly, "We went through all that last term. Remember? All that love conquers all stuff. Well, it doesn't."

"I know."

"You just broke promise after promise. You were never there when you said you'd be. I went crazy changing plans, never knowing what was happening, or when you'd decide to ignore me."

"It's the work, Ellen. I can't help it."

"I can't help it either. I need reliability. Commitment. Why can't you leave me alone?"

"Because this is killing me," he said miserably.

She hated him, sitting there reminding her of the worries, of the last-minute disappointments, of the anger. Of the comfort in his arms. She hated him. Or something. Damn him. She drove wordlessly past the dorm and turned into the parking lot.

He said, "I just wanted to know if, I mean, is it really better for you without me?"

"Yes!" cried Ellen, swinging recklessly into a parking space. Before she could switch off the ignition she was snuffling stupidly. He reached over timidly and touched her hair. She shook her head wildly. "Damn you, Jim!"

"Yes," he said soothingly, not timid anymore. "Yes."

He broke another promise that night. He didn't leave right away. Not at all.

VII

There was no fun in Maggie's demeanor tonight, no laughter in those eyes. "What's wrong?" asked Nick. He and Lisette had stepped into the hall during a short break in the rehearsal to find her waiting by the drinking fountain.

"Another one," she said.

"Hell. Where? We checked her things. Nothing there."

Last week Lisette had picked up her script after a court scene to discover one of her photo-résumés tucked into it. A black spider—real but dead—hung from a fake web that reached from her ear to her nose.

"Maybe our joker is going public," said Maggie. "It's in the costume room. It's not pretty."

Nick and Lisette followed her down a flight of stairs from the rehearsal room floor to the empty costume room. Maggie indicated the bulletin board that usually held Cheyenne's sketches of the *Hamlet* costume designs. Tonight they were gone, replaced by Lisette's photo. Above the smiling face, the hair writhed eerily, a Medusa-like mass. Earthworms. Most of them still alive.

"Oh, shit," said Lisette.

"Wonder where they got live ones in February?" Maggie, with admirable nonchalance, began to unpin the creatures and drop them into a styrofoam cup. "I'll pop these fellows into the woods behind the gym before the costumers come back."

Nick stroked his chin, stubbly now with a two weeks' beard. "There's a sort of pattern," he said dubiously.

"What sort of pattern?" asked Lisette.

"The photos were stolen at the cut rehearsal. The scorpion was at the dean's reception. The drugs were at the restaurant. Last week's spider was at the blocking for the court scenes. Tonight we're working the crowd into the Players' scene."

"Crowds," said Maggie. "There's never been an incident when only a few of you were rehearsing."

"You mean it's someone in the crowd scenes?" asked Lisette.

"Could be. Or it could be someone you see every day who wants to keep us guessing."

"The smallest group was at the restaurant," said Nick, "but fourteen people is pretty close to a crowd."

"Brian is only calling one full-cast rehearsal a week, right?" asked Maggie.

"Yes. The next one is Friday, the first week in March," said Lisette, checking her book.

"Friday. Okay. Let's set a trap," suggested Nick. "We could arrange things so that Lisette's things will seem to be unguarded, but we'll really take turns spying all evening. Okay? I'll get Rob to help. Maybe it'll be pointless and the joker will find another public room like this one. But all the other times involved her things."

"Or her," Maggie reminded him, capping the cup of worms and sticking it into her parka pocket.

"Maybe you should leave me unguarded too," said Lisette. "Spy on me. Ever since the restaurant you've been hovering around like a big hairy hen with one chick."

Nick smiled and shook his head. "No, Blossom. That we won't risk. We're guessing that this is a basically harmless person with a sick and angry sense of humor. We're guessing that the drug at the restaurant was a miscalculation, and the real goal was to get you embarrassingly drunk. But the problem is, it's just guessing. And even if we're right, the idiot might miscalculate again." He picked up the photo and crumpled it into his pocket.

"Lisette is right, though," said Maggie thoughtfully, following them into the hall. "Watching her things might not work unless we've got bait. Pardon the expression, fellows," she added, addressing her pocket.

"Bait?"

"Something to attract our joker to whatever we're watching. Something irresistible to put with her things."

"Irresistible," mused Lisette. "What?"

"We'll think of something by Friday." They started upstairs as Maggie made her way down. Behind them they heard voices approaching the costume room. "See you soon."

"Okay, Jason, let's do climbing stairs," Nick said on Friday afternoon.

Jason, in black exercise tights and tank top, with a new beard like Nick's, moved into the middle of the classroom and began to mime going upstairs. His movements were angular and jerky. Nick watched carefully a moment and said, "Freeze." Jason did. Nick moved to his side. "Okay, look. You want to get more of a mismatch. See, your thigh and your arm are working together." He demonstrated. "Break the line more. The Man of Dreams is out of touch with his body. Usually you work for harmony; here you want to destroy it." Nick adjusted Jason's arm. "Okay, slowly now. Good. The trunk is still a little rigid. Try more translation of the shoulders. Yes, good. That's got it." He watched in satisfaction as Jason, his tall limber body controlled to the point of seeming uncontrolled, different forces pulling it different ways, wavered his angular way up the nonexistent set of stairs. "Okay. Good. But I'm afraid our time's up for today. We'll work on it again Monday."

The students stretched and started for their next class. Most were going to a tumbling class in the gym across the parking lot, but Jim Greer lingered a moment.

"Nick, I had a question."

"Sure."

"It's sort of personal."

"I'll try." Nick smiled, and Jim took courage.

"It's just, well, is it really fair to be married if you're an actor? You and Lisette seem very happy. But isn't it hard?"

"God, Jim." Nick was taken aback. He smoothed back his thin hair. "Yeah. It's hard. What can I say? You know that actors have a lousy domestic record."

"Yeah. That's why I was asking. Because Chester and Rob seem like terrific people, but they're divorced. The current Mrs. Morgan is supposed to be the fourth."

"Well, marriage can be hard work even for people with normal jobs. And ours is such a crazy business. You have to be totally committed to what you're doing, or you won't have a chance at all. And you have to expect some jealousy of that commitment."

"Jealousy?"

"Anyone who cares about you is going to feel abandoned at some stages of your work. Not everyone can be understanding."

"Jealousy." Jim gnawed at the idea, brows mobile in the tanned, sensitive face. The reason for his concern was obvious to Nick; every night now, he waited to leave rehearsal with Ellen. Jim continued: "Because you're so focused on your work. It really is a rotten life to offer anyone, isn't it?"

"Yes. A rotten and wonderful life. Best and worst. She wants to be a lawyer, doesn't she?"

"Yes. She's really bright." Jim kicked the table leg unhappily. "I keep thinking it might be better if I got out of her life. Better for her, I mean."

"God, I wish I could say something useful," said Nick. "But I can't, really. Typical day: you work out all morning. Voice lesson. Your coach says at the rate you're going, you'll be lucky to play frogs. Off to work, a commercial if you're really lucky. Four hours of being part of the crowd behind some famous jock who can't even pronounce the words, much less remember them. Afterwards you call your agent. None of the fifty auditions you just did is working out, and he hasn't heard of anything coming up. You learn that the one solid contact you had, a top director who liked you in an Equity showcase, is moving to Europe for tax reasons. You call the restaurant that's always let you wait table and they're under new management, going cafeteria-style. Okay. Home at last. Your wife says, 'Boy, Jim, have I had a rough day!' Are you ready to listen to her?"

Jim smiled sadly, shook his head. Nick added, "It's great when it does work, Jim."

"Yeah." He seemed grateful. "Well, thanks, Uncle Nick." He picked up his gym bag and left.

Uncle Nick. Rob's nickname had stuck, and seemed as good a term as any for what he felt for his students. Closer than a professor, older and wiser than a brother. Maybe his advice was worthless to them, but he was warmed by the respect and the confidence they placed in him. Clayfooted though he was. Well, he tried to be honest. The Ann Landers of Elsinore.

He turned, feeling athletic in his black tights, and began to rearrange the room for his next class. His seniors were studying dialects, and he had asked Grace to work with them for a few minutes at the beginning of the class. As he set up the chairs, he wondered again at his own sense of well-being. He was worried about Lisette, of course. There was the problem of the jokes—he hoped their trap would work tonight—but there was a much bigger worry. Lisette's greatest enemy was herself. Was Ophelia going to be a danger to her? She was still resisting work on the mad scene, although her other scenes were going well and she was generally pleased with it. He knew her battle with herself would come to a head when she faced Ophelia's death and madness.

"Hi, Nick." Grace came in, set down a small stack of books, and leaned back against a table, half-sitting. "Any special instructions?"

"None at all. You know what they've done already. Take them wherever you want from there."

"I thought I'd work a little on upper-class British."

"Great. That's very useful, and not easy for them."

"The vowels are hard when you've been doing something different all your life." She was wearing a white blouse and a gray wool jumper that set off her gray eyes and sun-streaked hair. A pleasant, competent woman. Nick was working with her closely on the play, and despite her lack of physical training, she was finding a genuine emotional base for Gertrude, a warm and loving woman too easily swayed by the manipulating politicians around her. Vocally, at least, she was going to be good.

"What do you do besides teach, Grace?" he asked suddenly.

She was a little surprised. "What do you mean?"

He leaned against the table next to her. "Well, as a speech professor. I know you spend a lot of time seeing students, and coaching plays even if you aren't in them."

"Oh, there are a million things. Committee meetings. Research. I'm up for tenure year after next, and I need to get some more publications. Professional meetings." She smiled. "My parents were amazed to hear that I only spend twelve hours a week in the classroom. They don't realize that with everything else, a sixty-hour week is an easy one in this business."

"And doing this play must add another twenty hours a week."

"Yes. But . . ." Her gaze, unexpectedly soft and open, met his. He was suddenly pleasantly aware of the muscular lines of his own body in the tights. She put a warm hand on his forearm and said, "Nick, I'm enjoying every bit of it. I'm learning so much from you."

"Well, thanks." Nick was flattered, and warned. This complication he could do without. He crossed his arms. "We're learning a lot here too. Lisette was just saying the other night that it's useful to communicate to students. It forces you to become clear about concepts you thought you grasped, but really hadn't thought through."

"Yes, that's true." There was a trace of regret in her warm rich voice. "It encourages you to be very rational."

"That's important too," he said firmly, and was thankful to hear some of his students approaching down the hall.

"I may need a blackboard," she said.

"Sure. I'll pull one in from next door." He hailed one of the students to help him. In a few minutes he was pleased to see Grace take charge—capable and, of course, rational—and instruct his students in some of the subtleties of the language of Wilde and Shaw.

Brian had asked him to work with the Players. The flowery language, the sense of ensemble, the careful timing were all new and difficult for the undergraduates, and the extra hour they spent three times a week with Nick was much appreciated. It made his days long, though. They didn't finish until after six, and rehearsals started at seven-thirty. Today was worse than usual, because he had promised to meet Rob before rehearsal. "We'll have a picnic first," Lisette suggested to Nick. And as the last Players left the rehearsal room, here she was, warm and beautiful, with a huge sparkling gift box filled with fruit and cold cuts and a fresh loaf of pumpernickel. He closed the door and kissed her thoroughly.

"You know, Blossom," he said into the scented hair, "on top of your other virtues, you are a most satisfactory wife."

Amused, she ran a finger along his bearded jawline. "It's only fair, Nicky. You're a pretty good wife yourself, when I need one. Though a bit hairy."

"Can't be perfect."

"Oh, it is perfect! If Rob weren't coming, I'd ravish you right here on the rehearsal room floor."

"Mmm. Mind reader." He smiled, and took the box from her. "Let's eat before we both need cold showers."

She pouted impishly but obligingly changed the subject as they began unpacking the big box. "How was your day?"

"Crowded. Grace gave a good talk to my seniors. And the grads are really responding to the corporal mime unit. How was yours?"

"Fine. The beginners are a mixed bunch but some of them are doing well. Sheila did a fantastic reading from Miller today." She shook her head. "Poor old Paul is no actor, though. He works very hard in class and gets some of the technique things, vocally at least. But his coordination is zero. He should stick to staging."

"He'll get his C, won't he?" After some discussion, the acting teachers had agreed that any student who worked hard and attended regularly would get a C, at least. But some talent would be required for an A or B.

"Oh, sure. He's very faithful," she said. "Also, I think he has a crush on me."

"Probably does." Nick smiled fondly at his wife. Their relationship with its complex dependencies was beyond ordinary jealousy. But Nick could still remember the first weeks he had known her, when he had been a young instructor smitten by his dazzling student, and he sympathized with Paul and with the many others who had been similarly affected by her over the years.

Lisette had spread a red-checked cloth in the middle of the floor and was taking out the pumpernickel. "No ants," she said happily.

"Maybe all picnics should be held in rehearsal rooms."

"Maybe not all. Just until spring comes." She surveyed the dull scuffed walls, the taped floor, the mismatched chairs, the grimy windows partly opened to the surprisingly mild March air. "Shouldn't be long now."

Nick declaimed, "Winter slumbering in the open air wears on his smiling face a dream of spring," and fed her a grape with a romantic flourish.

When they had finished Lisette packed up the cloth and plates, replaced the ribboned top on the gift box, and pushed it aside. Rob appeared, as if on cue, holding his violin.

"Hi, Nick, Zetty. Hey, what a gorgeous gift! Wish it was for me."

"Maybe someday, if you're a good boy," said Lisette.

"Thanks for coming, Nick. It gets boring, practicing all by yourself."

"Unhealthy habit, too. Solitary practicing. I hope you aren't hitting it before lunch."

Rob grinned. "It may come to that. Okay, you want to give me what passes for an A on that thing?"

The rehearsal room piano was battered but had once, early in its career, been a reasonably good instrument. Nick had often played it, briefly, in odd moments between classes or before rehearsals. He thumbed through the music while Rob tuned the violin. Lisette settled into a chair, prepared to listen. Nick said, "Let me run through a couple of these sections, okay? Parts of this Beethoven sonata look tough."

"Okay. I'll play along with you."

They worked the more difficult sections a couple of times, then Nick said, "Well, I won't be any readier than this tonight."

"Okay. Let's go."

They played it through. Nick almost lost it in a couple of places, but Rob had been working on it and pulled him through, and in many sections it went surprisingly well.

"Not bad, considering your crummy choice of accompanist," said Nick when it was over.

"Rob, that was great!" Lisette was enthusiastic.

"Thankee, thankee, Zetty," said Rob, putting on a country accent. "Just what me old mammy used to tell me in North Carolina. 'Chile,' she would say, 'keep a-workin' and you'll be the best country fiddler in these here hills.' "

"And you ignored her!" said Lisette tragically.

"And became as dissipated as you two instead. Listen, Zetty! This was her favorite piece." He lifted the violin, and she smiled as he played the opening phrase of "Turkey in the Straw," then paused, surprised. The same phrase was floating, silvery, through the open window. A flute.

"Nice effects you country fiddlers get," said Nick.

Rob played the next phrase and stopped. Again, the flute repeated it. He frowned and shifted to a bit of Mozart.

The flute repeated and added a few bars, accurately. He grinned at Nick.

"Apparently we have become a trio," he said. He played a bit of Tchaikovsky's Chinese dance, the flute part. This time the response mimicked the violin part of the Kreutzer. Rob laughed out loud. *"Touché!"* he said. The flute played a few bars of a Paganini caprice. Rob concentrated fiercely and repeated it, faster. Nick, tired of the sidelines, did it on the piano.

There was no response.

"Have we broken its spirit?" asked Rob. He looked toward the window anxiously, then smiled in delight. "No—soft! What light through yonder window breaks?"

Maggie pushed the sash further open and climbed in to straddle the sill, four floors up, flute in hand. She was wearing her usual jeans and baggy sweatshirt and amused expression.

"It is the west, actually," she informed him.

"And Juliet is the ingenue. Shucks, I keep forgetting." Rob's blue eyes sparkled. "But welcome all the same."

"*Merci.* Play something else, okay? I really came to spy. But I'd like to hear more."

Rob turned to Nick. "How about the Schubert?"

"Right." They launched into the new piece. Maggie and Lisette listened with enjoyment, and applauded at the end. Maggie swung herself on into the room.

"That was good."

"Thanks," said Rob. "We're saving up for tuxedos so we can join the Philharmonic."

Nick cocked an inquiring eyebrow at her and played a few bars of the Humoresque. She nodded, and they played it through with few bobbles. Nick said, "Rob, let's add a flute to our musical evenings."

"By all means." Rob smiled at her. "Now you've been officially invited. You won't have to sneak in through windows."

"Good. It's hard on the ivy."

Ellen came in and plunked down her prompt book. "Hello, people. What are you doing here, Maggie?"

"I'm leaving, chief. I was distracted by these wandering minstrels." She saluted them with the flute and went out, calling over her shoulder, "Get them to do 'Turkey in the Straw' for you. Their specialty."

Rob lifted his bow and played Ellen a chorus. Nick watched Maggie swinging down the hall, tall and slim as Lisette, but heartier, bigger-boned, more full of life and laughter. Lucky the man who would share that joyous life. That joyous bed. He turned quickly back to the piano and closed it. He thought of Grace, and of Lisette, and smiled at himself. Spring was coming indeed. A middle-aged fancy lightly turning to thoughts of universal horniness.

Jason, just coming in, was looking after her too with a gentle, hopeless hunger. Poor Jason, thought Nick. Poor Grace. Poor Rob. Poor Paul. Loneliness came in many flavors. He suddenly felt a need for Lisette and went to where she sat in a chair backed against the wall, reading over her lines. She smiled at him as he sat down next to her, then her eyes returned to her book and she continued with her work. But her slender ankle moved a few inches and hooked around behind his, and he sat quietly for a few minutes, feeling lucky, until everyone had arrived.

"Excuse me, Lisette, is this yours?" Ellen held up the beribboned box. "Judy and I have to clear the rehearsal area."

Lisette looked up from her book. "Oh! Sorry. I'll just put it out by the prop room." She grabbed up the box and ran down the hall and around the corner to drop it on the bench by the prop room door. As she came back in, Laura handed her a rehearsal skirt, and she buttoned it on over her jeans.

The rehearsal began with the graveyard scene. David Wagner was getting better as Laertes, thought Nick. His young voice already had range and flexibility, and even at this early stage a brother's grief and anger were communicated as he stormed at the priests. He was not so convincing when Hamlet bounded into the grave with him. Their fight was still just a shoving match, but that could be worked out. And Rob was already damn good. As Horatio and the others pulled them apart, he glared at Laertes. "Why, I will fight with him upon this theme/Until my eyelids will no longer wag!"

"O my son, what theme?" asked Grace in her rich voice.

And the heartbroken answer came. "I loved Ophelia. Forty thousand brothers/Could not, with all their quantity of love,/Make up my sum."

Yes, in fits and flashes, Nick could glimpse an exciting

production emerging from this odd collection of cynical professionals, bright-eyed graduate students, and untrained, hardworking youngsters. What a peculiar and fulfilling business he was in.

They moved on to the Hamlet-Players scene, and Nick was no longer needed. "I'll be down the hall," he whispered to Ellen. "Just yell if you need me." He walked past the drinking fountain and stairs to the corner of the hall, glanced down both deserted corridors, noted the gift box on the bench, and slipped into the prop room where the two halls joined.

"Changing of the guard," he said to Maggie. "Anything?"

"Nope. The Players were clowning around out here for a while, but none of them touched it. Nobody else even walked down the hall. But the *Blithe Spirit* folks will be back in the dressing rooms when their performance is over."

"Thanks. Sorry if it was boring."

"Glad to help. If you leave the door ajar, you can see the box clearly through the crack. And if you move over to the hinge side, you can see down the other corridor past the exit and the drinking fountain to the rehearsal room door."

"Fine. See you later, then."

"Hey, Uncle Nick, good luck." She checked both halls and then, flute case in hand, slipped through the door and down the exit stairs.

Nick settled onto the chair in the dark prop room, surrounded by dark shelves with the shadows of goblets, candlesticks, papier-mâché food, stuffed animals, lamps, prams, and a million other dusty objects. He kept his eye on the gaudy picnic box on the bench outside, the top with its big bow fitted loosely over the box. He could hear the muffled sounds of the rehearsal as Brian worked through the scene. It was peaceful. Hell, it was dull.

Once, the costume and properties heads came up the stairs; Nick shifted sides and peered through the hinge side to watch them, but they just walked quietly to the rehearsal room door. He went back to watching the box.

Finally there was a commotion at the end of the hall. He heard one of the Players say, "How long? Ten minutes?"

"Yeah. Let's hurry."

He looked through the hinge side to see most of the actors pouring out of the rehearsal room, some hurrying to the exit stairs, others sauntering along the hall, stopping at the drinking fountain or just stretching their legs. Nick switched sides and watched the box attentively, but few people came around this corner. Grace and Judy walked past it toward the dressing rooms, then started slowly back toward the rehearsal room. Ellen and Tim, the props head, met them and they stood and talked for a moment, then went back with them. Nick was relieved; it wouldn't do for Tim to decide to fetch a prop now. He'd have to disguise himself, as a stuffed bear, maybe, or a giant hassock. Nick the potted palm.

The minutes wore on; people began to drift back into the rehearsal room.

"Yes, that's true." It was Lisette's voice; and the underlying tenseness in it caught Nick's attention. He moved to the hinge side.

"It's just that there hasn't been much genuine emotion yet." Brian was talking to her near the water fountain. Lisette was nodding in agreement, but Nick could tell that she was strung tight.

"I'll work on it, Brian," she said. "But probably not by tomorrow or Monday. I need more time."

"Sure. You know best how you work. But it's a crucial scene."

"I know, Brian."

"Well, don't rush things if you're not ready. The other scenes are wonderful. I'll trust you."

"Thanks." But she stood for a moment, rigid by the water fountain, after Brian went back to the rehearsal room, and Nick knew that she didn't trust herself. And that he was helpless to help her.

He realized suddenly that there had been a soft click down the other hall. He jerked around to peer out the other side of the door, and saw that the door at the end of this hall was closing slowly. Where the hell did that door lead? Another storage room? He couldn't remember. But the same glance told him that the lid of the big gift box had been moved. Damn. He flung himself down the hall, past the dressing rooms, and pulled the door open before it had closed all the way.

Darkness, vacancy. As he braked himself, his foot

slipped over the threshold and rang on metal. The upper catwalk gallery. He was high above the stage, the pulleys of the gridiron only a few feet above him. He thought he could feel the metal platform quivering in rhythm with silent steps descending its ladder. From far below came a voice. "Elvira?" The lead actor in *Blithe Spirit.*

And from far below, too, the anguished whisper of someone backstage. "Jesus Christ, keep that door closed! There's a performance going on! What's with you people?"

Nick recoiled as though burned, pushed the door closed as fast as its pneumatic arm allowed, closed his eyes. Terrific. Great plan, O'Connor. Let the joker escape, burst into the middle of someone else's show. Hargate was sure lucky to have professionals working here. Bozo O'Connor himself. The original Keystone Kop.

"What's wrong, Nicky?" Lisette had heard his step, was coming toward him from the other hall.

"I'm what's wrong. Christ! Me and my James Bond delusions."

"You blew it," she deduced.

"I blew it. Got distracted for a minute." He didn't tell her why. "And when I looked back, someone was disappearing through this door. I went blundering after and almost fell into the middle of a *Blithe Spirit* performance. The séance, I think."

"Oh, Nicky! Did the audience see you?" She was distressed.

He thought. "No, I think this upper level is masked by the velours. But there was probably some light spill."

Amusement crept into her eyes. "Well, maybe they would have thought you were a spirit, called back from above."

He grinned. "Yeah. I'm the ethereal type, all right. But anyway, our joker got away."

"You're sure he was here?"

Nick walked back to the gift box. A last mob of actors and technical workers was coming up the exit stairs, and he waited for them to reach the rehearsal room door before flipping back the top. Inside it was a recent *Time* magazine, with the familiar title and red border, and a diagonal banner reading "The Polluted Air." But Lisette's photograph had replaced the cover photo of smoggy Los Angeles. Wearily, Nick said, "I'm sorry, Blossom."

She slid an arm around his waist and looked down at the cover thoughtfully. "It's okay, Nicky. Better than worms."

"It's not okay! It's damn upsetting! Damn unprofessional!"

"Well, this ain't Broadway. Anyway, I'll tell you a secret. I'm using it."

"Using it?"

"For Ophelia. She feels like this too. Something unknown, faintly threatening, breaking into her life." She smiled at Nick. "It's helpful."

Their eyes met, and he felt a rush of wonder, as he always did when he recognized himself in her. His soul's mirror. I'd do exactly the same thing, he thought. Welcome any emotion that could be used. How wrong the joker was to think these pranks would interfere with her acting! He clasped her to him a moment and said, "God, actors are weird people."

Hand in hand, they went back to the rehearsal.

VIII

Rob thought it was hilarious. "Look, up in the sky! It's a bird! It's a blimp! No—it's the spirit of Uncle Nick that usurps this time of night!"

"Couldn't help it," Nick explained solemnly. "They went into their séance, and I felt a mystic tugging. Irresistible."

"At least our bait worked," said Maggie.

"But we'll have to be more clever next time." Nick was serious again. "If I'd realized where that door went, I wouldn't have chased him. Her. Whatever. But now I've given the game away."

"Didn't the *Blithe Spirit* people see anyone?" asked Rob.

"Sort of. I found their stage manager afterward and apologized. Just told him I was new here and that I'd followed someone else through. He asked around, but the only person who saw anything was the girl who helps the actress get into the flying harness. She was standing right under the two catwalks, and said she had the impression that someone on the lower one went out just after I appeared at the upper door. She was the one who told me to get it closed."

"That's not a bad way to hide," said Lisette. "Dodge out the upper door, take the ladder down to the costume room floor, and then casually join the mob in the stairwell coming back up to the rehearsal. No one would see you in the hall with the gift box."

"Have we learned anything useful?" asked Rob. "I guess we know this person is familiar with the theatre."

"That eliminates me," said Nick wryly.

"Yeah. It's a certain kind of humor, too," Rob said.

"Bugs on the face. Making someone act drunk. Magazine satires. It's crude, opportunistic."

"Yeah." Nick nodded. "Not elevated humor. Like you and me setting up poor old Harmon."

Rob gave him a reproachful look. "That was in our misspent youth. Two whole years ago."

"In the full bloom of maturity, you merely set up French restaurants," observed Maggie. "But look, we really aren't any further along. I don't know anyone around here who regularly puts bugs on faces. And unless we want to bring other people into this problem, I don't know how to get a roll call of who was in the rehearsal room when it happened, and who was in that crowd of suspects you saw coming up afterwards."

"Wish I'd been thinking," said Nick. "But I was getting ready to open the box, and I was still in shock from gate-crashing *Blithe Spirit.* I hardly looked at them."

"I didn't either," said Lisette. "I think Jason was in the group. But I stepped back out of sight when I saw them, and he only registered because he's so tall."

"You were in the rehearsal room, Rob," said Nick. "Did you notice who was in that last group?"

Rob shook his head slowly. "No. David had asked me some profound question or other about the Laertes I played in summer stock. We were talking, and everyone else was just part of the hubbub in the background. I can't even vouch for Brian."

"I can," said Lisette. "He went back into the room just before Nicky started chasing the joker."

"Wow! Progress!" said Maggie. "We've eliminated the director and the dean's son. Two prime suspects."

Everyone was silent for a moment, discouraged. Then Lisette said stoutly, "Well, it's not all that horrible. Nicky has become my royal taster, and he's always been a good bodyguard. The photos aren't a real problem."

"Still, let's all stay alert," Nick said. "I've let the cat out of the bag, unfortunately. I don't think we'll trick the joker again that way. But the main object is to protect Lisette from these nasty jokes, and we can do that just as well by being obvious. Forget about catching the joker."

"Obvious?"

"One of the three of us with her or her things at all times. We can keep the jokes away from her, at least."

"Oh, God!" Lisette threw her arms around Rob and Maggie. "Now I'll have to put up with three mother hens!" But she seemed pleased.

Jim had reformed. Well, almost. In the weeks since the night in the dorm lot, he had met her faithfully after almost every rehearsal, even the times when he wasn't called. Ellen, wanting to trust him, enjoyed her time with him. But she still felt a nagging uneasiness that she was building on hope rather than certainty.

Her father phoned. "Hi, honey bunch!"

"Hey, Dad! How are you?"

"Fine. I'm coming through Jefferson Tuesday on my way to a meeting in Buffalo. How about lunch?"

"That would be great!" Ellen was excited. Thomas Winfield's corporate law practice kept him busy and often on the road. Lunch with him was a rare treat even when she was home on vacation.

"And why don't you bring along your young man?" he added casually. "We can look each other over."

"Oh. Okay. Sure. He'd like to meet you too."

Her father laughed. "If he's like me, he wouldn't. He'd be scared stiff. But tell him I don't bite."

Jim had agreed, hesitant and eager all at once. "He'll like you, don't worry," Ellen told him.

"I won't worry if you won't."

Her secret thoughts were flashing neon for him to read. She eyed him sternly. "How do you always manage to see through me? Everyone else in the world thinks I'm the calmest person around."

Jim smiled fondly. "You are. You ought to see the rest of us inside."

Well, these days were a test of everyone's calm, all right. *Blithe Spirit* had closed, *Hamlet* had moved down from the rehearsal room to the stage, and chaos had been heaped upon Ellen. As unexpected problems emerged, her clipboard became a mass of urgent notes about platforms, wheels, costumes, paint colors, light colors, and scene shifts. Tonight it was props. The new swords were fine, good-looking metal ones commissioned with the dean's money. Finally, rehearsals of the Hamlet-Laertes duel could begin. But Tim was panicking about Ophelia's flowers.

"Pansies, fine. Columbines, fine. Jane says she can get fennel," he reported. "But what the hell does rosemary look like? Or rue?"

"I don't know," admitted Ellen.

Rob, somehow looking elegant in dingy old rehearsal tights, was inspecting the rack of swords. He turned to them, smiling, balancing a sword in both hands. "Rosemary has blue flowers and leaves sort of like pine needles, dark on top and light underneath."

"Oh," said Tim. "And rue?"

"Rue is sort of cute. A weedy little plant with little yellow flowers, four petals."

"Our resident botanist," said Ellen.

"Your resident former Laertes," he corrected her. "Had the stuff handed to me every night for a month, that summer. Look, Tim, your library here is pretty good. It'll have pictures somewhere."

"Okay, thanks," said Tim, and left, preoccupied.

"An important point might be made here," said Rob, tracing a rococo swirl in the air with the blunted tip of the sword. "Even artists of the most applied sort should occasionally do academic research."

"Heresy!" declared Ellen. "Hargate is not yet ready for such great pronouncements."

The sword point, flashing, circled gently and disconcertingly a few inches in front of her face. "True," he said. "Tell me, Ellen, will your matchless roommate be here tonight?"

"She's up there already," said Ellen, waving generally at the flies.

"You know," he said, dropping the sword tip to the floor and looking up, his hair like gilt under the lights, "she is the most three-dimensional person I've ever met. Makes me feel as though we're living in an aviary."

"She'd probably be an astronaut if they allowed women, you know."

"Really? She'd be good!" He was more amused than surprised. He's turned out to be a good sort after all, she thought, easy to work with. The friendly eyes that met hers were suddenly as disturbing as Jim's. He hesitated an instant, then continued, "Didn't January's misfortune bother her? Those three fellows crisped in the Apollo capsule?"

My God. "She was no happier about it than the rest of us," said Ellen in a vinegary voice.

"Of course." He was still looking at her, eyes intensely blue, regretful. "Ellen, I'm an oaf sometimes. Try to forgive me. I admire your roommate enormously, and I'd like to be friends with you too."

"Well, sure." Damn it, he had her off balance again. She pushed back her hair with both hands. "Now really, I have to get that wagon schlepped into place."

"I'll help." And he did, pushing the heavy platform carefully into position. Ellen, grunting as she heaved her own end of the rugged construction, wondered at the contrasts in him. Sensitive and callous all at once. Exasperating man. Fascinating too. The same slim, powerful build that she found so irresistible in Jim, but without Jim's comfortable directness. She hoped that he and Maggie would continue to keep their distance. Rob's few spare hours were spent with the O'Connors or in New York, and Maggie seemed content to go to concerts or movies with her math department admirers or, rarely, with Jason. But Ellen still found herself nervous about the situation.

Jim arrived, but she only had time to wave before Rob pounced on him. "Horatio! Come on up, I have a question." He bounded up the ladder that led to the top platform of the half-finished rampart wagon. Jim followed.

"What's the problem?"

"Now that they've finished this platform, I don't know if we have room to do the 'swear, swear' bit the way we'd planned."

"I see what you mean. Shall we try it?"

"Well said, old mole! Canst work in the earth so fast?" Rob declaimed, and they began to go through the practiced steps. Rob was right, Ellen thought: the kneeling pushed him uncomfortably close to the brink of the platform, so very high above the stage.

"Ellen, have you seen my prayer book?" asked Lisette.

Ellen turned to her. "Props has to recover it. Can you use something else tonight?"

"Sure. Just wanted to be sure it wasn't lost."

"It should be ready tomorrow. Oh my God, Paul, stop!"

Unaware of the two actors high above, Paul and two stagehands had started to shift the ramparts wagon. The unexpected jerk had thrown both Jim and Rob off balance.

Jim was all right, sprawled on the platform, but Rob had been kneeling at the edge. They all watched in horror as he struggled wildly, half on and half off the platform, for a long moment. Jim's efforts to reach him were unavailing. Then, from the catwalks above, they heard Maggie's chuckle. The flailing stopped abruptly, and Rob waved to her.

Paul, still staring up at him, faltered, "You're okay?"

The brilliant Jenner smile shone down on him. "Well said, old mole!"

Everyone laughed in relief. Rob bounced up to sit on the edge of the platform. "All the same, Paul," he added, "we mortals should get together with you old moles soon to work out what life on this platform will be like."

"Oh, God, yes!" Paul was frantic to make up for his blunder.

Ellen stalked over to her book on the stage manager's desk. Overgrown children. This was not going to be an easy night.

She was right. They were rehearsing the final scene, and by the fourth time through, each repetition looked worse than the one before. And all her fault, it seemed. (The swords are awfully heavy, Ellen. The platforms squeak. Ellen, why didn't you tell us these steps were going to stick out so far?)

Well, maybe not entirely her fault. David Wagner was beginning to look a little panicked too. He had had a few fencing lessons, but as a mere senior he didn't get the regular training that the graduate program provided. On the second slow repetition of the duel, perhaps confused by the new sword, he had forgotten his blocking and struck Rob across the face with the side of the blade. ("Goddamn it, Ellen," said Brian, "why can't you people keep the first-aid kit where it belongs?") Since then, despite Rob's urging, David had been so cautious that no one could possibly believe a fight was going on.

Brian cut the scene short. "Look, people, this is rotten." Rob, the red streak flaming on his cheekbone, a constant reproach to David, nodded grimly. David seemed close to tears. Nick and Grace, waiting on the throne platform to die for the fourth time, sat down wearily. Jim and Jason, waiting for their entrances, looked miserable too.

Brian said, "David, you need a rest. Change places with

Nick and read the King's lines, okay? Let's see if we can at least get the blocking right once."

David grabbed his book gratefully and went up to the throne platform. Nick took off the ragged cape he was using as a rehearsal cloak and took David's place as Laertes, and they started again. It was much better. In Nick's practiced hand, Laertes' swordplay was convincingly fiery but did not damage Rob. They exchanged swords successfully. Rob leaped onto the platform, killed the King, and then died gratefully in Jim's arms. At long last Jason got to say the closing lines.

"Okay," said Brian, relief in his voice. "It will work. Nick, thanks."

"Sure."

"David, we've got to get you some more fencing time."

"God, yes! This is horrible." David was deeply embarrassed.

"Can you see Coach Prosser any extra time?"

"I've tried, Brian! But there is no time. I'm working with him once a week. But the only free time I have is in the afternoon, and that's when he's working with the fencing team or his phys ed classes. I really have tried, Brian, but there's no time. I knew I was in trouble, I tried." David was earnest and shaken.

"Rob," said Brian, "you're free in the late afternoon."

"Yes," said Rob unenthusiastically. He was inspecting the rack of swords again, his lean back turned to them.

"Maybe you could work with him. He needs confidence as much as anything."

Nick said, "I could help, Brian."

"Oh, come on, Nick. You're already working with the Players. And your classes run later than Rob's in the first place."

"It's all right." Nick regarded Rob's taut back with sympathy. "Rob has the longest part. And I'm good with a sword too."

Brian said impatiently, "Rob, speak for yourself."

Rob pulled a sword from the rack and held it up, running a finger along the edge from hilt to tip. "I'd rather not, Brian," he said mildly, without turning around.

"Oh, Christ!" Brian exploded, and Ellen cringed. "This is disgusting! We're trying to teach people here about professional commitment and devotion to theatre, and our

Mr. Bighead Hamlet is turning into a Hollywood starlet instead. Can't dirty his hands with any extra chores. Upsets the whole schedule so he can run off to the city every weekend. Needs contacts, he says. Can't wait to get away. So why is it the other three have been in once or twice and you've been gone every week? Why is it they're all working extra time with the students and you're—"

"Shut up, Brian!" Nick's voice rang with authority, sharper, colder than Ellen had ever heard it. "You know damn well that the length of the part is the difference. Rob is working harder than any of us. He's here every goddamn rehearsal. We aren't. He's got a hell of a responsibility, and he's doing a hell of a good job. You can't just keep loading him up with other things."

"I'm not loading him up, damn it! He's the logical one, he's in the damn fight we're staging!" All the frustrations of the evening were rising, focused on this problem. Ellen wished she could run away. Brian looked ready for violence. "We've all of us got a hell of a responsibility, as you put it. We've all got to pull our weight!"

Rob replaced the sword in the rack and turned deliberately away from it, raising his empty hands, palms out, in a gesture of surrender. "Okay," he said mildly. "I'll do it."

"You'll do it?" Brian seemed astounded, cut off in the midst of his anger.

"Rob, really, I can help," said Nick. He and Rob looked at each other.

"Thanks for the offer, Nick," said Rob lightly, smiling a little, the red slash vivid on his face. "But Brian is right. I'm the logical one. I should pull my weight."

"Well, I didn't really mean you weren't doing it," Brian said uncomfortably.

"I know. Look, we're all having a bad night. We all said things we shouldn't have. Let's just forget it."

"Well, okay, thanks. You'll find the time?"

"No problem. David's a fast learner. Can you give us two weeks to work on it?"

"Sure. Judy, Ellen, adjust the schedule for that, okay?"

"Sure," said Ellen, deeply relieved. "What about the run-through?"

"We'll skip the swords that night."

"Fine," said Rob, businesslike again. "Look, right now

why don't we work the end of this scene? I'm still not happy with how I kill Nick, okay?"

"Good idea." Brian too was very cooperative now. "From 'They bleed on both sides.' "

Things went better this time, almost as if they had needed to vent the seething little frustrations of the last several weeks before they could work harmoniously again. Ellen hoped fervently that it didn't have to happen too often. Brian was frightening in that mood. She'd never seen him so angry. She was glad it was over.

Rob came up to Maggie afterward, as they were getting their coats on, and edged her away from Ellen to speak to her quietly for a few minutes. He seemed tired and serious, and looked at her with a new sort of warm respect.

"What did he want?" Ellen asked Maggie when the brief, murmured conversation was over.

Maggie paused on her way to the door to zip her jacket. "He wanted to know about the requirements for becoming an astronaut."

"God," said Ellen, "I knew it was a rotten rehearsal, but I didn't think it would drive him to such drastic lengths!"

Maggie smiled, then added, "He also wanted me to go to the Philadelphia Orchestra concert next week, with him and the O'Connors."

"Saturday night?" asked Ellen, astonished.

"Mm-hmm."

"But that's when he's gone!"

"Mm-hmm."

"Well. Looks like Brian's little tantrum has brought about complete reform." Ellen was not at all pleased by this turn of events.

Unfortunately, her trials for the evening were not over. Jim was very late in joining her, and when he did there was grief in his dark eyes.

"What in the world is wrong, Jim?"

He took her books and followed her into the stairwell before he answered. "It's about lunch with your dad tomorrow."

Her heart winced. "You won't come."

"I have to work the ramparts scenes with Rob and the staging people. It was the only time."

She had explained how difficult it was to catch her busy

father. She slashed at him in pained reflex. "There are twenty-four goddamn hours in the day!"

"I made them go over every single minute. They've got exams, or they work. One guy is on night shift at the drugstore."

"Why can't you use rehearsals?" She trailed off. It didn't matter. She didn't even hear his explanation as she stared the monstrous truth in the face.

"Ellen, I had to," he added.

"Yes." Their eyes met, hers as bleak as his. "I know you did. Well, see you around."

She held out her arms for the books. After a moment, he handed them to her. She didn't know how long he stood gazing after her as she drove the lonely way to the dorm.

Maggie was toweling her damp hair at the sink, singing a lusty version of "Let the Sunshine In," but after one look at Ellen she said "Oh, dear." She took Ellen's books, fixed her a hot chocolate, then sat by her bed for two hours stroking her roommate's hair. At last Ellen dropped into a sad and choppy sleep.

IX

Nick, who was in Ophelia's mad scene himself, was increasingly worried each time they rehearsed it.

Usually she was all right, happy with her students, comparing notes with him and Rob and Chester about useful acting exercises and good ways to make points. The joker had not been heard from for two weeks. While they couldn't relax yet, it was good to know that their vigilance was paying off. And Lisette was enjoying their occasional breaks, too. Rob, apparently on impulse, had bought four tickets for the Philadelphia Orchestra concert one Saturday. He was taking Maggie, he explained, and insisted that Nick and Lisette come too, to chaperone, he said, smiling. After the concert they had stopped for a little while at Joe's to eat pizza and dance to the Rolling Stones, and after that went for coffee to the O'Connor apartment. Rob produced a joint and they all sat around on the anthropologist's African rug to share it. Maggie and Lisette leaned back against the front of the sofa, long legs in short skirts stretched out before them, and the lamplight fell on smooth skin and bright eyes. Nick felt immensely grateful. "You three are beautiful," he said.

Rob's mouth twitched a little, and it dawned on Nick that he was higher than he'd thought. But Maggie gave him a friendly smile and said, "Nick, you're beautiful too," and Lisette nodded seriously, so he felt pleased and benevolent again. After the others had left he and Lisette had agreed that college could be fun.

But not on mad-scene night. At best, she was edgy. A week ago he had come in to find her absorbed in an acting textbook, and had gone quietly to the kitchen to start the meat loaf. She appeared at the kitchen door a minute later.

"Damn it, Nicky, quit pushing! It's my day. I'll get it done."

"I don't mind."

"Of course not. You just want to make me feel as though I can't manage anything. Won't even give me a chance to finish the chapter."

"Lisette, it's been a long day. I'm trying to help."

"Oh, sure. You're trying to make me feel incompetent."

He washed his hands and turned to face her. "Do you want to talk about it?"

"Talk about what?"

"Okay. I'll be back in twenty minutes." And he left her and walked downtown to get a newspaper. Mad-scene night, he thought morosely. But it was okay, at least she was lashing out at him, not turning it in on herself.

But that came too. Two nights later, mad-scene night again, he opened the door to a silent apartment and saw her after a moment curled up on the sofa, brown eyes lost in grief. Her fingers were knotted tightly around the bottle of bourbon she clutched in her lap. He sat down quietly on the sofa next to her, uncertain. His heart was twisted in her fingers too.

The bottle was unopened.

After a while she seemed to notice him. She gave him a rickety smile, then looked down at the bottle as though puzzled. "Well, not tonight," she said suddenly, getting up and running to the kitchen. She opened the bottle and poured it all down the sink, and then turned on the water until all the smell was gone. Finally she turned to Nick and hugged him close.

"Not tonight. I'm not strong enough," she whispered.

"You're doing fine." He meant it; she was fighting hard. But he was worried too. If she lost, if it proved too much for her, what would she do? There was no Franklin in Jefferson. Where would she go? Would he find her in time? He felt far from home and civilization.

But then he noticed that she was smiling at him.

"Hey, Nicky. I'm getting tougher."

"I know. I can tell."

Nick put down his glass and said, "The problem with Claudius is that he's always playing to people."

"More than the others do?" asked Brian. They were sitting by the fireplace in Brian's living room, the party rumbling around them and under them in the basement rec room. Brian had decided to celebrate the halfway point of rehearsals with a short Friday rehearsal followed by supper at his house. Deborah Wright had boiled spaghetti and tossed huge amounts of green salad, and set out iced tubs of beer and soft drinks. Now knots of undergraduate actors and crew members eddied through the house in high spirits. Brian had surreptitiously pulled out a bottle of Chianti, and he and Nick on the sofa and Rob and Cheyenne in wing chairs were finishing it.

"Yes, more than the others," said Nick. "Don't you think so, Rob? Hamlet puts his antic disposition on, but usually he's sincere."

"God, I hope he is," said Rob. "It's hard enough to catch a few of the complexities without adding yet another level. Sure, in the Ophelia scene and a few others, but even there he keeps slipping out of character. He tries, but he's not really an actor. His natural response to stress is to joke. Too much in the sun. The politic worms. The games with Polonius. The manic side of his depression."

"Right," said Nick. "But that isn't Claudius's way. He's very rational, always looking for the best way to present his case. I usually trust death scenes. And Claudius's last two lines are lies. First he claims that Gertrude is just swooning at the sight of blood when she's actually dying of his own poison. And his very last line is that he is just hurt, when he knows that Laertes' poison is deadly. His very last line."

"Maybe he just doesn't want to believe it," said Brian.

"Oh, I could play it that way. Self-deception. But I think he knows, and his ingrained response is to cover up, to lie."

Brian was frowning. "We have to be able to trust what he says, though, Nick. From the point of view of the play, he's not just a character. He's also presenting half the exposition. Fortinbras, the trip to England, the plots to kill Hamlet. That's all straightforward."

"Not from his point of view," Nick insisted. "The first time you see him, he's playing to the court. It's more rational to marry than to mourn, he tells them. He makes a big production out of being a statesman, sending messages to Norway to avoid war with Fortinbras. He butters up Polonius. And when he talks to Hamlet, he's really playing to Gertrude, pretending love for her son."

"I see what you mean," said Brian. "But I don't understand why you want to change. I like the Claudius you're giving me now. We agreed that you were to work on the statesman aspects of the character. I still think that's the important thing."

"Oh, I don't think I'll have to change much of that," said Nick. "I think most politicians are pretty good at playing to people. The best seem the most sincere."

"True."

"It's just that in scene after scene now, I feel that I'm missing something essential. I'd like to try reading it this way for a while. A man of some ability, yes, but terrified and insecure in his position and his marriage. Constantly on edge, constantly plotting, constantly acting. I think I can make it work."

"Well, try it," said Brian. "We can always pull back again if it doesn't work."

"In his marriage?" Rob asked curiously. "I thought he and Gertrude were made for each other. Two cold fish. All that passion was just in Hamlet's overheated young mind."

Nick smiled. "Grace and I haven't worked that out yet. Maybe he feels real passion, maybe not. For now I'm assuming that her charm is in her inheritance." He became thoughtful. "You know, though, if he really did have a grand passion for her, not just for her power, he'd be in heaven, wouldn't he? The crown, sexual pleasure, peace with Norway. Paradise, except for this little matter of a murder, and all the supernatural powers being after him."

"Still," said Rob astutely, "you won't be able to manage any grand passions without Grace opening up more than I think she can."

Brian and Nick nodded in agreement. Grace, although a fascinating Queen to hear, was improving very slowly physically. It was difficult to play opposite her. The spontaneous communion that Rob and Lisette had created in their first reading of the "Get thee to a nunnery" scene, the electricity that ran under and beyond the dialogue, was completely inaccessible to Grace. Her readings were intelligent, and musical, but unconnected to what anyone else was doing.

"Well," said Nick, "one thing at a time. I'll try my new interpretation first. Time enough to worry Grace later."

"My worry right now," said Rob, "is getting Hamlet's thoughtful scenes and his impulsive scenes to be part of the same person. I feel schizophrenic. When he follows the ghost, or stabs Polonius, or jumps into the grave to fight Laertes, he's all action. But on the other hand he's got all those soliloquies, all those qualms. I haven't quite pulled it together."

"You're right," said Brian. "It is contradictory."

"He's a perfectionist," said Cheyenne from his wing chair.

"How do you mean?"

"It's his father who was killed, his mother who was led astray." The designer's dark eyes glowed over his wineglass. "He can move fast, he knows how to fight. But he wants his revenge to be perfect. Appropriate. Plan carefully, then, when it's time, act fast."

"He's right," said Nick. "Otherwise you'd stab me while I was praying, right?"

"Yeah, I could work with that," said Rob. "A bit like our own job, isn't it? Long preparation and then split-second decisions when we're finally on."

"Right," said Brian, and then grunted. A small human form in red overalls had rocketed into his lap, splashing his Chianti all over his jeans and even Nick's. "Jessie, you disgusting child! What are you doing?"

A tiny face, hot and unhappy, peered up at him. "Gary's pulling my hair," she said in her thin child's voice.

"Gary!"

Reluctantly, the second-smallest creature in the room came over to face his father. He was about six, Jessie around four. Brian said, "Okay, Gary, Jessie. Time to cut this out. It's past your bedtime, you know."

"But you said we could stay up for the party!" Gary protested.

"I said you could stay up if you behaved yourselves."

"She started it."

"I don't care who started it. Anyway, who's helping Mommy with the old beer cans?"

"Me!" shouted Gary, and escaped excitedly into the crowd. Jessie launched herself after him but discovered that Brian still held her wrist.

"Hey!" she protested.

"No. There's another job for us, kitten. There's someone at the door." Nick realized that there had been a bell a moment ago somewhere in the din. Brian took Jessie by the hand and they pushed through the crowd by the archway to answer it. Cheyenne drained his glass abruptly and followed them.

Nick dabbed at his jeans with a paper napkin. There were only a few drops of Chianti on them.

"You and Zetty going to have kids?" Rob asked, watching him.

"If George can come up with parts for them, why not? The Seven Little O'Connors. Lynn and Vanessa O'Connor. Wolfgang Amadeus O'Connor." He stopped. Rob was smiling at him gently.

"You know," said Rob, "we may end up playing each other in this show."

Nick smiled at the grain of truth. "Well," he admitted, "I don't really know about kids. Not soon." He glanced across the room to where Lisette and David Wagner were talking earnestly by the archway, their plates of spaghetti ignored on the shelf beside them.

Rob said, "Kathleen had a miscarriage once. But you know, while she was pregnant, I was probably the happiest man in the world."

Nick wadded up the napkin and threw it into the fire. "Yeah. Kids can be great. But it's damn hard work just being married. Worse to involve other little people in the mess."

"I know. Part of the insane choice we make when we become actors. Maybe I was lucky at that. If she'd had the kid, she'd probably have custody now. Filling its little head with stories about big bad Daddy." He smiled up at a point behind Nick. "Hey, how're you doing up there, Jessie?"

"Fine!" piped Jessie. She was riding on Maggie's shoulders, clutching the black curls for balance. Brian and Paul Rigo and Ellen followed them. Maggie knelt neatly on the hearth rug and helped Jessie down.

"Where have you people been?" asked Nick.

"Putting up posters. Paul's in a peace group," explained Maggie, straightening Jessie's red overalls.

"Draft-card burnings and such?"

"Yeah. Draft counseling," said Paul. "Except I really don't do much when there's a show to build, of course."

"First things first," said Nick, grinning.

"Well . . ." Paul looked a little uncomfortable. "You know, I sort of go by what Cheyenne says. If you can be an artist—well, you know, help create a work of art—then that should be the main thing. Because that's the purpose of life, isn't it? You try to save lives but you also have to have something to save them for."

Rob smiled at him. "Well said, old mole."

"What's your group doing now?" asked Nick.

"There's going to be a big peace march in the city. We're doing some local organizing, mostly putting up posters and things. But I signed up to make the Uncle Sam effigy too."

"To be burned?"

"No, no. Just carried along with a sign, something like 'Does America stand for life or death?' "

"Good question," said Brian. "But right now let's go get you people some food." He and Paul started for the kitchen.

"Maggie?" asked Ellen over her shoulder.

"Join you in a minute," said Maggie. She was sitting cross-legged on the rug, Jessie perched on one knee, and they were singing very quietly about an eentsy-weentsy spider, the long bony fingers and the tiny plump ones twisting and turning, parodies of each other.

Rob smiled at Nick. "Too much," he said.

Maggie finished the song and gave Jessie a hug.

"Say, Jessie," she said, standing up, "you know what I need?"

"What?"

"Food. Where's the food?"

"Over here!" Jessie seized her tall friend's index finger and pulled her toward the kitchen like a small tugboat.

"As for me," said Rob, "I'm going to fall fast asleep from this wine if I don't move."

"Is that the Beatles I hear in the basement?" asked Nick.

"Right! Dibs on your wife, Nick."

Nick laughed, and they went across to Lisette and David. "Deep conversation here," observed Rob.

David smiled at him. "We were talking about growing up together."

Lisette was wearing a silky cream-colored tunic that draped softly along the line of breasts and long back. She explained, "He means Laertes and Ophelia."

"Shop talk," said Rob severely. "Shame on you."

"Oh, it's the latest thing; everyone here is talking shop," she said.

David added mischievously, "I distinctly heard the word 'Laertes' from your corner. To say nothing of 'politic worms.' "

Rob, unembarrassed, said, "Well, we're stopping now."

"Actually," said Nick to Lisette, "Rob is trying to get up enough courage to ask you to dance."

"Hey, great idea!" Lisette was enthusiastic. "Let me just finish my spaghetti."

Nick took the paper plate from her. "Later. Rob needs to dance."

The stairs to the basement were off the kitchen, where Deborah Wright stood wearily in front of a stack of used paper plates. She was filling a plastic bag, held solemnly open by little Gary. Nick went to her, dropped Lisette's plate into the bag and put his arm around her waist.

"Deborah! Come dance with me!"

"What?" Startled dark eyes. "Me? But I have to clean up."

"Gary can tell Maggie what to do. Can't you, Gary?"

"Sure," said the boy confidently.

"Of course he can," agreed Maggie, mouth full. She was working her way like a tornado through an enormous pile of spaghetti.

"Come on, Deborah," Nick urged. "It's a great party. Join it!"

"Well, maybe just for a minute." She took off her apron and allowed Nick to escort her downstairs. A big room, dusky, banquettes around the edges, a table in the far corner. Lots of cigarette smoke, beams of light slicing through the haze, loud music. "Nice lighting," shouted Nick to Deborah over the beat.

"Yes. Cheyenne designed it for us."

"Where is he?"

"He left early. Never has been the party type."

Then they were at the bottom of the stairs. As Nick guided Deborah to a space on the floor, he saw Lisette and Rob dancing happily not far away. They had gravitated to a spot with golden cross-lighting that made their fair skin glow and struck sparks from the bouncing hair. Jason was nearby, tall and well-coordinated, dancing with tawny-haired Laura. Something had gone wrong between Jim and Ellen, Nick saw; they were both dancing with technical crew members.

The record ended and Deborah, giggling and relaxed now, returned to her post in the kitchen. Nick went to Lisette's side.

"Hi, kid. Remember me?"

"Uh-oh. The irate husband, sending me on my way to find another partner," said Rob cheerfully. "See you later, Zetty." He beat Jason to the foot of the stairs to meet Maggie and draw her to the middle of the floor. Then the music started again, and Nick threw himself into the dance, watching appreciatively as his rosy, sexy wife did the same.

An hour later, flushed and laughing, Lisette shouted above the music that maybe, as older folks, they ought to be getting home. Nick looked at his watch; eleven o'clock. He nodded and slipped an arm around her shoulders. Grace was watching them from one of the banquettes, and he was startled to see despair in her eyes. He waved goodbye to her cheerily, but he was relieved at the distraction when Jason and Maggie broke out of the hazy crowd and joined them at the steps.

"Nick, if you're leaving, could you give me a ride to campus? I've got an English paper due, and Ellen's left me in the lurch."

"Sure, Maggie. You too, Jason?"

"I'll go later with Jim. The idiot will need someone to drive," he said. Nick followed his gaze and saw why Ellen had left. On one of the banquettes in the corner, Jim Greer was in earnest conversation with a redheaded costumer, his arm around her shoulders, and the table by his elbow piled with beer cans.

Nick nodded. "I see. We'll be glad to drop you off, Maggie."

"See you," said Jason wistfully, and turned back into the smoky room.

Brian and Deborah were both working in the kitchen, which was almost spotless again. They thanked them and went for their coats in the front bedroom. Maggie's blue parka was on the top, and she shrugged into it and went to wait in the hall while Nick and Lisette burrowed through the pile to find their jackets. When they finally went back into the darkened hall, Nick became aware of a soft murmuring voice, and of Maggie standing quietly in the shadows a bit further down the hall, looking silently into another lighted bedroom. Surprised by the intensity of her mood, Nick and Lisette stepped quietly behind her to look in too.

It was Rob, sitting on a small bed, a book on his lap and the two small Wrights at his sides, following his words intently. Oblivious to the muffled party noises and to the shadowed observers, Rob held the children with his pleasant magnetic voice, his serious answers to their questions, his gentle open gaze. Nick was startled; he had never seen his friend with his guard dropped so completely. Once Jessie stood up suddenly on the bed beside him and then dropped to her knees again and wriggled closer, her eyes never leaving the pages he was making so fascinating for her.

Nick decided he didn't want to be seen, and touched Maggie quietly on the arm to urge her to come away. She blinked and turned quickly to follow him and Lisette out.

"You all right?" Lisette asked her at the front door.

She looked at them bleakly. "Can't win, can you? Doing the wrong thing haunts you. But damn it, doing the right thing can haunt you too."

Understanding only her grief, Nick patted her clumsily on the back. She fished up a smile from somewhere and said, "Look, drop me at the gym, okay? I usually feel better after a good workout."

"Sure. Can we do anything else to help?"

"No, no. The gym is the best antidepressant I know."

She talked about the show with them until they reached the gym, but before she got out she paused, hand on the door handle. "That plate of spaghetti you threw away," she asked. "Lisette's?"

She didn't miss much. He nodded grimly. "It was probably nothing. But it had been sitting on that shelf a long time. Lots of people around."

"You didn't actually see anyone do anything to it?"

"No. Just my own paranoia."

"Well, better paranoid than sorry."

He nodded agreement, and watched her run into the gym.

X

The week after Brian's party, Ellen stepped into the stall of the women's room and jumped back again, revolted. "Jesus Christ, Maggie!"

"What's wrong?" Maggie came to look over her shoulder. "Oh."

In the bottom of the toilet, held down by a broken brick, Lisette's photo smiled up sweetly, yellow in the stained water where someone had urinated and not flushed.

"God, that is disgusting!"

"True." Maggie had rolled up her sleeves, and now fished the brick and photo from the disgusting water. She wrapped the dripping cargo in paper towels and dropped it into the trash bin. Ellen flushed the toilet, and decided she would wait until she was back at the dorm.

"Who would do such a disgusting thing?" she demanded.

"I wish I knew."

"Well, I'm going to make an announcement before rehearsal tomorrow. This is awful. What if Lisette had seen it?"

Maggie was scrubbing her arms. She inspected Ellen for a moment, then sighed, "Winfield, old thing, there's something I guess I'll have to tell you."

She did.

Ellen was staggered. "Ever since the first week of rehearsals?"

"Yes. Though this is the first time in three weeks."

"Why didn't you tell me? Or Brian, or someone?"

"Because it's nasty, and there's already too much stress on this cast. Lisette didn't want that. Didn't want them upset."

"But what about her? How can she think about the show with this nauseating stuff going on?"

"It's not hurting her acting. And she doesn't want publicity."

"Well, I still think we should try to figure out who it is."

"Sure. But there are two other things that are much more important. One is Lisette's safety, and the other is the show."

Ellen added the joker to the list of things she had to worry about. A long list these days. Some news was good. Paul Rigo, despite a series of D's on homework, had managed a B– on his physics midterm, a cause for general elation among the technical crews. Maggie had gone to the concert with Rob and did not seem noticeably the worse for wear. Ellen's father had been a good sport about Jim's defection from the lunch appointment. "Yes, I used to act in amateur theatre. It's very seductive. Engrossing," he said tolerantly.

"Well, it's not serious anyway. He's just a friend," she said, overstating the case. She and Jim were avoiding each other now. There was a rumor that he had taken that redheaded costumer to a movie one night when he wasn't called. But that, Ellen told herself firmly, was good news too.

She was not so sure about her discovery that Rob and Nick were meeting occasionally in a rehearsal room during the dorm dinner hour to play music—and that her roommate had been invited to join them. Since Maggie was too poor to pay regularly for a second dinner, too proud to tell her co-musicians that the arrangement forced her to miss it, and too hungry to do without, Ellen was pressed into service. Her role was to take a paper bag to the dorm cafeteria those nights and smuggle out anything portable, which Maggie then devoured, gratefully and uncritically, after the evening rehearsal. One such night Ellen said, "Jason is miserable, Maggie. People are saying you're making a big play for Rob."

"I'm not Jason's keeper. I've never lied to him," said Maggie, her mouth full. "And you know they're saying that about half the unattached females working on this show. Except, of course, Ellen Winfield, who has convinced no one she's unattached. Not even herself, *n'est-ce pas?"*

"Shut up," said Ellen grouchily. "Anyway, you're the only one who's had more than a coffee date with him."

She shrugged. "We both like music."

"Don't you get enough music with your Sunday afternoon orchestra rehearsals? And all that practice?"

"I never get enough music."

"You never get enough food either." Ellen looked grumpily at her roommate's enormous if unbalanced meal of bread, boiled potatoes, and apples.

"My extravagant metabolic rate."

"Or maybe tapeworm."

Ellen was definitely not in a good mood these days.

The rehearsals, at least, were better. Paul Rigo, working tirelessly with Cheyenne, had all the platforms functioning smoothly and unsqueakily, and the arches were almost completed now. The curtains were being painted, elaborate careful designs that looked like tapestries and took hours of Paul's time. Jase, despite bitter complaints, turned out to be very surefooted on the lofty front wagon, at present still a skeletal structure of two-by-four lumber. At the actors' request, the four stagehands assigned to shift it, who were called the old moles, of course, rehearsed with them every time the ramparts scenes were done. The scenes grew smoother.

The acting was progressing too. David's growing skill was the most obvious improvement, but Brian seemed pleased too by the rampart scenes, and by Rob's soliloquies. And by Nick's simultaneously more suave and more uncertain King.

As April approached, more polish was applied. The night they worked the fight in Ophelia's grave, Ellen was exhausted. It was already eleven-thirty, and she still had her government paper to finish.

"This is I," cried Rob, bounding across the stage and leaping into the grave, "Hamlet the Dane!" Jim followed and knelt by the graveside.

"The devil take thy soul!" David lunged for Rob's throat.

"Thou prayest not well," said Rob, then, beginning to struggle, "I prithee take thy fingers from my throat;/For though I am not splenitive and rash,/Yet have I in me something dangerous." He tore David's hands away and began to bear down on him. "Which let thy wisdom fear. Hold off thy hand!"

"Pluck them asunder," said Nick.

"Okay, stop," said Brian. "Too early, I think."

"Wouldn't I be wheezing by then?" objected Rob.

"Maybe. But the King is waiting too long now. Try it on 'fear.' "

For the fifth time, they took their places. "For though I am not splenitive and rash,/ Yet have I in me something dangerous,/ Which let thy wisdom fear." Again he tore David's hands from his neck and began to gain the advantage. "Hold off thy hand!"

"Pluck them asunder," said Nick.

"Good," said Brian. "Let's set that, okay? The cue is 'fear.' Once more, from 'This is I.' "

Rob crawled out of the grave and crossed with Jim to his starting position. Ellen was bored and vividly aware of the minutes ticking away.

"This is insane," she said crossly. She tried to get comfortable on her tall stool.

Nick, standing nearby waiting for his cue, turned and regarded her kindly. "Yes, it is."

"Why do you bother? It's maybe two seconds on stage. We've been working on it for hours."

"Two seconds," he said thoughtfully. "But Ellen, that's all we need sometimes. The perfect detail, the instant that sends shivers down your spine. Sarah Bernhardt used to talk about the nights when the god descended." He smiled at her. "It is insanity. You're right. But that's what we're always chasing. Those performances when somehow for an instant or two we connect with the universal. With eternity. When it happens, if it happens, it's worth any amount of time. It's worth your whole life."

Ellen was staring at him, astonished. "But you're so reasonable!" she blurted.

He laughed. "I am reasonable," he said. "But unfortunately, that's my reason. An insane reason. Without it there wouldn't be much meaning to any of this."

Brian called, "Okay, let's go!" Nick turned back into the scene.

"This is I," cried Rob, bounding across the stage and leaping into the grave, "Hamlet the Dane!"

Jim followed and knelt by the graveside; and Ellen, who should have been following book, watched him thoughtfully for a long time.

* * *

Brian avoided the final duel scrupulously until Rob and David said they were ready, exactly two weeks after the first disastrous rehearsal of the fight. Things had improved enormously. Ellen could tell that David was very nervous, but despite that, he threw himself into the fight with convincing gusto, and did not miss a step. Finally, the choreography was set.

"Terrific!" Brian cried enthusiastically. "Keep it up, David, you'll scare the guts out of the front rows."

Rob looked pleased, and David glowed with his success. Ellen breathed a sigh of relief. Having the dean's son muff his big scene would not be good public relations for the theatre. Thank God David had some real ability.

After rehearsal, Rob stopped Maggie at the door.

"Cup of coffee with the O'Connors and me?" he suggested.

She was regretful. "Not unless you'll drink it at the laundromat. Ellen and I have chores tonight."

Inexplicably, he accepted, with delight. "Of course we will! I'm sick of coffeehouses with dark wood and mood lighting. Only a true soubrette would think of a coffeehouse so fresh and different."

It was a challenge. Uh-oh, thought Ellen, seeing the merry glint in Maggie's eyes. They pleased each other, Ellen saw; there was a sort of instant understanding and delight in the other's odd fancies. With a sudden twist of dismay, she realized that the relationship had moved past the playful acquaintance it still seemed on the surface. Maggie said, "*D'accord.* We'll be there in half an hour. On College Avenue. It's called, pardon the expression, Sudsy Duds."

"Ugh."

"And don't forget your fiddle."

He was a few minutes late, but it turned out that he had been home to collect some laundry of his own. Maggie and Ellen, lounging in the ugly plastic chairs that lined one side of the big humid room, looked up when he came in.

"Hi, Maggie, Ellen."

"Hello."

He looked around. "Had Dante known about this place, he would have created a special ring for it." He had to raise his voice a little. It was true, thought Ellen. The rumbling, swishing machines, the ugly fluorescent glare, the heavy, steamy air—all made this one of the experiences she dreaded most each week. But Maggie answered solemnly, "That's just because you have not yet been initiated into the true delights of the Sudsy Duds."

"Nonsense." He dropped his basket on a chair, watching her expectantly.

"Not at all. Sensible as a dictionary." She glanced at her watch. "It's not time yet. We have eight minutes."

"Eight." He looked at his own watch seriously. "A countdown?"

"Right. Meanwhile, they have a coffee machine."

"Fine. And I can put my clothes in." He picked them up.

"Use number fourteen."

"Fourteen!" Ellen protested. "But that's the one—"

"Exactly," said Maggie, smiling at her, and part of the pattern shifted into place for Ellen. Their own clothes were in five and sixteen. But why was Maggie picking the noisiest machines?

"Fourteen it is," said Rob, oddly encouraged by this exchange. He dumped his clothes into the appointed machine and pushed in the coins, but Maggie came up beside him and raised the lid, stopping the action.

"Six minutes more," she said with a smile.

"I can hardly wait. Look! Here come Nick and Zetty."

"Terrific! Come on, quick!" said Maggie urgently, taking the basket from Nick. "Number thirty-one. We'll have to get it going right now."

Nick looked at Rob, who shrugged in amused puzzlement, and followed Maggie around to thirty-one. Lisette sat down next to Ellen. There were only two other customers, sitting reading in a torpor at the other end of the row of seats.

"What's going on?" asked Lisette.

"I'm not sure," said Ellen, "but it's going to be noisy."

"Is that why Rob told us to bring the guitar?"

"Who knows? She brought the flute."

"Violin?" asked Maggie.

"In the car," said Rob. "And Nick brought his guitar."

"Great. You've got two minutes."

They brought in their instruments. Maggie closed the top of Rob's machine, and the familiar throbbing high-pitched hum of number fourteen joined the rumbling of the machines already in action.

"Sorry I can't give you an A. That's a B-flat," said Maggie.

Grinning, Rob and Nick tuned their instruments.

"Now, in just a minute, number sixteen will start its first spin. I would suggest 'The Impossible Dream.' "

She held up a solemn finger, and in a few seconds the low pulsing grind of Ellen's machine in its spin cycle joined the din, providing a dominating bass beat to the other noises. Maggie's finger fell, and the three of them launched into an enthusiastic parody of the song. Nick even managed to bellow out two verses of it before Ellen's machine moved on to its next phase. Despite herself, Ellen, like Lisette, was vastly entertained. She was embarrassed for a moment when a new couple came in with a load of clothes, but Maggie, with a polite face, asked them quite civilly if they would please use number twenty-four, and they shrugged, then obeyed.

By the time their clothes were dry, they had collected a small audience—customers as well as a number of bemused passersby. Some Beatles songs and many current musicals had been subjected to atrocious and delightful parody. Some had to be sung at peculiar tempos because of the inexorable mechanical rhythms in the background.

When they finished, their audience applauded ecstatically, cheering and whistling. For a moment Ellen had forgotten her own worries. It was, all in all, the best laundry she had ever done.

She turned to Lisette. "Is it always like this? Being married to an actor?"

"No, not at all," said Lisette, a little surprised. "In New York there never seems to be time to just play." Then she frowned at Ellen, puzzled, and said, "There's really no time for it here either, though, is there? It must be Maggie."

Ellen shook her head. "Not really. She's always clowned around a little, but not like this. I guess they inspire each other."

"She's probably never had such willing henchmen," said Lisette, looking at them fondly. "They needed an audience. I've hardly ever seen either Rob or Nick this happy."

Or Maggie, thought Ellen.

The next day, the first flowers came, a small bunch of daisies. Maggie picked up the little florist's package from the mail desk and opened it, and buried her nose and her smile in them.

Ellen glanced at her own mail and stuffed it into her bag, then inspected her roommate more carefully. "All right, tough girl," she said. "You can't fool me. You've gone all soft and runny inside."

Maggie peeked over the white petals at her and then handed her the little card. *"Pour ma soubrette—de ton danois,"* it said. From your Dane. Ellen looked back at her friend and shook her head, frowning.

"Too bad," she said regretfully. "Makes you act exactly like an ingenue."

Maggie laughed and raised her math book like a club, and, in a bubbling exuberance of high spirits, chased Ellen all the way up to their room.

Flowers came every week after that.

XI

The mad scene was still Nick's greatest worry. The joker seemed to have sworn off all but photograph jokes, and although they still watched alertly on the few occasions when he and Lisette ate with cast members, nothing serious occurred.

But spring vacation was approaching, and Lisette had still not come to grips with the mad scene. One night Rob sat in the auditorium with Brian and watched the scene. A few minutes later, when Nick could take a break, he went back toward the greenroom. Maggie and Paul Rigo were there, in a corner, working on some project or other in physics that seemed interminable. At the center table, a couple of costume people were working on hats. Rob, standing by a sofa, seemed to be ignoring them. As he came down the hall from the wings, Nick could hear his low voice.

"It shouldn't be that hard, Zetty," he was saying, a thread of anger in the quiet words. "Just pretend you've had too much booze. Or something."

Lisette was furious, Nick could see as he approached the door. She was standing in her rehearsal skirt, her head back, her hands clenched, her eyes dark with anger. But she spoke quietly too.

"You're hired to act, not direct, Rob Jenner. Don't you think Brian might like to know who you're directing? Or Dean Wagner?"

"Brian and Dean Wagner might be interested in what Arnie Hutton could tell them, if it comes to that," he said coldly. Maggie, caught by the tone of the quiet voices, was watching them now.

"Or in what Kathleen could tell them!"

"Lisette! Rob! For heaven's sake," said Nick, exasperated, finally reaching the door. They both looked at him angrily. Rob recovered first.

"Uncle Nick. You're right. You've interrupted a nursery quarrel, I'm afraid."

"Shut up, Rob," said Lisette furiously.

"I plan to, Zetty. I was completely out of line. Let's never speak of the matter again."

"Good plan, Rob," said Nick briskly, but Lisette remained stubbornly silent. He took her hand and led her upstairs and out to the parking lot. The nights were still chilly, and the air, not moving much, carried the smell of coal smoke from the college heating plant. They sat on the wall that ran beside the sidewalk.

"Nicky, he can be such a beast!" She was still angry.

"He isn't usually."

She thought a minute and shrugged. "I know. I guess I really started it. He just said that opening night wasn't too far off now. I thought he was criticizing my scene."

"He won't do it again."

"God, Nicky, he can draw blood." She shuddered.

"We all can when we want to. But we generally don't." He smoothed back her soft hair with the backs of his fingers. "Blossom, I really think you're stronger than you were."

"I'm still afraid, Nicky."

"Of course you are."

"Maybe in a few days."

But Brian didn't give her a few days. They ran the scene again the next night, and as she started offstage to wait for her entrance for the second time through, Brian stopped her.

"Lisette, just a minute."

"Sure." She turned back toward the auditorium. Her rehearsal skirt had a little rip in the side that someone had safety-pinned together.

Brian walked up to the edge of the stage from his seat in the center of the house. "Okay. When you read that scene for me in New York, it was intelligent and sweet."

"Yes," she said in a low voice.

"It still is," he said. "It hasn't gone anywhere. It's exactly the same. Ophelia has outgrown it."

Nick, still waiting in the wings for his own entrance, tensed a little. Help her, God, he thought.

She faced Brian, sad but composed. "I know, Brian."

"Everything else you're doing is wonderful. People are going to want something more from this scene."

"I know."

Nobody else seemed to realize what was happening. Ellen, long hair smooth down her back, was taking advantage of the pause to write out some scribbled notes legibly as she perched at the stage manager's desk near him. David was fidgeting behind him, practicing pulling his sword from the scabbard smoothly. Cheyenne was focusing a light from one of the side boxes. Grace and Jim were sitting calmly on one of the wagons. Some staging crew members were working on the slide that was to hold one of the elaborately painted curtains, running it back and forth, over and over. And Brian, calmly and competently doing his job, was opening a chasm in front of Lisette.

"I think the problem is with the death images," he said with terrifying accuracy. "You're relating very well to the King and Queen and your brother. Very appealing. The songs are okay. But there's no depth. I just don't feel that you give a damn about your father being stabbed by your lover."

"I'm horrified by it."

"Yes, okay, I'm overstating a little. What you're doing now would go. But it could be so much better. The horror is all intellectual, it isn't very real. 'The violets withered all.' Surely you've felt like that at some time or other, when someone important to you died or something. The insanity of it all?"

She had covered her face with her hands.

"Lisette?"

"Brian, you'll have to give me a minute."

She turned and walked upstage, head lowered, and leaned on one of the newly finished columns of the back level. Nick, in the wings, was gripping the velour of a black tormentor curtain in one hand, crushing it in silent terror. He ached to hold her, to encourage her somehow. Around him the inane noises of the theatre continued—the whisk of David's sword leaving its scabbard, the trickling sound of the curtain sliding on its rod, the faint scratch of Ellen's pencil. He couldn't bear to watch her lonely battle any longer and glanced away, and unexpectedly saw someone near him in the wings. Maggie, a coil of electrical cable looped over her shoulder, was watching her too, tense, lower lip gripped between her teeth, dark blue eyes intent and worried. Unreasonably comforted by the realization that someone shared his terror, Nick looked back at Lisette.

Brian at least had the sense not to push her now.

Another moment passed. Then she turned back abruptly, head high. "Okay, let's go. You want withered violets, you'll get withered violets, Brian. Hup, two, everybody!" She clapped her hands imperiously. "Move!"

Ellen, startled perhaps, but as always unflappable, calmly read off the cue as the actors scurried to their places. Jim and Grace gave the opening lines, and then Lisette entered, with her sad little song. "White his shroud as the mountain snow— /Larded all with sweet flowers; /Which bewept to the grave did not go /With true-love showers." That was his cue, and he came in anxiously. She was shaking, and the blank eyes she turned on him frightened him. But her lines were still coming accurately.

"Conceit upon her father," he said, and she stared at him in horror, as though "father" meant "Jennifer." Which, for now, it did.

At last, brokenly, she managed to push away her dread for a moment, and shifted to the cheerful and bawdy St. Valentine's song.

"Pretty Ophelia!" was Nick's line.

And then she terrified them all with something they had never rehearsed. Her line, referring to the end of the song, was, "Indeed, without an oath, I'll make an end on it." But this time the submerged mad thoughts overwhelmed her, and she sprang violently and unexpectedly at Jim, seizing the dagger in his belt and wildly pulling it up, ready to stab herself. Nick was there in an instant, wrenching it away from her, and the blighted eyes looked at him unseeing for a moment. Then, with a little shrug and an absent, chilling smile, she finished the song.

Nick, shaken and completely out of character, forgot his next line. "How long hath she been thus?" Ellen's calm voice prompted him. He repeated the line woodenly. Lisette gave her first exit lines, shaking as waves of horror overcame her and steadying as she pushed them away. She moved offstage, graceful and distracted. Nick started after her. In the wings, he saw her stumble into Maggie's arms. After a second Maggie looked at him over Lisette's shoulder and signaled "okay" with thumb and forefinger. "Follow her close," said Ellen, for the second time. Oh, God, that was his line too.

"Follow her close; give her good watch, I pray you," he said, as much to Maggie as to Horatio, and watched Jim join them in the wings. Nick stumbled through his next speeches and managed to complete them, but he kept looking offstage and had no sense of his character at all. Grace and David, a bit puzzled, held up their end well, though, and before long it was time for Ophelia to enter again, singing. She saw her brother, and her eyes went immediately to his drawn sword.

"Fare you well, my dove!" she said, and this time, although David was shocked, Nick was ready when she lunged for the blade. He pulled it away from her, and again she gave the little shrug and vacant smile and went back to the songs, and to distributing the flowers in her sash.

"Oh, you must wear your rue with a difference!" she said to Grace seriously. "There's a daisy. I would give you some violets, but they withered all when my father died. They say he made a good end." The slim body was shaken again by a wave of dread, and then she sang bravely, "For bonny sweet Robin is all my joy."

David said, "Thought and affliction, passion, hell itself,/ She turns to favor and to prettiness."

Ignoring him, Ophelia finished her song. "God have mercy on his soul! And of all Christian souls, I pray God. God be with you."

Nick followed her out this time, irresponsibly and unprofessionally, leaving the others onstage alone. She had walked to the fly rigging and was leaning back against the ropes, exhausted. Maggie was holding one of her hands.

"She's okay," Maggie said, her wide smile welcoming Nick. He picked Lisette up and held her to him a moment, off the floor.

"Oh, God, Lisette," he said into her shoulder.

She leaned back a little in his arms and looked down into his eyes. "Hi, Nicky," she said, and smiled.

"Hi."

"Looks like you've blown your concentration."

He put her down and inspected her carefully. "You're okay," he said, unbelieving.

"I was only acting." Impish, triumphant. Overwhelmed, he hugged her again.

Rob, who had been in the house again watching, came bounding up the connecting stairs and embraced them both.

"Zetty, there wasn't a dry eye in the house!" he exclaimed.

"Thanks, Rob." She beamed at him.

"You're exhausted," he said, looking at her clinically.

"Sure. Heavy scene," she said cheerfully.

"Well, honey, you've just left the rest of us gasping in your dust." He turned to Nick with a humorous look. "Especially Nick. Our admiration for Zetty's performance is equaled only by our scorn for Uncle's."

"Looked bad, did it?" asked Nick. He was grinning foolishly. He wanted to jump and sing.

"I was sent to tell you that Brian wants to see you all onstage as soon as you pull yourselves together."

"Okay." Lisette started out onstage promptly, and Nick followed.

Brian was no fool. "Lisette," he said, quelling the spontaneous applause from the scattered actors in the auditorium, "is that something you can get under control?"

"I'd like to try, Brian." Calm and quiet.

"I'd like you to try, too." Reassured by her attitude, as Nick had been, he still was a little cautious. "But the other actors have to be able to trust you."

She looked mischievously at Nick. "I didn't muff *my* lines." Grace, standing behind them, turned and walked to the side of the stage, arms folded.

Brian asked, "Do you want to run it again now?"

"Yes, I do. Very much."

"Will you be grabbing for the weapons again?"

"If you want me to."

"I do. I just want to know."

"Okay."

Brian started to say something else, then paused and looked at Nick. Nick said, "Could we try it exactly the same way? I'll try not to blow it again."

"Yes." Brian understood and nodded, and Nick had permission to seize the weapons that she grabbed from the others. Carefully blunted though they were, they could do real damage. He could still feel, with an inward shudder, the wild strength in those slim arms raising the dagger. He couldn't, yet, trust Jim or David with her in that state. Not yet.

It was not quite as good the second time, but more than good enough. Lisette seemed to tire during her second entrance, and the distribution of flowers and the final song were a little strained and fatigued. But the diseased frenzy was as powerful and frightening as before.

"Everyone onstage," said Brian when they were done.

They all trooped back and sat or stood on the forestage. Brian came to the front of the auditorium, by the orchestra-pit rail, and looked them over. Nick sat on the edge of the stage, legs dangling into the pit, and pulled Lisette, tired but not unhappy, close to him to lean on his shoulder.

"All right," said Brian. "We've got a new scene here, people. It's not set, and I don't want to set it yet. Right, Lisette?"

"It's still pretty fluid, I'm afraid," she agreed.

"Okay. That means everybody onstage—Jim, David, Grace, Nick—has to be alert. If she surprises you, good. Work it into your own character. But don't break her concentration."

They nodded soberly.

"As for Nick . . ." Brian looked at him, still serious. "We can hope you'll get used to it."

"Nothing I'd rather do," said Nick lightly; but only Lisette, and maybe Maggie on the catwalks above, knew how much he meant it.

They went up to the dressing rooms to change from their rehearsal clothes, and, because he was still absorbed in the joy and terror of Lisette's accomplishment, Nick blundered. He dressed quickly and was going down the stairs to the greenroom to wait for Lisette when he saw Grace, still in her rehearsal skirt, sitting on one of the bottom steps of the stairwell, face bent toward the wall.

"Grace! Are you ill?" Worried, he put his hand on her trembling back and crouched beside her, concern furrowing his friendly face.

"Yes." She was at the edge of tears, the gray eyes too bright.

"Can I do anything?"

She turned and looked at him a second, then kissed him, lips fierce and soft, hands gripping his broad surprised back with desperation. Nick held himself still, ignoring the answering warmth that was spreading up through him. In a moment she released him and turned away. "Oh God, oh God."

His hand was still on her back. He patted her clumsily and sat back on the same step, leaning against the pipe that held the handrail. Well, boor, he told himself bitterly, neatly done. Nick O'Connor, artist- and stud-in-residence. Let's see you get out of this one. "Grace, it's all right," he said lamely.

"It's not all right." Her voice was low and husky.

"You didn't mean it."

"But I did, Nick."

"But not in any permanent sense."

She gave him a quick glance. "You don't think so?"

"When we work on shows, we all fall a bit in love with each other."

Another quick glance. "Maybe."

"I always do."

"But you stay with her, with that child!"

"Yes." His voice was gentle. "Because a show doesn't last very long. But my commitment to Lisette is for good."

"I know." She nodded miserably.

"You're outgrowing Jon a little."

"He's so rigid, Nick! With his sports, and his lectures, and his endless research articles! I'm sick of it!"

"Dear friend, all theory is gray, and green the golden tree of life."

She looked up at him then, helplessly. "See?" she said. "You understand. Instinctively."

"Goethe understood."

"Jon's read it all too. But he'd never think of saying that."

"Grace . . ." Nick rubbed his hand across his thinning hair. Everybody's goddamn uncle. "Look. Do you ever quote anything to him?"

"No. He wouldn't understand."

"Maybe not. But maybe he thinks you wouldn't understand." She was startled. Nick added, "Actors say things like that. It's our business to say them. Gives us an unfair advantage."

"Yes." She was a little better, embarrassed now. That he could cope with. She said, "Oh, God, how can I look you in the face?"

"Grace." He stretched his arm across the step and turned her face toward him. "It's the most wonderful compliment a man could ever have."

She shook her head, still miserable. "But you think I won't feel the same in a year."

"No, you won't. So I should probably tell you right now, Grace. On this show, you are one of the people I've fallen a bit in love with."

Gratitude and, thank God, a bit of suspicion. "Maybe," she said. She flexed her hands, looking down at them where they lay on her knees. "Nick, what'll I do?"

"Same thing I'll do. I'll live with it a while. Build it into myself. Understand a little more, grow a little more. Look at it again a year from now."

The quick glance she gave him this time had a touch of resentment. "Use it for one of your damn emotional memories."

"Maybe. That doesn't make it any less genuine, you know."

Jim's voice, muffled, echoed down from the floor above, and they heard footsteps approaching the stairs. They stood up, and Nick smiled at her and blew her a quick kiss. She turned and went up the stairs, head bowed. Jim and Judy passed her on their way down.

Nick went into the greenroom. Rob, still in his tights, was inspecting the stuffed effigy Paul had started. He put it down.

"Safe to use the stairs now?" he asked mildly.

They looked at each other. "Sure," said Nick.

"Well played, Uncle."

"Thank you. I appreciate that, from an expert."

Rob shrugged. "Not so expert at that stage. I specialize in nipping such fancies in the bud."

"Wish I had. How?"

"I use the occasional flash of unmotivated viciousness. Keeps down ninety percent of them."

They looked at each other again. The cut on Rob's cheek

had faded to a dusky red line. Nick found himself feeling very sympathetic toward this bright handsome man. Clearly being godlike had its disadvantages. He said, "Cruel only to be kind."

"Well . . ." Rob shrugged again and started for the stairs. The pleasant face was weary. "One does what one must. Let us all ring fancy's knell."

"Ding dong bell," said Nick.

Lisette had come down to join Nick, and the two of them were starting up the stairs to the exit when Cheyenne's angry voice exploded through the stairwell.

"What the shit is this?"

He was in the scene shop. Nick and Lisette hurried down through the greenroom again and found him staring at the big double door that led into the stage. On it was taped a cheap target for a dart game, and on the target was Lisette's photograph, tinted in rings to match the background.

In the center of the target, a steel-tipped dart had been pushed carefully through the pupil of her left eye.

"Damn," said Maggie. She and Ellen appeared behind them.

Nick strode over to the door, pulled out the dart, and ripped down the target. Cheyenne said, "What the hell is going on?"

"Somebody around here thinks it's a big joke to abuse Lisette's photos," explained Nick.

"Goddamn it! You mean there were others?"

"Several," Maggie told him. "At first they were tucked in with her personal things."

"Jesus! Fucking amateurs!"

Lisette said, "Don't get upset, Cheyenne. It's not so terrible."

"You sound like a goddamn amateur yourself," he said.

"Yeah. Professionals do their hating after hours," said Nick. "But look, this is probably just some unhappy kid, Judy or one of her friends, maybe. We'll be gone at the end of the term and everyone can get back to normal."

Cheyenne stared opaquely at the spot on the door where the target had been taped. After a moment he said, "I'm not going to graduate people under my signature unless they know what comes first in this business. We'll set a trap."

"We tried that," said Maggie. "We gave Lisette a big gaudy gift box and pretended to leave it unattended. We thought the joker would put his latest effort there."

"What happened?"

"Worked like a charm," said Nick, "except that the person watching, namely me, looked away for a couple of minutes and missed seeing whoever it was. And then I gave the game away by chasing after the joker and not even coming close."

"So now this creep knows you're watching."

"Right," said Maggie. "And it's sort of worked. It's been weeks since the joker has touched Lisette's personal things."

"So you've managed to push this person into crapping up the whole theatre now."

"A spreading cancer," said Nick. He had to agree with Cheyenne; it was pure luck that only Ellen and the designer had stumbled across the jokes, now that they were being left in public places. But he found himself angered by the lack of human concern for Lisette's feelings.

Cheyenne stood for a moment, hands in pockets, frowning. Then he said abruptly, "We need a better trap. I'll tell Brian. But here's what we'll do."

XII

The Thursday rehearsal was supposed to be the last complete run-through before spring vacation, but Cheyenne had announced that it was the only time he could get the floorcloths painted, so the actors would have to work elsewhere. Brian, grumbling a little, finally announced a line rehearsal in the upstairs room they had used before. Ellen had arrived a minute or two early to find Nick playing a cocktail-bar tango and Rob dancing with the Uncle Sam effigy. He had removed its hat and borrowed a rehearsal skirt from Laura's stock for it to wear. Everyone was giggling as he stared deep into its flat painted eyes and dipped and whirled it suggestively around the room. Overgrown children, thought Ellen. She noticed that her mouth was smiling and straightened it out firmly. The last chords sounded, and Rob bowed gravely to his stuffed partner, tucked a fake flower behind its ear, and then ran out to dump it heartlessly in the hall.

Brian and Cheyenne came in a minute later. "Ellen," said Brian, "Cheyenne wants to go over the book with you for light and sound cues. Why don't you do that now? Judy can manage the line rehearsal."

"Okay," said Ellen, and left. She was glad for the excuse. Ignoring Jim was much harder in the small room.

Cheyenne led the way downstairs and into the stage area. As they passed the pin rail, he adjusted a couple of the tied-off ropes. In contrast to *Blithe Spirit*'s arrangement, tonight the framing velours were pulled up very high; at the moment, even the front teaser, which formed the top of the proscenium arch, was flown high. Below, the damp floorcloth was spread across the stage. They went down the side steps and through the auditorium, then upstairs to the light booth behind the balcony.

"Hi, people. All set?" asked Maggie.

"Right. Kill 'em," said Cheyenne. Maggie pushed a couple of switches, and the stage and house were thrown into a velvety darkness broken only by the red glow of the exit signs.

"Well," said Maggie, "we've got time. Let's go over these cues." They settled down to work, writing the proposed light and sound cues into Ellen's master book. They were in the fourth act when Maggie suddenly stood, eyes fixed on the stage. Ellen and Cheyenne followed suit.

High above the stage, a glimmer had appeared. Someone had opened the upper door to the catwalks, the door Nick had once stumbled through. With the velours pulled high, they could see the light-rimmed edge.

Ellen, squinting, tried to make out what was happening. It looked like the silhouette of a tremendously fat child pushing its way slowly onto the catwalk. No, not a child, an adult bent over. Pulling something bulky. The door closed again, and she could see nothing. Then another light appeared, a flashlight beam. It gave her glimpses of folds of pale fabric, curly brown hair, glossy paper. Then, briefly, the beam hit the grid above, searching, and settled on a spot lower down, near the catwalk. The top of a sandbag, hooked to a flying harness. They watched a rope push through the hook while the light bobbled, then switched off.

"Crap," said Cheyenne admiringly. "We were right."

"Too bad Rob and Nick can't see this," muttered Maggie. "Should be spectacular."

The light glimmered twice more, but Ellen could not make out what was happening. Then the beam shot across the stage, and below the catwalk level it caught motion, something swinging, something with brown curls.

Maggie hit the switches, and the stage flared into sudden noon. It was a repellent scene. Slowly, rhythmically, the body in the long cream-colored dress swung back and forth, its neck in a crude noose that hung from the flying harness, its head at a grotesque angle. The face, smiling a dead smile, was Lisette's.

On the catwalk, staring up at the lights in shock, stood Laura.

The tableau lasted only an instant. Then she reached down to her bag on the catwalk, jerked out a sheaf of pages, and fumbled for a moment. A cigarette lighter. She was lighting the papers.

"What the hell?" said Cheyenne.

Laura ran toward them on the catwalk, the blazing roll of papers held high like a torch, her eyes intent on something high on the wall beside the proscenium opening.

"Merde!" Maggie wrenched open the door and was gone, crashing through the doors that led back down to the auditorium.

"Fuck!" Cheyenne followed her out, but he ran the other way, toward the fire exit to the outdoors.

Bewildered, Ellen stayed in the booth. What was worrying them? The body still swung, but that was no problem. Even from here you could see it was only Paul's Uncle Sam effigy, outfitted now with Lisette's mad-scene costume, a brown wig, and Lisette's smiling photo for a face. Unpleasant but harmless. Laura was out of sight now, but that was no problem either. They knew now who it was; they could always find her later.

Maybe she meant to start a fire.

But even that wouldn't be a major problem, would it? The sprinkler system would come on, the asbestos curtain would fall, and no major damage could occur. Yet Maggie was flying down the aisle toward the stage as though a life depended on it.

In the next instant calamity fell. Ellen heard the hiss of water, the first clanging bell, saw the fire curtain plummet before Maggie could get up the steps past it. Without breaking stride, Maggie shifted direction, up the side stairs to the outside exit. Ellen realized that no one could get into the stage area now; it was sealed off, though Laura could use the emergency bar of the catwalk door to escape. And the bells were ringing, and water was slucing down. Ellen came to her senses, hit the stage-light controls to turn off the power. Theatre lights were not made for immersion.

In the clanging darkness, she fumbled her way downstairs. Only the emergency lights were still burning. She stumbled out to the parking lot. Cheyenne was there, giving a last twist to a big outdoor water valve and cursing. The actors and crew members were pouring out onto the lot from other exits, calling questions to each other above the clangs. As Ellen hurried toward them, sirens screamed. A campus police car skidded into the lot, and just behind, grinding up the hill, came a big hook and ladder.

Cheyenne said something to the firemen, but they shoved him back rudely and ran into the building. Ellen, dazed, walked on with the others to a distance where the clanging was not quite so unbearably loud. Brian began grilling Cheyenne, who answered in sullen monosyllables.

"God, we should never have tried it," said Brian.

The others stood quietly, watching the activity. It was not quite real, the clanging bells, the cool night, the festive lights pulsing, the tense silent friends, the busy shouting strangers, the occasional sputters of metallic radio voices. No smoke. No lights from the building, except the bouncing circles from the powerful flashlights carried by police and firemen.

They waited. The clanging stopped, but still the firemen and policemen bustled about the building. Dean Wagner, summoned by his son, joined them. He looked very old, the slack jowl dismayed. He kept saying, "I can't believe it. I just can't believe it."

Maggie reappeared, looking tired, and went to talk to Rob and Nick. Rob put a consoling arm around her shoulder. Ellen joined them. "Did you catch her?" she asked.

"No. I tried to head her off but she must have come out another door. I went to her dorm room, but she didn't show, so I came back." She sounded exhausted.

Nick said, "God, if I'd only caught her the first time. Goddamn it."

"Do you think it's on fire in there?" asked Ellen. Her stomach was crawling around uneasily.

"Oh, probably not," said Maggie wearily.

Eventually the firemen started doing something different. They seemed to be rolling up the hose, collecting around the truck. Ellen frowned at them, not quite understanding. Then a campus policeman came up.

"Dr. Wright?"

"Yes?" said Brian.

"They've got things under control. It took a while to check all the rooms, but apparently there was no fire, just a small paper fire by one of the detectors on stage. You're very lucky. It'll be safe to go in soon."

"No fire?"

"Looked like just what your designer told us. A torch. Seemed to be made out of a bunch of large photographs rolled together, then lit."

Brian asked, "Is the stage all right?"

"Sure, no real damage. The automatic fire curtain and the sprinkler system worked perfectly. Everything was under control by the time it was shut off." He looked resentfully at Cheyenne. "You were lucky. Only authorized personnel should turn it off."

Dean Wagner said, "So things are basically all right?"

"Absolutely, sir. You can see for yourself in a few minutes."

"Thank God," said Dean Wagner. "You open the twenty-eighth, right, Brian?"

"We were supposed to," Brian replied unhappily

"That gives you three and a half weeks."

"Except that we have to get everything done by tech rehearsal or we can't pull it together. And spring break starts Wednesday."

"Not for us," said Cheyenne.

"We'll get the custodial staff to help," said Dean Wagner. "Support you however we can. All the alumni activities are scheduled around this show and the fair."

"All right," said Brian, depressed.

Rob said uneasily, "We'll play it in the parking lot if we have to, Brian."

"We'll play it anywhere," said Jim. Brian didn't answer them.

The hook and ladder went away. A moment later the lobby lights came on. "You can go in now, sir," said the policeman, responding to a signal from a fireman.

Cheyenne said, "Maggie, take a fireman up to the booth and see if anything works." Ellen realized the implications suddenly, the weeks of work that might have to be redone if the circuits had been damaged by the water.

Maggie ran on ahead, and the rest of them filed into the lobby. Through the doors, the auditorium was inky except for the beam of a fireman's flashlight. Then, startlingly, the houselights blinked on. One circuit okay. So far, so good. They filed in and looked around.

The main thing was the wetness. Seats and carpeting were soaked. A little pool glistened at the foot of the sloping aisle.

"How about switching to *The Merchant of Venice?*" suggested Rob flippantly. "We could bring in the audience on gondolas." No one answered him.

Ellen walked a few steps ahead of the others, down the soggy carpet. It would dry out, she told herself, pausing to inspect a damp seat.

There was a creak ahead of her, and she looked up to see that the gray asbestos fire curtain had begun, slowly, to rise. She watched it hopefully, not quite knowing what to expect. She could see that the stage floor was glistening, sprayed protectively by the sprinklers. No real damage. But as the curtain rose slowly, Ellen's stomach cringed, and her ears began to roar.

Water.

Gallons of water flushed all over the stage.

Gallons of water on the painted surfaces of the platforms. Water on the floorcloths. Water in the heavy velour of the tormentor curtains that masked the sides. In the canvas and gauze of the giant cyclorama. In the instruments and sockets and electrical cables of the onstage lights. And on the fragile curtains of the platforms, the curtains painted so carefully over the weeks to look like tapestries.

The bones of the *Hamlet* setting, columns and arches, stood forth in the murky light from the auditorium, erect and sturdy. But the life and flesh of paint and fabric drooped sodden from the arches, the colors puddling and sagging like candle wax into the gleaming pools on the floor. Weeks and weeks of work dribbling away like blood onto the stage.

Above it all, twisting slowly, the grotesque effigy still dangled.

Through the roaring in her ears Ellen was faintly aware of the others around her, a little moan from Lisette, a string of curses from Rob, most standing silent and appalled. She could not look anymore. She turned and fled for the only shelter there was in that glaring roaring night. For a moment he stood rigid, unbelieving; then his arms came around her, stroking her hair, and she clung silently to him, the unmoving point in her lurching world.

Brian said, "Dean Wagner, it's hopeless, sir."

There was work to do.

Her stomach was all right again, and her ears. She released Jim and said, "Guess it's time to get to work," and even sounded calm.

"Okay," he said.

He followed her up the side steps to the forestage. Maggie and Cheyenne and Paul, who had an electric lantern, joined them there, and they stood on the sodden floorcloth and looked things over.

"Number one," said Maggie, "let's dry things out. Two, let's start making lists of what needs replacing."

"We'll need people," said Cheyenne.

"I'll get that organized," said Ellen.

"Right now," Paul said, "I'll get the vac."

"We could use some fans too," Cheyenne said. Maggie thrust her flashlight into Ellen's hand, and Jim and Ellen went to get them. By the time they returned Maggie had strung cable from the working outlets in the house, and they could plug in the big fans and the commercial vacuum cleaner fitted with its wet nozzle.

"What's the broken glass?" asked Ellen, looking at the fragile shards scattered thinly on the puddled floor.

"Cold water on the hot bulbs," Maggie explained. "Didn't help my gels much, either."

The gels. Those carefully tinted transparent colored sheets that made the lights warm or cool, human or supernatural, gay or sombre, and that were so soluble that even high humidity in the air could wrinkle and spoil them. Ellen said, "God, Maggie."

"I'll manage, roomie," said Maggie confidently. "You look after Paul. And Brian."

Ellen went back into the auditorium to see Brian, who was leaning on the back railing looking miserable and stubborn. Rob, Nick, and Lisette, troubled, stood near him. Dean Wagner and David were a little apart, despondent, watching Paul use the vac on the stage. On her way up the aisle Ellen passed Judy. She gave her the flashlight.

"Go up and see how the rehearsal room looks," she said. "We can't let the actors back on the stage for a while."

Ellen joined Brian and the others.

"I just don't see how we can," Brian was saying.

"We've got to try, Brian," urged Nick.

"But look! No place for the audience. No place for the play. No lights. How can we?"

Ellen said, "Brian, it's a mess. But you're supposed to give us until tech rehearsal to finish things."

He looked at her, surprised. "Are you kidding?"

"Look, it's just a technical problem, right? Nothing's wrong with the actors."

"We're as frisky as ever," agreed Nick.

"So let us techies work on it a while. We haven't given up."

Brian looked skeptical.

Nick said, "You can always cancel later, Brian. But once it's done there's no turning back."

"Well, I'll talk to Cheyenne," Brian conceded. From the relief evident in Nick's brown eyes, Ellen realized that it had been a close thing.

Ellen said, "Why don't we have a meeting in the rehearsal room in the afternoon? For everyone's progress report?"

Brian nodded slowly. "Okay. One o'clock. I'll tell Cheyenne."

"Okay. I'll contact everyone else." She turned back to the ruined stage and got to work. It was two a.m.

Eventually the sun came up. Ellen, armed with her clipboard, had started making notes. She and Paul had stripped off the painted curtains from the rods, a cold job with the fans going and their clothes and hair drenched with the sprinkles of colored drops that fell every time the curtains moved. With the help of the campus policemen, they cordoned off an area of the parking lot and spread things to dry behind the barriers. Tim had carefully dried off the new swords and the flagons, but Ophelia's flowers and the books and other props on the prop table had been soaked. Cheyenne was everywhere—checking instruments with Maggie, ripping up the sodden floorcloth with Paul, requisitioning towels from the student union to dry the big power saws and lathes in the drenched scene shop, meeting the building custodian to arrange for cleanup of the auditorium. Brian, to everyone's relief, had gone home.

At about six-thirty Lisette, who had disappeared for a while, came in with a huge coffee urn and stacks of foam cups from the student union. Ellen called a recess, and they all collected in the lobby for a brief break.

"How are we doing?" asked Ellen. Everyone looked tired and muddy and eager for the coffee.

"No chance," said Judy wearily.

Cheyenne said, "Get out of here."

"What?"

"We've got no room for amateurs now. Get your ass out of here."

Grace said, "Come on, Cheyenne. We're all pretty discouraged."

"I'm not talking about discouraged or not discouraged. I'm talking about doing what has to be done."

"Professional commitment?" Judy's voice trembled. "Well, breaking your neck on a hopeless job is not professional. It's stupid."

"Professionals have one goal, and they do what's necessary," snapped Cheyenne. "No matter what sacrifices have to be made."

"That's stupid!" Judy was near tears.

"So get out. Move."

"Damn right!" Judy ran out the lobby door, slamming it behind her.

"All right, Ellen." Cheyenne turned to her as though nothing had happened.

"Yeah." Ellen, who felt she suddenly understood the universe, gathered her stunned forces. "Um, let's have a rundown on how everyone's doing. Paul?"

"We're going to need a lot more of the parking lot to dry things out," reported Paul. Like Cheyenne, he was now focused on the task, his usual friendly interest in everyone around him evaporated.

"Okay," said Ellen. "I'll get some more of those barriers. Tim?"

"Not bad. A lot of work to do, but if we can get some money it can be done. Thank God we saved those swords."

"Maggie?"

"Cheyenne's going to call New York first thing to order bulbs and gels. We may need instruments and replacement outlets too. Won't know till it's dry enough to test."

"Cheyenne?"

"We need velours. The act curtain is shot, but we

weren't going to use it anyway, it can wait. But the teaser and tormentors can't."

"A lot of stuff to get from the city."

"Yeah. And I don't know about the cyc. It may stretch dry on its own pipes. Or we may need a new one."

Nick said, "If you can get them ordered, Lisette and I will be in the city a couple of days over spring break for auditions. We can bring them back."

"You don't have a truck."

"We'll rent a trailer."

"Okay. I'll stay here and work."

"What about the house?" asked Ellen. "The carpets and seats?"

"Gone," said Cheyenne. "Buildings and Grounds will throw them out and bring in folding chairs."

"Sounds like high school again," said Ellen. "Okay. Anything else?"

"What about breakfast?" asked Maggie pragmatically.

Rob, who had been standing near her silently, musing into the plastic cup he was gripping, looked up at her now, astounded. Then he broke into helpless laughter. "The ravenous Miss Ryan!" he exclaimed, and kissed her streaky forehead enthusiastically. "I volunteer for your crew, so I won't miss any meals!"

"Well, take a break whenever it's convenient," said Ellen shortly. "Remember, people, be in the rehearsal room upstairs at one o'clock for the meeting."

They finished their coffee, talking quietly together. Ellen caught her roommate's eye and smiled a little. There were muddy smears all over Maggie's face and hands and clothes, but the blue eyes were still cheerful. Maggie smiled back. Guess I look like that too, thought Ellen, touching her hair. It was stiff with slowly drying scene paint. But the coffee helped, and her sweater had dried out a bit since she and Paul had taken down the curtains, and she really did feel hopeful again.

The others were drifting out, and Ellen quickly poured herself a last half cup and began to gather up the discarded cups in a trash bag. Maggie and Paul left together. As they pushed open the doors, Ellen heard Maggie speak quietly to him, and for the first time her roommate's voice was grim.

"Well, Paul. Guess we go to Plan B, huh?"

And Paul answered, sadly but firmly, "No choice."

Puzzled, Ellen was looking after them when Jim came back in and said tentatively, "Ellen."

She turned. She owed him an explanation, didn't she?

He said, "You don't have to explain. I know it was just stress. It's okay. Don't worry."

"You think I'll be fretting because I gave you the wrong impression?" She was tired and smudged, and full of new wisdom.

He was a little embarrassed. "No, not fretting, it's just that I know it's no good for you, so don't worry."

"Jim, I know something now too. Cheyenne just explained."

"Cheyenne?"

" 'Professionals have one goal, and they do what's necessary,' " she quoted. "I kept thinking you were a student. Like me."

"I see. But that doesn't change anything, Ellen. You're right. I know it's a hell of a life. I don't want to trap you in it. I thought about quitting acting. But I can't, it runs so deep. Don't worry, Ellen, I understand, it's better if—"

"Listen, you goddamn pro, if you quit acting you won't be you. And it looks like nobody else will do. Hell of a life or no."

Jim let out a whoop and spun her around the lobby, making her spill coffee all over her soggy jeans.

XIII

"Who would these fardels bear?" called Nick through the big doors to the loading platform. Down on the main floor of the shop, Maggie looked up with a wide grin. She was stirring paint, and looked as lively as ever and much better scrubbed than the last time he had seen her.

"Come on, everybody, it's the fardels!" She led a small stampede up the stairs to the platform and out through the giant doors to Nick's car and his rented trailer. With appropriate exclamations about grunting and sweating under a weary life, they carried the boxes of lighting cable and bulbs, the bundled new velours, and the enormous packages of the new cyclorama into the theatre. Cheyenne appeared in a moment or two, looking as close to pleased as Nick had seen him recently.

"Let's get that cyc up, Paul," he said, and a group of them carried the bulky parcels across the shop to the stage beyond. Nick followed.

They had made real progress in the three days he had been gone. About half the cast and crew had canceled their plans for spring break in order to stay and help. Dean Wagner had arranged to keep the dorms open for the students. He had also rushed through emergency authorization to purchase the new velours and cyclorama, a risky administrative move because the insurance report had not been completed. But it had meant that they could order the new ones in time for Nick to bring them back. The dean's interest also was inspiring Buildings and Grounds to amazing custodial feats. The auditorium had already been stripped of soggy chairs and carpets and supplied with racks of folding chairs. Judy Allison was back, on probation, having groveled before Cheyenne. She was working hard to complete the costumes Laura had left behind, and was keeping accounts for Cheyenne, separating production expenses from those caused by the water damage.

The set, of course, remained the biggest problem. Only now, after four hard days of work, had they finished stripping and scrubbing the units. Several wheels had rusted enough to become sticky and had to be replaced. The rampart unit, which had been covered with canvas, was back down to a scaffold on wheels. Today, Nick saw, they were almost where they had been four weeks ago.

They had two weeks left.

Looking around now as he walked through the stage and shop, Nick realized that ordinary responsibilities had been abandoned in favor of joining the staging crew. Maggie and Rob had been mixing paint for Paul. Chester and his wife were removing tacks from platforms. Ellen was keeping track of everything, translating Cheyenne's curt comments into directions that willing but inexperienced hands could understand. Cheyenne was admirable; tough and wiry, he seemed to be working everywhere, encouraging and inspiring his crews far more than vocal comments ever could.

Nick returned to his rented trailer, which had to go back that afternoon. Maggie popped out of it to perch on the bumper a moment, balancing a big box of lighting gels on her lap. "You remembered everything," she said, patting it.

"It's my training as a waiter," he said gravely.

"*Sans doute.*" A breeze lifted her hair. "How did the auditions go?"

"We'll eat this summer. Lisette has a part in a soap, and I've got a slot in a musical stock company in Connecticut if I want it."

"You'd rather stay in New York?"

"I'd rather stay with her. Maybe I can adjust the hours."

She folded down the flaps of the cardboard box on her lap thoughtfully. "It's sad to think you won't be around here anymore," she said.

"Yeah. That's probably the worst thing about this business. You make such good friends and then lose track of them."

"Yeah. Unless you're married or something."

"Even then, if you're not careful."

Her voice was edged with a little sadness. "Listen, Nick, I still think she's a lucky woman," she declared, then stood up briskly, hoisting the heavy box. "Well, back to work. Thanks for all these terrific fardels."

"Sure. Tell everyone I'll be back as soon as I turn in the trailer. I'll pick up Lisette too—she's changing."

It took a little longer than he expected, because when he got back to the apartment, Lisette was not ready.

"Hello?" he called. There was a smell of gardenias today.

"Hi, Nicky." Muffled voice. She was in the bedroom, standing by the dresser with her back to him, tying a dark string behind her head. She was naked, the fair skin smooth over the delicate bones and thin muscles of her back and rounded hips. She said, "This is a test. Do you love me for my pretty face alone?" She turned. She had borrowed one of the anthropologist's African masks from the wall, a painted grimace of black and yellow stripes, the bold, artful ugliness incongruous against her soft hair and light, fragrant flesh.

He scooped her up onto the bed with one arm, unbuttoning with the other hand. The leering directness of the atavistic mask was contagious, although he lifted it after a moment from her flushed face, in order to kiss and lick and nuzzle her into a primitive enthusiasm matching his. She made him feel feral, exuberant, today. Tarzan, Dionysus, and Romeo all in one package. One balding package.

A little later, dozing in her arms, he roused himself from a gardenia-scented stupor to mumble, "Did I pass the test?"

"You moved the mask," she said judiciously. "I'd say B-plus." She giggled when he poked her.

They dressed and went back to the theatre to work.

That week the actors continued to help Cheyenne in the shop. Rob appointed himself chief assistant to Maggie, whose job was enormous. Nick could sometimes hear Rob and Maggie singing or talking on the catwalks as he painted platforms below, but he knew that, like all of them, they were working hard, dawn till midnight every day.

Then spring vacation was suddenly over. Classes and rehearsals began again. Midway through the first week Brian put his foot down.

"You people are exhausted," he informed his assembled actors at nine o'clock one night. "Go home and sleep. And don't let me catch you in the theatre doing technical work again."

Nick, who wanted to help his busy friends, knew that Brian was right. The actors also had lost time, and needed to concentrate to regain their momentum. They were all delighted when Cheyenne announced a few days later that they could rehearse on the stage again, naked though it still was. There was so much yet to do, so little time.

Laura, they heard, was at home with her parents.

One day only, they did not work.

Even Paul emerged from his subterranean existence early that Saturday and joined the Hargate group and a hundred thousand other people in New York City for the peace march. The vast crowd in Central Park was old and young, black and white, blue-jeaned and business-suited. Uniformed policemen were everywhere, and daffodils, and folk music. But under the songs and flowers and warm sense of community was the somber undercurrent that was so much a part of life now, the despair of being a citizen of a country that seemed to be entangled in the wrong war at the wrong time.

After a while the march started. Placards came out. Stop the Bombing, Children Are Not Born to Burn, and, in black groups, No Vietnamese Ever Called Me Nigger. Pete Seeger and some children were on a float, singing. Behind the Hargate group, chants began.

"Hell, no, we won't go!"

"Hey, hey, LBJ, how many kids did you kill today?"

It was not cold, but still the skies threatened, and the crowds that lined the streets were not always friendly. Some shouted "Escalate!" and some threw red paint. Maggie pushed a tissue into Nick's hand from where she was marching behind him.

"Better wipe off your shirt," she said, "unless you like red."

"Thanks. I didn't know we were under fire."

"Well, they're worse off than we are, really."

"What do you mean?"

"They put the counterdemonstration over by the U.N. wall. The one that says 'They shall beat their swords into plowshares' in granite letters two feet tall."

Nick laughed. "That'll make nice photos in the papers."

At the U.N. Plaza they heard Dr. King and others speak. Then at five o'clock the downpour finally materialized. Drenched and complaining, the massive crowd disappeared abruptly into the interiors of the city. The Hargate people ran into the jammed subways and headed for their cars again.

They stopped for hamburgers just outside the city and sang songs during most of the dark, damp drive back to Hargate.

The next day, *Hamlet* engulfed them again.

Lisette was not yet happy with her mad scene. While the others were already overwhelmed by its power, she felt a lack, an inconsistency. Waiting in the wings near Ellen's prompt desk one night, Lisette complained to Nick and Grace.

"It's so hard. It comes over her like a fever. You know, malaria or something. And then I have to push it back each time. Like waves. But it's so exhausting."

"Too exhausting for Ophelia?" asked Nick.

"I think so. When I go for the dagger it's like a release. I stop fighting it, I'm going with it instead. I'm just riding the wave."

"You mean she needs to be restrained? A straitjacket?"

"Something like that. Or something to fight it with, an opposing force."

Grace opened her mouth, and closed it again, and then as though she was ashamed of her indecision, she said, "Sex," firmly.

"What?"

"The opposite of death. Life. Procreation. Sex."

The honey-brown eyes widened. "That's why her songs are bawdy! Grace, you're right!" Lisette looked excited. "I just discarded that earlier because this Ophelia is so political. Not like the Ophelia at Minneapolis. But you're right! Because if she didn't have that counterforce she'd be dead already. That's what was wrong." She threw an arm around Nick's neck and rested her smooth cheek against his beard. "Nicky, I'm going to be most indecent, and you must blame Grace for it."

"No. I'll blame Ophelia," he said, smiling at her.

Even with this warning, she surprised them a little. The opening part of the scene was as before, Lisette's slim proficient body shimmering with the effort of mastering the powerful dread within her. But this time she fought back harder. The beginning of the St. Valentine's Day song was almost obscene; then she rucked up her skirts in front of the King.

"Pretty Ophelia!" Claudius was shocked; and his words interrupted her lascivious thoughts, sobering her, and again she was prey to the desire for death.

"Indeed, without an oath, I'll make an end on't!" She pounced on Jim's dagger. He grasped her raised arms, those slim strong arms, and there was the usual brief struggle. Suddenly, to Jim's surprise, she gave a little smile, and one hand trailed sensually down his strong straining arm and shoulder and back to curl behind his waist, her shapely body molding to his, pressing against his crotch. He stepped back, amazed, dropping the dagger in surprise, and she laughed in lewd delight and finished her song. David in his turn received the same treatment; appalled, he turned away from her, hiding his face as he said his lines. At the end, when she left forlornly, saying "God be with you," it was clear that she was searching for another dagger.

Brian was ecstatic.

"That's it! Lisette, it's great! It's all of a piece now. Are you comfortable with it?"

"Yes. That's how it is for her. That's how we want it."

"Jim, David, wonderful reactions. Keep them. But Jim, don't drop the dagger. David, yours is just right, the horrified brother invited to incest."

"It's scary," said David.

"Oh, God," said Brian. "Your father?"

Rob said, "David, he'll have to get used to that sort of thing someday, if you're an actor."

"Yes, but this is his college. His alumni," said David doubtfully. "Well, I'll try to warn him."

"Let me know if he hits the ceiling," said Brian. "But it's good, David, it's honest."

Nick glanced at Lisette, sitting quietly on a platform.

What a beautiful and talented and lovable and disruptive wife he seemed to have. She sensed his eyes on her and looked up with a little smile. With a sudden jolt of wonder Nick thought, she's done it, she's found her way out. Then his natural caution reasserted itself. Better wait, said his objective self, see how she does back in the city. But at some deep level he was convinced, and jubilant.

He and Rob, separately or together, were onstage for all but a couple of scenes. During the run-throughs, which were scheduled most nights now toward the end of April, they often spent their offstage time in the house watching the other scenes, absorbing a sense of the whole play. Arriving a minute late at the back of the house one night, Nick leaned on the back railing to watch the first scene. Jason was really not bad as the Ghost, lanky and sepulchral, and Jim was excellent as Horatio, a warm, intelligent reading that made it clear why he would become a prince's special friend and support.

Rob and Maggie were watching too, sitting on the side near the back, his arm thrown carelessly across the back of her folding chair, exchanging an occasional whispered comment. After a while she stood up, gave his hand a squeeze, and went back through the door that led to the lighting control booth steps. Rob left soon too, and Nick joined him and the rest of the crowd that entered for the first court scene. When it was finished, Nick exited; but he was a little uneasy and waited by the door to the stage-left wings until Rob completed his scene with Horatio and exited after him.

"Rob. A word?" he said. David and Lisette were onstage now for their first scene.

"Anytime, Nick."

They were alone in the little hall that buffered the greenroom and shop from stage and wings. Nick said as lightly as he could, "I assume you always make sure that your undergraduate friends are aware of the facts of life?"

Rob hesitated before he answered, also lightly. "Always, Uncle. They know everything they should know. My whole boring autobiography, entitled *From Cradle to Kathleen, and After.*" But he seemed a little disappointed in Nick, and Nick regretted now that he'd brought it up at all. Then Rob grinned, not unfriendly, and added, "Not that it's any business of yours, but I couldn't teach these modern children anything that they don't know already."

"Well, good," said Nick, relieved. "I wasn't suggesting that. It's just that they're very young."

The shrewd blue eyes gave him a calculating look. "Young or not, you can't seriously be worried about our soubrette! She's far more sophisticated than you or I, Nick. She tells me she was thoroughly deflowered in Paris."

"Goddamn it, Rob! That's what I meant!" Nick was surprised by his own vehemence, and lowered his voice again. "You're right, it's none of my business. So don't tell me, or anybody! You shouldn't spread stories like that."

Rob looked hurt. "I'm not spreading stories. I haven't told another soul, and I won't. I was just trying to ease your troubled mind."

"Okay. Fine. Good. Consider it eased."

"Okay." Rob looked at him, puzzled, and then jerked his thumb toward stage right. "I have an entrance in a few lines, if you'll excuse me now."

"Okay." Nick made an effort and met his friend's gaze. "Excuse me too, Rob. I was out of line. The subject is closed."

"Sure." Rob clapped him once on the shoulder and disappeared.

Well, meddler, thought Nick, let that be a lesson to you. Thou wretched, rash, intruding fool. Rob knew his responsibilities. Nick vowed to stay out of it.

The developing mad scene helped all the actors. Nick had been working on Claudius's political playacting, his ability and insecurity, his constant weighing of every situation in terms of maintaining his shaky throne. Now, with this basic line of the character as natural as breathing, Nick realized that Claudius was taking on a life of his own. He was deeply afraid of damnation not only because of the murder, but because of his passion for his Queen. With trepidation, Nick decided he'd better do some work with Grace.

He knew it might hurt her. She wasn't professional. But it would help her performance as much as his. Nick liked to think of himself as a kindly man, but he had to admit that Ellen had been right; in the quest for a strong performance he was a bit insane. He would sacrifice himself, and if need be, he would sacrifice Grace. Ruthlessly.

She listened in silence. Nick explained to her, carefully, his reasons for what he wanted to try; and, calmly, she agreed. Then, with a flash of bitter humor, she added, "It's all right, Nick. Don't protest too much. I'll help you tune your damn piano."

They went over their scenes together that afternoon, alone in the rehearsal room, and expressed the feelings behind the lines in exaggerated physical action. When Claudius felt fond of Gertrude, he kissed her passionately; when he was irritated by her attachment to Hamlet, he shoved her angrily away. Even when he was urging Hamlet to remain at court, Claudius's hands moved sensually over her responsive hips and thighs and hard-nippled breasts, his lips murmuring the lines against her throat, in demonstration of his hidden motive of pleasing Gertrude. Grace too exaggerated Gertrude's actions, fondling him and kissing him; and during some of his long speeches to the court, she knelt by him, running warm hands along his legs. Then, in the later scenes after Hamlet scolded her, she gave her lines from far away; as he approached her, searching for comfort, she would recoil, backing away, dodging his attempts to reach her. They worked the scenes several times until, finally, they were satisfied with the interplay.

Nick checked his watch; he had thirty minutes before he was scheduled to meet with the Players. He'd been ruthless long enough. Hoping the session had not hurt her, he asked casually, "Do you want a quick coffee or something?"

She was buttoning her suede jacket, and smiled and shook her head. "No, thanks, Nick," she said. "Not today."

"Appointments? The busy professor?"

"If you must know," she said pleasantly, "the busy professor is going straight home to teach her husband about the golden tree of life. Today's lesson includes screwing before cocktails." And she left.

Nick stared after her, rubbing his head, amazed and rather pleased.

That night their scenes were full of life. Nick's well-trained body remembered the afternoon's work, and while he stood in the same places and did the same things he had done every night, he could tell that the work was paying off. There was a quality to his voice and movements that betrayed the new emotional weight of the lines, a sort of electricity in the exchanged glances and light touches that had never been there before. When they assembled in the house afterward for notes, Brian said, "Nick and Grace. Interesting development tonight in the Claudius–Gertrude relationship."

"Yes," said Nick. "I thought it was much more intense."

"I liked it. You might look for just a couple of places to physicalize it—stroke her arm when no one's looking, that sort of thing."

"Okay."

"Grace, good work tonight. Keep going in that direction, okay? Nick will help you."

"Yes, I'm sure he will."

Rob, sitting next to Nick, leaned over, hand hiding his mouth, and murmured, "Nick, old man, has the bloat king been giving that woman reechy kisses again?"

Nick looked at him innocently. "One does what one must," he said. Rob chuckled.

Rob's performance too was changing subtly, in part because of the strengthening performances of the others. The aching vulnerability that had first been glimpsed in his scene with Ophelia was more and more apparent now, in stark contrast to the politicians—Claudius, Laertes, Polonius, Fortinbras. In scenes with them he seemed younger, a brave boy standing up to his sophisticated elders. With Horatio, as with Ophelia, he hungered for companionship, a lonely prince who yearned to be loved for himself. In the soliloquies especially, the vastness of destiny, the enormity of his supernatural assignment, seemed to overwhelm him—the young man shrinking from his fate. Nick admired what Rob was doing; to take a strong six-foot frame and project that kind of human frailty was quite a feat.

"It's looking good, Rob," he told him one night. "You're appealing to all our mother instincts."

"Thank your wife," said Rob. "She gave me courage to let go. Hamlet wants to die as much as Ophelia."

"You've been there too?"

"Sure. When my marriage was breaking up. Not re-

cently." He shrugged. "I've pretty much come to terms with myself. Has she, Nick?"
"I think so, Rob. I think she finally has."

In the midst of their frenzied preparations, one interesting bit of information sifted in from the outside world. Laura, said Brian, was coming back to school. Hargate officials had agreed to allow her to finish the term, with the understanding that she would continue in psychotherapy, and that she would stay away from the theatre except for necessary classwork. If this probationary period worked, charges against her would be dropped.
"What are the charges?" Ellen asked Brian.
"Damaging the theatre, and stealing and defacing the photos."
"There was more than that," said Nick.
"Yes, but the Hargate legal counsel says we only have real evidence about those things, and that's all she'll admit to. It should be enough to keep her in line, I think. Nick, we're all furious about this, but obviously it's worse for you two. When she's back in your class, will you be able to hide your feelings?"
Nick shrugged. "That's how I earn my living. Besides, she's more sick than evil. I want her to get well."

It was going to be a damn good show, thought Ellen. A damn good show, but strewn with the discarded husks of hardworking techies such as Ellen Winfield. Dry tech tomorrow. A perfect name. It meant a rehearsal of technical effects without the actors, but this time it described the state of the exhausted crews as well. Paul and Cheyenne were haggard, the other crew heads not much better off. The old moles seemed older every day. Even her energetic roommate had been to the clinic, and now collapsed every night in cheerful exhaustion.
Still, Ellen had to admit she was almost grateful to be so busy, because Jim was gone again. Ignoring her half the time, wrapped up completely in the play. His Horatio, of course, was thriving; he and Hamlet had developed a genuine, palpable relationship, an honest friendship that projected warmly. She had never felt so proud of a show before, and Horatio was part of it.
But the Jim who was so alert to every nuance of her life

had disappeared. Again. She missed him desperately. But that's how things had to be, she knew now. He'd be back again.

Others had problems too. Judy, struggling to prove herself to Cheyenne, had a chronic cough these days. Three members of the staging crew had flunked a big biology exam, one of Maggie's follow-spot operators had quit when he realized that working on the show would mean failing calculus, and Ellen herself had received a mere B-minus on her history paper, completed at four a.m. one night last week. Not the way to get into law school. But the worst off was probably Paul Rigo, although he was not complaining. He seemed to have stopped going to classes altogether. He was there, painstakingly reworking the curtains, every time Ellen arrived or left. He was tired but oddly cheerful, though Maggie occasionally gave him a sad glance. They never worked on physics anymore.

One day Lisette sought him out where he was adjusting one of the new velours. "Paul," she said, "you've missed three classes this week."

"I know, Lisette. But I have to finish this." He waved vaguely at the stage.

"The problem is, I can't give you a passing grade if you don't come. Acting class isn't like other classes, where I can just give you a test to see if you know the facts. The whole process is important."

"I know. But I don't have time."

"You've worked so hard in class up till now, Paul."

"Thank you." He gave her a shy, pleased smile. "I know I'm not much good at it. But I liked it. You're a good teacher."

"Thank you, Paul. But really, I want to pass you if I can."

"Oh, I know you do!" He looked concerned. "I don't blame you, Lisette. Honest. Don't think that."

"Okay. But please come. Someone else can fill in for you here a few hours a week."

Cheyenne materialized suddenly next to them, his steely fingers closing viselike on her forearm. "The hell they can!" he snapped, black eyes angry. "You leave my crews alone!"

Startled, Lisette stared at the clamped fingers, then at his glaring face. "I was trying to help, Cheyenne!"

"Bullshit. He's got work to do. You're supposed to be so professional, you know that."

"But Paul isn't professional. He's still a student."

"Listen, lady, you wouldn't be here if it weren't for me. You've got one purpose, and that's Ophelia. Period. Now leave my crews alone!"

"Cheyenne, you're hurting her!" Paul jumped up, grabbed Cheyenne's arm in protest. The designer's attention shifted to him; then, with an effort, he forced himself to release her arm and stalk off. Paul turned to her anxiously. "Are you okay?"

"Yes." Lisette rubbed her arm, looking after Cheyenne, bewildered.

"It's just that we all care about the show. And he's tired," Paul explained apologetically. "So I'd better stick with it."

She gave up. "Well, think it over, Paul, if the grade is important to you."

Ellen went up to him when Lisette had gone. "Is that true, Paul? You're going to fail acting?"

"Well, sure. She can't pass me if I'm not there."

"Don't you give a damn about the draft anymore?"

"Ellen," he said, and for once he did not smile, "they'll never send me over there to kill people. Don't worry. They can't force me to do that."

"But Paul, you don't want jail either! It would be so much easier if you kept your deferment!"

"Don't worry, Ellen. Please."

Ellen ignored his instructions and went on worrying. She asked Lisette if he could be given a grade of incomplete in the course, but Lisette had already checked the requirements for all possible non-failing grades, and Paul's case simply did not qualify. And his other professors, physics for example, could not ignore his complete abdication either. "Jim, I'm so worried about him," Ellen said one night after rehearsal.

"He feels he has to do it," he explained.

"But he could ruin his whole life!"

"Abandoning the show right now might ruin his life too."

"Insane! You're all insane!"

"Is that supposed to be a news flash?"

Paul got his work done. Ellen stayed late Friday night,

helping him get the last tapestry curtain hung before Saturday's dry tech. Then she dropped him off at his dorm before driving back to hers. These last two weeks she had hardly noticed the outdoors; now, abruptly, she was aware of the new growth, vigorous young leaves on the trees and bushes, opening to the mild air.

The lot was nearly full, and she had to park at the far end. She walked back to the dorm along the edge of the woods. The lights from the parking lot did not reach very far into the trees and she might not have seen them if it hadn't been for the gleam of the flute, a shock of silver in the dappled darkness. It hung down from her dangling arm as she stood, body stretched a little to meet his height, the two slim forms merged in the leafy darkness. One of his hands cradled her head; the other moved gently down the length of her back and then, lean and masculine and expert, caressed the blue-jeaned buttocks. His pale hair, like distant flame, mingled and was lost in the feathery dark curls of hers. Ellen, unwilling voyeur, hurried past without indicating that she had noticed anything; but the image haunted her as she climbed the stairs to their room. She did not know what she had seen. Apollo, finally mated to a creature suited to his bright and airy realm? Or merely dallying with a poor doomed Icarus? She looked sadly at the daisies in a water glass on Maggie's desk as she brushed her hair and got into bed. Cut it out, Winfield, she told herself, you're just being fanciful. They are mere human beings like all of us. Get some sleep before tech.

But she waited till Maggie came in a little later, humming, and demanded, "Maggie, you aren't getting really serious about Rob, are you?"

"What's the matter, eldest oyster? You think you're the only person in the world who likes actors?"

"Come on, Maggie. Don't mock."

Maggie was smiling a little. "Okay, Ellen. Look. Super secret." She had a thin gold chain around her neck, under her shirt. She pulled it out. There was a gold ring on it, with a little diamond.

"Maggie!"

"Secret. Okay? He's afraid the dean would freak out."

"Well, he probably would." Glad, and worried still, Ellen watched her drop the ring back between her breasts. "Maggie, what's he really like?"

"Bright and funny and thoughtful and loving. And complicated. And gloriously unboring. The beauty of the world, the paragon of animals!" She bounced exuberantly into her bed and looked owlishly at Ellen. "Sound familiar?"

Ellen grinned grudgingly. "Yeah. Sounds like Jim."

XIV

"House to half."

Ellen sat alone in the dark, perched on her stool. The carefully framed light that fell on her book was the only light in the wings. The murmuring and rustling of the audience slackened as the lights dropped.

"Warning, Sound three, Electric one, two, three."

She spoke quietly into the headset. The stage was lit at a low level, the bulky ramparts edged with faint light, the new cyc a deep gray-blue. The music, a rumbling ominous piece, moved to its conclusion.

"Electric one. Go."

The houselights blacked out, and the stage darkened as the music ended. The audience grew silent. There was an almost noiseless flurry of actors moving in the darkness.

"Electric two, go. Sound three, go."

Three muffled shots sounded as low lights came up again on the darkened castle. A spotlight above Ellen's head and to her left picked out Horatio's profile as he stood by the stage-right rampart, wrapped in his cloak and looking left as some soldiers rolled a cannon across and off left.

"Electric three, go."

The ramparts above grew faintly brighter as a man toiled up toward the highest level and, sensing the sentinel nearby, cried, "Who's there?"

"Nay, answer me. Stand and unfold yourself."

Hamlet was underway again.

It was difficult to believe that this was already the last performance, the tenth time through. It had been a success, even from Dean Wagner's point of view. Perhaps impressed by the play, perhaps by the sight of the naked auditorium filled with folding chairs, the visiting alumni had responded to the special theatre-fund drive with great generosity. Brian and the dean had not tried very hard to dispel the illusion that the age of the equipment was somehow to blame for the damage, and so even the unglamorous maintenance fund received support. And Judy, who was keeping careful accounts of the show expenditures for Cheyenne, reported that they would come out a little ahead despite the water damage.

"Electric four, go."

A blue follow spot from low in the left wings shot up to catch the ghost stalking across the highest level of the rampart. The three others, panicking, pushed Horatio to the front to speak to him.

Jim was damn good, thought Ellen with vicarious conceit. She had watched him ignore her through dress rehearsals and opening night with a new, fond tolerance. And once the show had been successfully launched, he'd had time for her. Almost too much time.

"Warning, Electric forty-nine, forty-nine A."

Ellen remembered working out this cue at the cue-to-cue technical rehearsal Sunday, the first time the actors had worked with the lights. It had not gone badly for a show with over a hundred light cues, and they had worked their way fairly smoothly all the way to Cue sixty-one, just before the solitary act break. Rob had been standing onstage, patiently waiting for Brian to decide how rapidly the lights behind should fade for his soliloquy, "'Tis now the very witching time of night."

"Let's try a five-count," Brian had said.

"Right," said Maggie. They tried it.

But Brian hadn't liked that. "Fade's okay. But he needs more light," he said. "Can you get another instrument in there? On the side?"

Rob, stoically, had pulled out his broad dagger and was inspecting it; for the moment, he knew, he was not Hamlet, not Rob, but merely an object that reflected light.

"We've got the Horatio special," said Maggie's voice in the headset. The light from the side joined the others, adding shine to Rob's hair and bouncing from the dagger to hit the curtain. "God!" said Maggie on an indrawn breath.

Brian was saying, "That's better. Try that. Five-count."

The lights behind Rob faded out slowly, leaving only the front and side lights as he gave the soliloquy; then Ellen said, "Electric sixty-two, go," and they too blacked out. The act was over.

"Brian?" said Maggie's voice.

"Yeah, that's fine, set it."

"I want to do Cue forty-nine again."

"But we've set that already!"

"No, I want you to see this. Ellen, are you there?"

"Yeah?"

"Put Rob on."

Ellen called Rob over and handed him her headset. He listened intently a moment, then asked, "Where should I be?" and then, "Full front? No, probably three-quarters front, facing left," and finally, "Gotcha, celestial and most beautified!"

He grinned at the headset's reply and handed it back to Ellen. She put it on in time to hear Brian say plaintively, "Okay, we'll try it, but it better be good, Maggie."

"Ellen?" Maggie was all business.

"Yeah?"

"Act Three, Scene One, after Cue forty-eight. Call Claudius and Polonius."

The lights went up onstage. Paul's crew reset the scene, and Nick and Chester, patiently, came out to take up their positions. They began their lines, Ellen gave the warning for Electric forty-nine, and Nick and Chester disappeared behind the curtain to eavesdrop. Ellen said, "Electric forty-nine, go." The stage lights blacked out; and this time, instead of the front areas remaining lit as Ellen remembered, they went dark too. Only the Horatio special from the side came up. Rob was standing further forward than Jim did, so the light came from a little behind him, turning his pale hair into a gleaming corona and flashing from the broad shining dagger. His face was in shadow.

"To be, or not to be, that is the question." The familiar words were transformed, magical, in the dark. As he said the next few lines, he turned the dagger slowly; and suddenly, chillingly, his face was illuminated by the reflected light of the dagger. As the speech went on the other lights came up, imperceptibly slowly, so that by the end they were ready to move into the scene with Ophelia as before.

"Hey, Maggie!" said Brian's voice.

"Yeah?"

"You're right. Set that."

"Okay. Thought you'd like it."

"Rob?" Brian called from the house, headset off.

"Yes?"

"Great effect. Tomorrow hold the dagger reflection until you get to 'and by opposing end them.' "

"Right."

And now, as they went through it for the last time, Ellen felt again the power of the moment. As the lights fell for the end of the scene, the audience rustled a little, shifting on the folding chairs, coughing occasionally; but when the special came up on the golden head and silver dagger, shining in the dark, they checked, suddenly silent. Rob's pleasant voice, thoughtful, aching, gave the familiar lines; then his gentle grieving face was revealed in the awful reflected light of the blade. A silent shiver ran through the attentive, motionless audience. Ellen felt humble, and ferociously proud, that she was part of this show too. Whatever mysterious thing they were doing was the most worthwhile thing there was. Nick was right, and Cheyenne, and Paul. And Lisette, who, Ellen suspected, had risked real danger for the sake of her art.

And Jim.

"Electric eighty-five. Go."

The lights rose again. Then Lisette, delicate yet strong in her pale sacking costume, came on for the mad scene. This had been the most controversial scene, for both playgoers and reviewers. Dean Wagner, at first shocked but then pleasantly titillated, had taken to bringing important alumni backstage every night to introduce them to Lisette, to show them that she was really sweet and innocent in real life, not a lascivious bawd.

The reviews, too, had been mixed. Everyone's favorite had appeared before Friday's show, when Rob strode into the greenroom waving a New York weekly newspaper.

"Margaret Mary Ryan," he had announced, "they love you in the Big Apple."

"Really? Let me see!" Maggie flew to his side and peered at the paper. The three New York agents, after mighty efforts on all fronts, had managed to convince a solitary critic from the city to accept free travel and accommodations to go upstate to review this centenary *Hamlet*. The result was finally out.

"Hey, look at that!" Maggie was beaming. " 'Lighting, by M. M. Ryan, gave a fresh look to familiar scenes.' Whoopee!"

The others in the greenroom crowded around. Rob had brought two copies, and several clumps of people jostled for position to read the review. They tossed each other phrases: "A *Hamlet* for the sixties, focusing on the implications for the entire nation"; "Rob Jenner's Hamlet is humorous as well as melancholy, determined as well as hesitant, skillful as well as vulnerable"; "Nicholas O'Connor's strong and interesting Claudius, a skilled statesman with a foul underside of murder and lechery"; "One of the high points was Lisette O'Connor's beautifully conceived Ophelia, adorable when sane and intensely moving when mad"; "Competent performances by Jason Vandervere as the Ghost, David Wagner as Laertes, and Grace Halliday as Gertrude"; "Jim Greer brought an unusual warmth and definition to the often thankless role of Hamlet's friend"; "Evocative, flexible setting."

Nick grinned at Rob. "Too bad we close in two days. In New York a notice like this would extend the run."

"Won't hurt the old portfolio in any case."

It was a pleasant change from the local reviews. The Jefferson newspaper had praised the production, but devoted most of the space to a plot summary and an account of the centenary. The student paper had been negative—its young reviewer had found the play too long, the Ghost and Hamlet's hesitation unbelievable, but did praise Ophelia, the Gravedigger, and the climactic swordplay. "Well," said Rob kindly, "old Will put those scenes in for the groundling mentality."

The other two critiques had been in Buffalo papers. One complained about the traditional production, wondering why some of the innovations introduced by Guthrie or others had not been followed, and only grudgingly admitted that the actors were competent. The other deemed the production too innovative, mentioning "distracting lighting" and "an uncomfortably explicit mad scene" as drawbacks to a potentially brilliant production.

So the New York review delighted them. The professionals and the graduate students knew that a favorable notice from even a small New York City weekly looked better in their files than a rave from Buffalo or Jefferson. The undergraduates could wave it at their friends as proof of the incompetence of the student reviews. And it was pleasant to find that someone had noticed their efforts to emphasize Hamlet's role in the state, the broader implications of this particular family's tragedy.

"Warning, Electric one-oh-four."

"Hamlet, thou art slain./ In thee there is not half an hour of life./The treacherous instrument is in thy hand,/ Unbated and envenomed." David, falling, touched Rob's calf in supplication. "Lo, here I lie,/Never to rise again. Thy mother's poisoned./I can no more. The King, the King's to blame."

"The point envenomed too?" cried Rob. "Then, venom, to thy work!" He lunged for Nick, who leaped off the throne platform. The courtiers shifted. Like a lion tamer, Rob stalked him around the stage, thrusting twice and missing, and finally leaping down on him from the platform, running the sword through. The courtiers gasped and fell back.

"O, yet defend me, friends!" pleaded Nick. "I am but hurt!" He pulled himself onto the platform next to Grace's still, white form and turned to face Rob, who had snatched up the poisoned cup and now leaped up next to him, forcing the cup to his lips.

"Here, thou incestuous, murderous, damned Dane,/ Drink off this potion!"

Nick stumbled back, weakly, and grasped the red curtain behind him; then, as Rob backed away, still watching him, Nick fell forward, the red curtain ripping from its supports above to reveal the one behind, a steely Fortinbras blue. The red fabric billowed from the King's suddenly stilled hand, spilling crimson across the stage.

"Electric one-oh-four. Go."

The long slow fade to the end began.

That curtain effect had taken Paul long enough, Ellen thought. Cheyenne had suggested it; but Paul was the one who, on top of everything else, had to get a new blue curtain, and attach the painted red one with strips of Velcro, exactly enough so that it would stay up when necessary, and rip off when necessary. Hours of Paul's life had gone into those few seconds on the stage.

And, beaming, he had said enthusiastically to Ellen, "Doesn't it look great?"

The audience tonight, silent, gripped, seemed to think so too.

"Electric one-oh-seven, go."

Fortinbras was speaking as the special lights on him began to fade slowly. "Take up the bodies. Such a sight as this/Becomes the field, but here shows much amiss./Go, bid the soldiers shoot."

Hamlet's limp body was removed gently from Horatio's arms, and the soldiers carefully began to carry him off. Horatio stood slowly and pulled his cloak about him as the stage darkened.

"Electric one-oh-eight, go. Sound nine, go."

The Horatio special spotlight above Ellen's head picked out Horatio's profile as he stood by the stage right wagon, wrapped in his cloak and looking left, watching the soldiers carry off his friend. Three muffled shots rang out.

"Electric one-oh-nine, go."

The stage grew black.

There was a long silence, then the explosive surge of applause from hundreds of moved and grateful people. Ellen found that there were tears running down her cheeks.

"Call. Go," she said calmly, if a bit huskily.

The lights brightened, and the actors, smiling, ran on to form a line. Courtiers and ladies and soldiers, then Players and Rosencrantz and Guildenstern, the First Player and Osric. And then the larger roles—David, Jason, Jim. The applause was louder now. Someone out there was yelling approval. And Chester and Grace and Nick and Lisette. More yells and bravos. And finally Rob, to a general clamor. He bowed, and reached back for the others, and they all bowed, and bowed again. Ellen gave them one more bow.

"Call down. Go. House up. Go."

The stage blacked out, and the auditorium lights brightened. The applause faded into the muttering of hundreds of conversations, the scraping and shuffling of hundreds of people moving slowly to the aisles and outdoors.

It was over.

Forever.

* * *

They collected afterward in the greenroom, filled with the bittersweet elation of a difficult and strenuous job well done. Brian congratulated them and then left to pick up Deborah and bring her to the cast party at the Oasis. Rob stuck his head in and said not to wait for him, he'd see them at the party. Dean Wagner came down, smiled at his son briefly, and told him not to be too late as David started upstairs to change. Then the dean headed straight for Lisette to introduce her to tonight's batch of important alumni. She stood smiling in her rough-textured cream costume, holding her bouquet tightly and answering questions patiently. Many of the other actors changed quickly and joined Ellen and the others in the greenroom. Finally, proudly, the dean gave her a little peck on the cheek and left. She started across the greenroom and toward the stairs, then paused where Nick was sitting, her gentle hand on his shoulder.

"Are we all going to the Oasis?" she asked.

"Right. Back room. We'll leave when we're sure everyone has a ride," said Judy.

"It'll take me a few minutes. Nicky, wait for me."

He turned his head to kiss the hand on his shoulder. "Sure," he said. She ran up the stairs.

Cheyenne came down past her and looked around the greenroom. "Maggie around?" he asked.

"I haven't seen her yet," said Ellen. "She'll probably be along." Paul wasn't here yet either, or David, but he probably had to go home. Tim came in and sat down.

"It's great weather tonight," he said.

"I don't care. My mission is indoors, at the Oasis, getting pissed," said Jason with determination. There was a chorus of agreement from the undergraduates.

After a few minutes' chatter, Grace said, "Shouldn't we let them know we're coming? I told Jon I'd meet him there."

"Good idea," said Judy. "I'm not sure how long they'll hold the room. Grace, you and I can go on over. Maybe Paul and the others will be here soon."

"I think I saw Maggie and Rob driving off when I was in the parking lot just now," said Tim. "They may be there already."

"Or somewhere. He said he'd be late," muttered Jason sadly.

"Well, Grace and I can go on ahead," said Judy. "Cheyenne, I've got the account book finished in the car. I'll give it to you at the Oasis, okay?"

"I'm not going," said Cheyenne. "I'll get it now." The three went out.

"What are you going to do with all your spare time?" asked Tim.

"What spare time?" said Ellen. "I've got a whole term to make up this week."

"Still no time for the flying harness?" teased Jason.

"Not for me. I'm a grownup now."

"Speaking of grownups," said Chester, "did anyone notice that lady in the second row? The one with the laugh?"

"The dirty-minded one? God, yes!" said Rosencrantz. "When Rob asks us if we live in fortune's secret parts, you know that gesture he uses? She had a fit. I loved her."

They continued discussing the audience reaction. Eventually a couple of property crew members drifted in from clearing the final scene. Cheyenne returned with Judy's account book and slouched against the doorjamb, asking if anyone had seen Paul. No one had. Nick leaned over to Ellen and said, "Ellen, excuse me. Lisette really ought to be here by now. Would you mind checking, making sure there's no zipper stuck or anything?"

"Sure."

"I'd go, but I don't know if everyone else is down."

"Looks like they are. But I don't mind," said Ellen. She jumped up, pushed past Cheyenne, and ran up the stairs, wondering vaguely why her roommate had gone off so early when she knew perfectly well that they were to meet in the greenroom first. Well, she and Rob probably wanted some time together first.

The dressing-room floor was deserted, the cement hall still brightly lit but noiseless except for the quiet padding of Ellen's sneakers on the hard floor. She knocked, then opened the door of the women's dressing room, and for an instant was exasperated. Lisette had taken off her outer costume but was lounging on her makeup table with only her slip on, nowhere near dressed. Words were scribbled in greasepaint on the mirror that reflected her bright hair. Then something about her posture silenced Ellen, and she hurried in to her, concerned. She was too still. Ellen felt her forehead, cool and damp, and picked up the limp wrist. There was no pulse. She raced to the hall phone and dialed the campus police.

"Emergency!" she said. She was screaming. She brought her voice under control. "We need an ambulance at the theatre. Stage door, second floor. Real fast. Somebody collapsed."

She hung up and hurried back to her. She couldn't remember her first aid. Head down, wasn't it? And blow in the mouth. She started to pull her back off the table, holding her by the waist, and saw the hypodermic syringe, lying partly under the still hand on the table. No time to worry about that. She dragged her off the folding chair to lie on the floor and began artificial respiration, hoping she was doing it right. After a few breaths she heard footsteps running on the stairs. Nick and a campus policeman, probably from the traffic-control car that had been outside, came in simultaneously.

Nick didn't pause. He took over Ellen's job and said to the policeman between breaths, "Can we use your car?" The policeman nodded.

"I'll radio for someone else to come here, to make the report," he said over his shoulder. "Young lady, don't let anyone else in until the officers arrive." He and Nick rushed out with her, and a second later Ellen heard the siren. She went back into the hall and closed the door behind her and stood there, stunned, listening to the rise and fall of the siren fading into the distance.

Jim was coming up the stairs. "Nick said he thought something must be wrong," he said anxiously.

"She's awfully sick," said Ellen. "The police said not to let anyone in there. God, Jim!"

"What happened?"

"I just don't know. There was a hypodermic."

He took her hand and they stood quietly together. Other people drifted up from the greenroom to investigate, and she answered their questions briefly, as best she could. Then a pair of officers arrived and entered the dressing room. They looked around, and one of them used his radio to call for technicians and detectives. The lighter-haired one went down to the outside door and politely stopped a couple of people who were leaving.

"Please," said Ellen to the other. "What's happening? Do you know how she is?"

The darker-haired officer looked at her, a glimmer of pity behind his professionally neutral expression. "Dead on arrival," he said.

XV

The next few hours went by in a daze. A courteous, gray-haired man, Detective Sergeant Hawes, arrived with another plainclothes detective to take charge. The police technicians photographed and fingerprinted the dressing room, collected dust and scraps of paper, and inspected the message that had been printed in grease pencil on Lisette's mirror. Sergeant Hawes called the hospital, where someone was still with Nick.

"Fred? Listen, we've got what looks like a suicide note here on the O'Connor case. Would you ask the husband if she's made threats or anything? Yeah, I'll hang on." There was a pause, and then he said, "Really? That definite? Well, okay, we'll treat it as murder. But listen, tell him we'll want him to look at it. Doubt if he'll recognize the writing. It's printed. Okay. It says, 'Nicky, goodby. I can't live with what I did to Jennifer.' No, that's all." He listened a moment. "Bruised arms? Okay, I'll ask."

Nick, poor Nick, thought Ellen, and wished she could be with him to help. Help! What a stupid thought. She found herself gripping Jim's hand as though she would fall off a precipice without him.

Sergeant Hawes, replacing the receiver, noticed Ellen's dazed stare. "Miss Winfield?" he asked.

"Yes?"

"I'd just like to go over what happened tonight—carefully."

He asked her about everything, in great detail, from the last time she had seen Lisette hurrying up the stairs to the moment he himself had arrived. He was especially concerned that nothing had been moved in the room. He made her sit at a table to demonstrate exactly how Lisette had been lying when found, before being pulled to the floor.

"I'm not sure about her legs," Ellen said, keeping herself analytical and detached. "Her head was on her right arm like this, turned away from the door. I had to walk around to her other side to see her face. Her left arm was bent like this. The hypodermic was under her right hand."

He nodded and made careful notes and sketches. Then he said, "Would you say Mrs. O'Connor ever gave any indications she might commit suicide?"

"Never," said Ellen firmly. Then she shrugged. "Of course I only knew her this one term. She seemed hardworking and easy to get along with. My roommate knew her better, I think."

"Your roommate?"

"Maggie Ryan. She was dating Rob. Rob Jenner. They went around with the O'Connors a lot."

Sergeant Hawes had a program. He said. "Jenner. That would be this Hamlet?"

"That's right."

"He's from New York too?"

"Yes. He might be able to help you even more than my roommate. He knew the O'Connors before. They'd worked together."

Sergeant Hawes, attentive, wrote it all down. "Was there any enmity between Mrs. O'Connor and any of the others?"

Ellen paused. What could she say? But someone in that huge cast would talk if she didn't. She could at least put it in context. "Well," she said, "there was Laura Eisner."

"Yes. I'd heard about that. The kid that vandalized the sprinkler system."

"Yes. She was jealous of Lisette, I guess. Defaced her photos, drugged her one night. But she hasn't been in the theatre since we found out she was the one."

"I see," he said, writing busily. "What's her address?"

"Buckley Hall. 3058, I think."

"Was she here tonight?"

"No. She's been coming to classes and leaving instantly."

"We'll check. Any other friction?"

"No. Even Judy came around."

"Judy?"

"Judy Allison. She or Laura probably would have been cast as Ophelia if they hadn't hired Lisette."

"Did she get along well with her husband?"

"Yes. Very well."

"I'm told she was a very beautiful woman. Sexually demonstrative."

"When she was acting!" said Ellen indignantly. "In one scene she had to be very seductive to Jim. But that didn't mean anything."

Sergeant Hawes's kind eyes moved to Jim. "This is Jim?"

"Jim Greer," said Jim.

"Did it mean anything?"

"No," said Jim. "Of course Lisette is a very beautiful woman, and in that scene she was very blatantly sexual toward me and toward David Wagner. But it was just acting."

"David Wagner?"

"He was Laertes in the play."

"Did he have any jealous girlfriends?"

God, thought Ellen, this can't be real. But Jim was answering calmly, "I doubt it. He dated a couple of girls in the undergraduate acting program. But none of them were especially serious."

"He's also the dean's son," said Ellen acidly.

That, at least, made the sergeant pause. "Dean Wagner?"

"Right."

Hawes nodded soberly and made a note.

"Can you think of anything else? Any attachments? Quarrels?"

"Not really. Both O'Connors are really very pleasant. Talented, and good to work with."

"She is reported to have bruises on her arms."

"Damn. I was afraid of that," said Jim.

"What?"

"In the mad scene. She was really into it tonight. I had to grab her arms very tight, or I think she really would have stabbed herself."

"I see." Hawes wrote it down. "We'll want to talk to everyone who was here. They're speaking to Mr. O'Connor at the hospital. You said Miss Allison went early to the Oasis?"

"Yes, she and Grace Halliday."

"Okay, we've sent a man over there. And Mr. Jenner?"
"Rob left, said he'd be at the party later."
"How about Miss Ryan?"
Ellen found herself becoming nervous. She said, as calmly as she could, "She wasn't there either."
Jim said, "Didn't Tim mention he had seen Maggie and Rob driving off right after the show?"
"Oh, that's right," said Ellen, relieved. "Maggie must be coming later with him."
"Who's Tim?" asked Sergeant Hawes.
"Tim Anderson. He's in charge of the properties."
"Is he here?"
"Yes."
"Let me just send someone to check on Miss Eisner's dorm, and then you can point him out to me."
Thankful to be able to comply at last, Ellen led the way to the greenroom and introduced Sergeant Hawes to Tim. The sergeant then dismissed Ellen, asking her not to leave the building. She and Jim found seats on the greenroom sofa.
She had little sense of time passing. Every now and then fragments of the real world would crash into her churning thoughts; one policeman quietly asking another, "Is it suicide, then?" and the reply, "Husband says not, poor sucker. But that loony kid was in her dorm with two witnesses. And even the husband says the note must be hers, something about a Jennifer Brown. Shook him up," and the first policeman again, "Probably doesn't want to believe it." Or Sergeant Hawes, quietly, to a member of the costume crew, "You say she was arguing with Mr. Jenner?" "Oh, it was nothing serious. Just once. They were in a bad mood or something." Or Cheyenne, curt as usual, "I heard nothing at all from that floor. Ask Grace and Judy. It was silent." Through it all, there was Jim, quiet but warmly present.
Rob came in, sometime late, slipping into the crowded room without Ellen noticing until he spoke quietly, leaning over beside her. "Ellen, I saw the lights still on and came back. What's happened?" He knelt by the arm of the sofa.
"It's Lisette. She . . . I guess she's dead."
"What?"

"They took her to the hospital. They said, dead on arrival."

"Oh, my God. Poor Nick. Goddamn it!" He struck his knee violently, and then ran a hand through his blond hair. "Where is he, Ellen?"

"He went to the hospital with her. I guess he's there. I don't know."

"What happened to her?"

"I don't know. There was something on the mirror, a suicide note. But Nick says it can't be suicide."

Rob's worried blue eyes settled on Sergeant Hawes across the room. "If it isn't . . ." He paused.

"Yeah. He's been asking to talk to you."

"Oh, God."

"Rob, where's Maggie?"

"I don't know." He was still looking at Sergeant Hawes thoughtfully.

"But Tim said you left with her."

"Oh." His look switched to her, alertly. "Right. But I don't know where she is right this minute. Probably back at the dorm."

"Maybe I should call."

"Tell her I want to talk to her too, okay?" He shook his head. "This is unbelievable. Poor Nick!"

Ellen went into the hall and rang her own room, but no one answered. She looked at her watch on the way back; two-twenty. Sergeant Hawes was talking to Rob, both of them quiet and polite.

"I'm glad you came back, Mr. Jenner," the sergeant said. "We just want to get an idea of where everyone was. Just routine."

"I understand."

"Could you tell me what you did?"

"I was with Maggie Ryan. A special friend."

"Yes, fine." The sergeant seemed satisfied. "You did not go to the Oasis, I'm told?"

"No, we wanted to be more alone. We did stop for a minute at Joe's."

"This was right after the show?"

"As soon as I could change."

"Fine. You knew the O'Connors, I believe? Can you tell me anything about Mrs. O'Connor?"

"A wonderful woman. I've always been fond of her."

"You're a friend of hers? Or his?"

"Both. More his, I guess—we worked together once before. Nick and I get along well, and here at Hargate we spent a fair amount of time together."

"Would you say Mrs. O'Connor was likely to commit suicide?"

He hesitated. "Sergeant Hawes, I really don't know."

"Just your impression."

"I thought she was a lot more stable than she was in New York a couple of years ago."

"Stable. I see." Sergeant Hawes looked at him thoughtfully.

"Nick is the one to ask."

"Mr. O'Connor is more or less in a state of shock. You can understand that."

"Sergeant Hawes, can I see him? He's my friend." Rob was almost pleading.

"Of course, in a minute. Can you tell me more about Mrs. O'Connor's former problems?"

"Look, Sergeant Hawes. Why are you asking? Because as far as I know it's irrelevant."

Sergeant Hawes was courteously brutal. "We're proceeding on the assumption that it was murder, Mr. Jenner, until we're sure it was not."

"I see." Rob was silent a moment, his face unreadable. Finally he said, "When I knew her before, she was alcoholic. Possibly on drugs too. But I'd swear she was off both this whole term."

So it was true, then, thought Ellen. She had wondered why Lisette never drank.

Sergeant Hawes was nodding. "Thank you, Mr. Jenner. That's very helpful. Her husband knew of this too?"

"Nick? God, yes! He's the only reason she lived this long!" He caught himself and shook his head. "I'm just guessing, Sergeant Hawes. I don't know. My impression then was that she was a beautiful, talented, sad lady. But all this term she's seemed beautiful, talented, and happy."

"A happy marriage?"

"Very. Look, where is Nick?"

"Our officers are taking him back to his apartment."

"Please, can I go to him?"

"In a moment. I understand that you and Mrs. O'Connor quarreled sometimes."

"Quarreled? No."

"She accused you of directing, I believe."

Rob looked confused. "Directing? Oh!" He nodded. "I wouldn't really call it a quarrel. Letting off steam, maybe."

"I see. Now, Mr. Jenner, did Miss Ryan come back with you?"

"Maggie? No." He turned to Ellen. "Ellen, Maggie's in the dorm, isn't she?"

"No," said Ellen. "Not answering the phone, anyway."

"Strange," said Rob. He looked worried. "I'll try to call her."

"Thank you, Mr. Jenner. You can go now. You'll be with Mr. O'Connor?"

"Right. If he'll have me."

"Fine." Sergeant Hawes, looking a bit weary, watched Rob go dial the telephone and hang up again in a moment without having spoken. Then the sergeant glanced around the room. "How many of you have I already talked to?"

Most people raised their hands.

"Good. Okay. Those people can leave. Check out with the officer at the door. Tell him where you'll be. I'll try to finish with the rest of you as soon as I can."

Jim and Ellen joined the file of people moving up the stairs and out into the pleasant night. In the parking lot, Rob was waiting for her. "Ellen?"

"Yeah?"

"I've got to go to Nick. But I have to talk to Maggie as soon as I can. Could you give her this?" He handed her a note.

"Okay." She looked carefully into her bag as she put the note in.

"It's important."

"Okay." Ellen hesitated, looking around the lot, then added, "If she isn't there I'll put it on her pillow."

"Thanks." He ran to his car and drove off toward Nick's. Ellen started slowly along the sidewalk toward the end of the building, thinking.

"You didn't drive tonight?" asked Jim.

"No, the weather is so nice. God, Jim, I want to see Nick."

"Yeah. Poor guy."

She glanced at him. "I hope Maggie's there when I get

back. She probably doesn't even know about this yet. Rob didn't know."

"Right. And that detective wants to talk to her."

"Yes." She pondered a minute as they turned the corner to cross the union lawn. "What Rob said makes it sound like suicide, doesn't it?"

"Yes. I never would have thought that," said Jim.

"Same here. But there was that note on the mirror."

"Yes."

"Poor Nick. I wish I could help."

"Rob's probably the best person right now, Ellen. His oldest friend around here. We'll see Nick tomorrow."

"I guess you're right."

Jim walked her back and kissed her gently and watched her start up the stairs. Ellen felt a little guilty that she had not yet told him her new worry. But she had to talk to Maggie first.

Because the car keys in her bag were gone. And her car, which had been parked near the theatre door, was gone too. The key ring held only a note: "Thanks. Don't tell a soul. M."

She was awakened from a restless nap at six-thirty. The blasted phone was ringing. Why didn't Maggie get it? Maggie! She jerked upright, alert all at once, and snatched up the receiver.

"Hello?"

"Hi, Winfield. Sorry to do this to you when you're hung over." Cheerful voice.

"Oh, my God, Maggie! Where are you?"

"What's happened, Ellen?" The cheerfulness was gone, instantly.

"It's Lisette. She's dead, Maggie."

"Oh, Christ." There was a fractional pause. "Nick. How's Nick?"

"I haven't seen him. Rob is with him, I think."

"Good. Oh, Christ, Ellen, I thought she'd be okay. Oh, Christ. Poor Nick. Did they find Laura?"

"Laura was in her dorm. They're sure."

"Then how did she die? An accident?"

"I don't know exactly. There was a hypodermic, and a suicide note."

"A suicide note. She wrote it?"

"Nick seems to think so."

"Goddamn it, Ellen. Poor Nick."

"Maggie, where are you? The police want to talk to you."

"To me?"

"To everybody. Not you especially. Except that you spent more time with Nick and Lisette than most of us."

"Yeah, okay. I'll be back later, Ellen. Probably not till the middle of the afternoon."

"Where the hell are you?"

"About two hours' drive," she said evasively. "Your damn cylinder head gasket gave out and nobody in this burg, population seventeen, sells the right kind. I'm going to have to wait for someone named Willy to go to . . . um . . . to go get one and bring it back."

"Sheesh. Where are you?"

"Take my word for it, Ellen. You don't want to know."

"I do too. So does Rob."

"Rob?"

"Yeah. Left you an urgent note."

"Read it to me."

"Are you sure?"

"And quick. I don't have the coins to keep feeding this phone forever."

Ellen took Rob's slip of paper from Maggie's pillow and removed the tape. "It says, quote: Soubrette, dash. Horrible unbelievable news. I'm with Nick. Apparently it happened while we were at Joe's, right after the show. Please see me before you talk to anyone. Love, dash, *ton danois.* Unquote."

"God," said Maggie. "Joe's."

"What?"

"It seems a million years ago. Listen, Ellen. If the police ask, tell them I'll be back tonight sometime. Okay? I'm having car trouble. You don't know where. And I think my time is up now."

"Wait, Maggie. How can I get in touch with you?"

The line was dead.

"Damn stupid bitch," said Ellen, in despair.

XVI

Nick, numb, was picking up her makeup jars and packing them into her little case. The dressing room was still disordered, with jars scattered across the dressing table, some still open, papers and clippings scattered, the bouquet of Ophelia's flowers still on the table, clothes tossed on hooks or in corners. The police had photographed and measured and dusted everything, and then had given him permission to clear it out. They had taken the syringe and the mirror with her note. He decided to start with the makeup. He focused carefully on each little pot to make sure it was hers and not Grace's, or one of the court ladies', and to make sure that the question trembling under the surface of his consciousness did not erupt. Later he would deal with it, if he could. Now he must not think about it.

Rob had come over last night, a few minutes after the officers took him home—and he had been a source of strength. Nick hadn't wanted to talk or think. Rob, understanding, had just been there, an undemanding warm background. He had made coffee, and eventually suggested that Nick might want to lie down and rest. He himself dozed on the living room sofa, alert whenever Nick stirred during that horrible blank night. The next morning Nick awoke from a thin agonized sleep to the smell of bacon and coffee, and dutifully ate what Rob gave him. He washed and dressed as Rob instructed him. On some level he knew he had to keep functioning, although it seemed pointless, and he was grateful that someone was there to remind him.

After breakfast, Rob gently directed his attention to all the things that had to be done—calling Lisette's mother, a funeral director, their agent George, and their other New

York friends. Nick talked to them, and made the decisions he had to make. Soon his friends began to come by. Ellen and Jim, Brian and Deborah, Grace and Jon, Jase and Chester and David and Judy. Even Dean Wagner stopped by, and a surprising number of students from the show or his classes. They helped pack up Lisette's things, quietly and efficiently. He was grateful and spoke to them about unimportant things with the surface of his attention. Somewhere inside, though, something horrible was growing, and the guardians of his mind were closing things off, warning him not to examine his feelings too closely. I have that within which passeth show. Don't think. Don't feel. Do things, and wait.

Rob stayed all morning. Sergeant Hawes came in right after lunch to tell Nick it was all right to remove Lisette's things from the theatre. Then he cleared his throat apologetically and said, "Mr. O'Connor, I thought I should tell you, Miss Eisner was in the presence of two other people from dinnertime till we arrived."

"You're sure?"

"We checked very carefully. And also, we didn't find any fingerprints on the hypodermic syringe except for Mrs. O'Connor's."

"I see," said Nick. He was glad Rob hadn't left yet for class. Rob responded to his mute appeal.

"Nick, Sergeant Hawes thinks it was suicide. Just say yes or no, do you know of any reason he should continue investigating?"

"No," said Nick after a moment, and snapped the doors shut on his thoughts again.

"Fine," said Sergeant Hawes. "We'll just get in touch with these last two witnesses, for completeness, and wrap it up, then. Thank you both. We appreciate your cooperation."

By midafternoon Nick had told Grace and Deborah that he wanted to be alone for a while. Brian would be arriving at ten to stay overnight with Nick; Rob had consented more for Brian's sake than his own or Nick's. Nick had walked around, then had taken Lisette's case to the theatre. As suppertime approached, the building was nearly abandoned. It was soothing to have a job to do, to take his mind off everything.

"May I come in?"

He found that he was not startled; his reactions were numb too. "Sure," he said. He looked up dully as Maggie came in.

"Can I help, Nick?"

"I'm probably the only one who knows which ones are hers."

"Yeah." She pushed a couple of pots within his reach. He continued sorting. There were a couple that might belong to either Grace or Lisette. He started a third collection for these ambiguous jars. Maggie said, "I know you don't want to talk. I'll try to be quick."

"It's okay." He made an effort and looked at her again. "I'm switched off now. I think I want to stay that way."

"I need an explanation of something," she said apologetically.

"I'll try."

"Okay." She moved past him to the little slot window and looked out. The last rays of sun streaked horizontally across the gym and through the window, rimming her profile with light.

"The police are still asking questions," she said. "You told them it wasn't suicide."

"That was my first reaction. Not now." He felt the anger and shame surging up within him and took command again. He looked fiercely at a jar of cold cream, decided it was Grace's, and smacked it firmly down on her side of the table.

"If it wasn't," she continued implacably, "we're all of us in trouble."

"It's got to be true, damn it! The prints on the goddamn syringe. And I saw the goddamn note. But . . ." No. Stop. Stay away from that. The wise young eyes were watching.

She said, unshocked, "You're angry at her. She left you and didn't give you a chance to try."

The unspeakable, spoken.

Nick stared, horrified, and then forced the thought away. It couldn't be. "No," he said, unconvincingly, guiltily. Her hand, comforting, touched his shoulder. She changed the subject.

"I just got back an hour ago and Ellen told me everything. She says most of you were with her in the greenroom. But Lisette, David, Paul, Rob, and I were not."

A safer topic. "That's right," he said. "We were waiting

for the rest of you. Eventually Grace and Judy went on ahead to meet Jon, and we were going to follow in a few minutes. Then Cheyenne came back, and then I asked Ellen to see if Lisette was ready—" Stop. No further. He rubbed his head. "I want to stay switched off. Please."

Her hands rested gently on the back of a folding chair. "I'm being brutal," she said. "But I have to know something."

He didn't look up. He wanted her to go away.

"You see, Rob asked me to say I was with him," she explained.

"You weren't?"

"No."

So that was the problem. His mind left his own agonies and inspected this distraction gratefully. He was a little exasperated with Rob.

"He shouldn't ask you to do that."

"I know. But I wonder why."

"Rob prefers taking the easy way out. And, well, you weren't there either, he might view it as a favor to you. I mean, when the police were interested."

"That could be. I'd like to think that, of course. But still . . . Forgive me, Nick, but I know that Lisette threatened once to tell about Rob. I don't understand how he could be hurt."

"Well, he couldn't really be hurt in the city, you're right." Nick stopped sorting and tried to concentrate on explaining, his dull eyes fixed on the capable young hands resting lightly on the back of the chair next to him. "It's really neither advantage nor disadvantage to his career these days. But he was concerned about disrupting the show. The department. I mean, this is an educational institution, and this project was aimed at the alumni. They're pretty conservative, not very broad-minded about homosexuality. And especially—"

He broke off. The hands he was watching had clenched involuntarily on the chair back, knuckles thrusting white under the skin.

"Maggie, you didn't know!" Astonishment scoured him of all other feeling. He jumped up and turned her face gently from the window to him. For an instant he glimpsed in the depths of the blue eyes the collapse and wreckage of half-formed young hopes and dreams. Then the eyes closed for a moment, and opened again cool and cynical.

"It's all right," she said, pushing his hand away. Her voice was almost steady. "Naive college girl learns about life in the real world. That's what you pros are here to teach us, right?"

"That bastard!" A rush of anger followed his surprise. "He told me you knew!"

"I should have guessed, maybe. It explains a lot of things. An awful lot of things." She was still gripping the chair, but he saw that the mind behind the veiled eyes was working again. "It's David, isn't it? The dean's son, for chrissake."

"That bastard!" Nick sat down again and looked at her helplessly.

"Who also wasn't there in the greenroom," she continued, ignoring him. "And Rob wants me to say I was with him." She closed her eyes again and drew a long breath. "I ought to hang out a shingle. M. Ryan, professional smokescreen. Scandals hushed. Deans misled. Morals charges averted."

"He said he had told you," Nick repeated miserably.

"Well, he hadn't. *Au contraire.*" One corner of her mouth twitched. "It wasn't just a sin of omission, if you're interested. He overcame his revulsion a couple of times, you know? Fooled me completely. Better performance than Hamlet. And then—oh, Christ, that's why he said he had the clap! Damn him!"

"The clap?" Nick repeated stupidly.

"He said he thought he'd been cured but the retest was positive. Sent me off to get shot full of penicillin. For nothing! And of course he was deeply repentant. So responsible he wouldn't do more than cuddle until his cure was confirmed. Of course it never was."

She glanced at him bleakly and fished down the neck of her shirt to pull up a thin gold chain. From it dangled a ring with a single small diamond. "He told me not to wear this until school was out. He said—get this—he was afraid the dean would not approve." She jerked at it violently, breaking the chain, and thrust it at Nick. "Return it, would you?"

"If I'd only known . . ." But she had already pushed past

him toward the door, blinking a little. He asked, "Where are you going?"

She didn't answer. He heard her light, rapid footsteps on the stairs. Through the little window that looked out over the parking lot, he watched her run across to the darkened gym. In the twilight he could see the lights go on.

He was furious, and helpless. But at least it was okay to be furious about this.

He finished packing the case, looking out the window occasionally at the lighted gym windows. He didn't think very much except every now and then, angrily, of Rob. In an odd way he was grateful to be angry; he needed a focus outside of his own ugly feelings. That poor kid. He was going to talk to Rob.

When he came out and headed for his car, the gym lights were still on. Disturbed, he went into the building and peered through the little window in the door of the brightly lit gym.

She was on the bars, all alone, twisting and pulling and swinging from one to the other, effort obvious in the power and skill required by the moves she was executing. He could see her arms trembling with exertion. After a moment, concerned, he went out to the phone booth and called Ellen. "I can't tell you the problem," he apologized, "but she needs a friend." Ellen promised to come right away.

Then he started home. Thank God Brian would be there soon to protect him from his thoughts. His foul and shameful thoughts. With a brand-new foul and shameful thought that had just now bubbled to the surface.

If she hadn't been with Rob, where had she been?

Rob burst in on him before eight the next morning, frantic, just seconds after Brian left. He must have been watching. Nick, who had remembered to put on pajamas but hadn't slept, of course, opened to the pounding and looked at him. Rob's blond hair tumbled around his anxious face. His eyes were pleading.

"Nick, you've got to help! She's found out. I mean, I guess you don't know. But you've got to help us."

"Come on in, Rob. We'd better talk." Nick could hear the coldness in his own voice. He wanted to ram his fist into that handsome deceitful face.

He closed the door and watched Rob cross to the end of

the sofa, gathering his thoughts, and turn back finally, still standing.

"Nick, I wouldn't bother you now, honest, but you're the only one . . ."

Nick didn't help, just looked at him flatly.

"You know about David." There was a trace of uncertainty in the pleasant, worried voice.

"Yeah, I'd guessed."

"Maybe you didn't know—I mean, he was the dean's son, we had to be careful. For him, for the sake of the show."

"You needed a smokescreen."

"Nick, for God's sake!" Rob turned away again, hands grasping the back of the sofa. They were both still standing. "Okay, look. I don't expect sympathy. It's a mess. But Nick, she attacked David this morning."

"Good for her."

"Come on! She hurt him! He's got bruises all over! She forced him to admit everything."

"He blabbed, huh?"

"Look, Nick, it doesn't matter what we say, really. We were nowhere near the . . . um . . . other thing. But we can't let people know we were together. And now she knows."

"Afraid you'll lose your reputation?"

"Nick, no." Puzzled by Nick's hostility, he pushed back his tousled hair. "If it were just us, we could just head for the city. No problem. But it's all the other people who could get hurt too. David can't tell his family. And you know it would ruin everything Brian's been working for. And the other thing is the cops. You've never seen cops with the likes of us, probably. Especially provincial cops. I've got to save David from that." He paused, looking at Nick's hard face. "What's wrong, Nick? Why so antagonistic? You never seemed like a straight prig. You never gave a damn before."

"Still don't."

"Well, then, what?"

"It's the way you used Maggie. Like an old Kleenex."

"I know." Rob accepted it. "It was wrong. But I had to. Don't you see?"

"Don't you see? You think only fags have feelings?"

"Of course not." Sorry and lonely, he met Nick's eyes. "Look, you'll probably hate me for this too. But I really did think about marrying her. She's got that spirit, that odd sense of humor—you know what I mean. You've got it too. And I thought, she's damn understanding, maybe she'd go along. We had a lot of fun.'"

"Nirvana according to Rob Jenner," said Nick viciously. "Entertained by little Maggie's sense of humor all day, and by little Davy's asshole all night."

"All right, damn it! I know! Give me credit for a little sense!" Rob was controlling himself with an effort. "I know it's unfair to her, I couldn't keep her happy, that's why I pulled back. All I'm trying to say is, it went further than I meant it to because she was pushing. Worse than Kathleen. But I was as honest as I could be."

"That's just bull, Rob! What's honest about the clap?" Nick took two strides across to the brass coatrack and pulled the chain and ring from his jacket pocket. He hurled them at Rob's feet. "What's honest about that?"

Rob stared at them and then, in furious comprehension, at Nick. "You! You told her! Goddamn it, Nick!" He lunged across the room. Eagerly, Nick met him, and for a moment they grappled, straining savagely against each other, struggling for advantage. Nick was heavier, but in agility and conditioning and frustrated rage they were well matched. Then Rob suddenly relaxed, blocking Nick's attack but no longer fighting. "Nick, stop. I'm sorry. This is dumb."

Reluctantly, still wanting to hurt him, Nick let go and stepped back. After a silent angry moment he said, "Okay, you're right, it's dumb. But I want to smash you, Rob. It was the rottenest thing you could have done."

"She wasn't supposed to find out. Why the hell did you tell her?"

"I didn't. I'm so thick-skulled, I believed you when you said you'd told her. So I just mentioned it casually, almost in passing. Thinking she knew."

"And David? Did you tell her that?"

"Look, two seconds after I gave her the clue, she had the whole picture. Characters, motives, the works. The only thing I did after letting the cat out of the bag was curse you."

"Yeah. She's sharp. Yeah, that's the way it would be. That's why I had to do those things, Nick. But look, really, do you think you can calm her down? I mean, after what she did to David—"

"What did she do to David? Be a little more specific."

"She was waiting for him this morning when he drove up to the theatre lot. He comes up early, to go to the library, he says, and if the coast is clear he lets himself into my office." Nick had a sudden unwelcome glimpse of Rob's hidden, furtive life. "He was surprised, but she asked him very sweetly to help her because she'd sprained her elbow, and she led him into the woods behind the gym, and lit into him. He said it was so unexpected he didn't have a chance."

"And what's all this crucial information she got?"

He hesitated. "Nick, I don't want to give you more problems. I'd leave you out of it if I could."

Nick answered his meaning, not his words. "Oh, hell," he said, "you can still trust me not to tell." He sat down on the sofa and put his face into his hands.

"Well, he admitted we were lovers. And that we were together Sunday night at my place, and that he told the police he was driving along the lake road all by himself. That was our agreement, you see. If anyone ever got nosy, he was supposed to be taking a solitary drive, and since I have more experience I could figure out something else."

"What was the something else?"

"That's the problem. I knew the police would be really critical, not like a parent or friend asking casually where you were last night and believing your answer. So I said I was with her at Joe's. I'd stopped there a minute on my way home. And I left a message with Ellen and waited for her. She didn't get back until the middle of the afternoon. Where the hell was she? And when I asked her to say she'd been with me, she was a little guarded, but she agreed. Sort of. Said she'd have to think of exactly how to put it."

"She thought maybe you'd murdered Lisette."

"Oh, God!" Stricken, Rob sat down at the opposite end of the sofa. "You're right. She must have. I didn't think of that. Oh, God, Nick, I'm sorry. It never occurred to me."

"And now she knows you didn't. Tell David his bruises are in a good cause."

"But Nick, listen, what'll she do next? Right now she could wipe out David's future and Brian's department."

"Whose fault is that?"

"It wasn't supposed to be this way."

"Jesus, Rob."

"Okay, you've made your point. But look, you must have some influence over her. Good old Uncle Nick. She's furious now, of course, but she's a reasonable kid. Bright. Couldn't you talk to her?"

"No." Nick was surprised at his own certainty.

"Nick, why not? Isn't it worth a try?"

"Rob, look, I don't want anyone else hurt. Well, you, maybe. But not David, not Brian, not the dean. But right now I could no more interfere in Maggie Ryan's life again than I could fly. We've messed it up enough. I don't think you realize yet the damage you've done. Why couldn't you have waited?"

The blue eyes, angry again, blazed at him. "You know damn well I tried, Nick! Ran back to the city every weekend, ignored him when I was here. It was hell, but things were under control until Brian pushed his fencing lessons onto me. You knew that. You even tried to help, back then."

"You were quick enough to turn down my help. Never saw anyone so eager to be led into temptation."

"Well, you're a hell of a one to talk about waiting! David's a senior. You married a freshman!" His face changed. Nick jerked away from his sudden contrite touch. "Oh, Nick, damn it, I'm sorry."

After a moment Nick hauled his mind back to the problem at hand and said, "You still haven't said why you picked on a good kid like Maggie."

"It had to be someone. Everyone's a good kid."

"All right, all right. But why her?"

"Well, first of all, she was fun. As I've said. She liked being with me, okay? We had to spend time together, we might as well both enjoy it."

"Oh, Christ."

"I swear to you, Nick, we had good times."

"That's supposed to make it better?"

Rob ignored him. "Second, she's strong."

"My God, Rob, no one is strong enough for that kind of betrayal!"

"So who would you pick? Judy, maybe? She'd have broken into pieces. The little stage manager, with her little beau mooning after her? Is that your idea of a good choice? Hell, I would have asked you and Zetty to play along, maybe, but Zetty seemed to be fighting demons of her own. Or would you suggest one of the other married ladies? Grace? Deborah Wright, maybe? Seriously, Nick, what else could I do?"

"Why did you have to do it at all?"

"Damn it, Nick!" Rob jumped up and walked to the window, then turned back to him. "I thought you of all people would understand. You force me to spell it out. Look. If it had been Zetty's reputation, and Zetty's future, and Zetty's family, and keeping Zetty out of the hands of the brutal cops, wouldn't you have done it to Maggie? For love? And because she is stronger?"

Nick couldn't answer. His pajamas had blue stripes and he counted them silently, seven across his left knee. He would think about the question later.

Rob, more softly, asked, "Won't you talk to her, Nick?"

And Nick, clinging to the one truth he dared look at, shook his head and repeated, "No. It's up to her, Rob. I've meddled too much already. I'm going to trust her."

"But she's not herself. I mean, when she's back to normal, she won't want to hurt Brian either."

"I don't know, Rob. I'm not exactly normal right now either. But I just can't. You've hurt one of the splendid creatures of God's earth. And if she has to take us all down to try to save herself, so be it."

It was final. Rob knew it. He looked out the window again, then turned back with a shrug. "Well," he said, "guess there's nothing to do now but wait for her next move. Hell hath no fury like one of God's splendid creatures." He picked up the ring and broken chain as he crossed the room, and with a last sad glance behind him, let himself out, leaving Nick alone and ashamed.

XVII

Ellen was worried. Maggie was acting very odd. After Nick's call last night she had found her roommate in the gym, working on the bars, palms bleeding, thighs and hips striped raw from hurling herself against the bars, an elbow sprained. She had scolded Maggie and put her to bed, the elbow packed in ice. The first thing she thought of when she awoke was her roommate. But when she sat up, full of solicitude, and looked across the room, the other bed was empty. All kinds of bad thoughts crowded into her head. Okay, she told herself sternly, she's not really suicidal. And even if she is, it's not your fault, Winfield, you did what you could.

She hurried down to check the cafeteria, but Maggie was not there either. Ellen grabbed a quick coffee and toast, then, back in the room, decided to try to get organized for finals while she waited. Lisette, Maggie, it all meant nothing to the inexorable university calendar. She laid out a schedule carefully on a yellow pad, then stared at it disconsolately, knowing that most of the times meticulously labeled "study for history" or "write gov. paper" would be spent worrying instead. About Maggie and Nick and Lisette. Or about what that policeman had said. Or, more happily, thinking about Jim. Maybe she should study with him, distracting though he was. Maybe he would help chase the bogeys away.

"I suppose that silly smile means you're thinking about Jim."

Ellen jerked around at the unexpected voice. "Maggie! Where have you been? I was worried!"

"You didn't look very worried." Maggie regarded her

fondly a moment; but the face was drawn and exhausted, and the wide smile was nowhere to be seen.

"Where have you been?"

"Around. One place you'll approve of. I got the clinic to strap my elbow." Her left arm was in a sling.

"Good. That does look professional."

"They say the bones are okay but the ligaments are torn. I'm not supposed to use it for three weeks."

"Better take up exercycling."

"Or I could do one-handed cartwheels." Maggie looked ruefully at the damaged limb, and Ellen's heart lightened a little. Sad, yes, but not suicidal.

"Are you going to tell me about the places I won't approve of?"

"No."

"Well. Okay."

"But I guess I should tell you why, loyal old Winfield."

"It's Rob, isn't it?" Last night Ellen had noticed that the ring on its chain was gone.

"Yes." Maggie firmed her chin with bravado. "All those daisies, Ellen. I thought they were marguerites. Special for me. But you know what they meant to the Elizabethans?"

"What?"

"Infidelity. My philandering Dane was in love with someone else all along. From the goddamn beginning."

"Oh. God, Maggie!" Ellen hugged her. For a moment Maggie stood rigid and proud, and then suddenly, trembling, hid her face in Ellen's shoulder. Ellen held her for a long moment. Then Maggie straightened, blew her nose, and looked at Ellen bleakly.

"Anyway, you've got to forget what I did in the gym last night."

Ellen frowned. "But it shows! Am I supposed to tell people you ran into a door?"

Maggie regarded her seriously. "Actually, I fell down a cliff."

"Oh, Christ, Maggie." Then Ellen shrugged. "You're right, I guess. No sense in a scandal."

"This has nothing to do with sense!" said Maggie violently. The fingers of her good hand drove back angrily through the black curls.

Ellen backtracked as fast as she could. "Okay, okay,"

she said soothingly. "My lips are sealed. Hear no evil, see no evil, speak no evil. You're rooming with all three monkeys, okay?"

The hurt, strained face softened a little. "Glory be to God for unflustered things," said Maggie; then, apologetically, "But I'm afraid I have to ask for your help again. I don't want to see the police yet."

"Oh, hell, Maggie! I've held them off too long already."

"Only for another hour or so. You can tell them I'll be in the greenroom at nine."

"Shouldn't you call? They're looking for you. You and Paul."

"But not very hard. It's suicide, not murder."

"They're sure?"

"She'd tried before. And anyway, Laura's the only one who really hated her, and Laura was definitely in her dorm."

"Wouldn't have been Laura anyway," said Ellen wisely. "Even Jim would be more likely."

"Jim? Why?"

"The timing. Laura didn't give a damn about the show. She wouldn't have waited around till closing night. Jim would have."

"I see what you mean. But Lisette cared as much as Jim, so that points to suicide too."

"True." So what the policeman said wasn't important.

"Anyway, tell the police I'll be there at nine."

Ellen sighed. "Okay, I'll try, Maggie."

"Good."

"Listen. Are you okay?"

The bitter blue gaze shamed her. "Since you ask," said Maggie, "my left ear, right knee, and ability to reason mathematically are all unscathed. The rest is a shambles."

"Poor Icarus!" The words escaped Ellen unedited. Maggie stared at her a moment, and for the first time something like a smile flickered across her face.

"Why can't you be like normal people, Ellen? Just say 'I told you so.' "

"It's all this higher education, I guess." Ellen was a little embarrassed.

"Yeah." There was affection in the sad face. "Well, now I really must leave your delightful presence."

"Okay." Ellen gave her a pat on the rump. "But listen, before you run off, I need your advice about something the policeman said."

The phone rang. Ellen turned to answer it, and when she looked back, Maggie was gone. And a good thing.

"Hello, is Miss Ryan in?"

"No, I'm sorry. Can I take a message?"

"Is this Miss Winfield?"

"Yes."

"Sergeant Hawes. I'm still trying to reach Miss Ryan."

"She isn't here." Ellen took a deep breath and wished she'd studied acting. "She left early this morning to go to the clinic. Had a fall. Hurt her elbow."

"Okay, thanks, we'll check there."

"She said she'd be at the theatre at nine."

"Okay. I'm sorry she didn't call us."

"Well, I told her you were looking for her. I guess her elbow was giving her a lot of pain."

"All right. Thank you, Miss Winfield."

"Sure." She replaced the receiver. She was shaking. Accessory after the crime, that would get her into law school all right. False reporting of an incident. What incident? She didn't even know. But she had to help Maggie. That came first.

Well, she decided, she had something to tell Sergeant Hawes too. At least she wouldn't compound her guilt by withholding information. Not that it was relevant anyway.

She threw a couple of books into her bag for form's sake and hurried down the stairs, homing for Jim.

A number of actors and crew members were already in the greenroom as Jim and Ellen entered, others who could not yet quite cope with the void in their lives caused by the closing of a show that took five hours a day, and by Lisette's death, and by Paul and Maggie's disappearance. Jason was there, and David, favoring his right shoulder, and Judy Allison, who smiled at them.

"Hi," said Jim. "What's the crowd here for? Decompression?"

"Yeah, I always feel lost after a show closes," Judy admitted.

"You get to where you can't even study without a whiff

of greasepaint," said Ellen. They talked a few minutes, carefully not mentioning Lisette. Then Nick came in. He looked haggard, his dark eyes flat and dull. Saddened, Ellen went to meet him.

"Nick."

He focused on her, and concern livened his eyes. "Ellen, how is she?" He spoke very quietly.

"Sad. Better this morning, I think. She got the clinic to fix her elbow."

"She really did sprain her elbow, then." For some reason he was looking at David Wagner.

"Yes. That's the worst thing, physically."

He looked back at her sharply. "And otherwise?"

She shrugged. "A shambles, she says."

"Hell. But she said she'd be here at nine."

"She called you?"

"She just said to be here at nine if I could."

"God. I wish I knew what was going on."

They walked back to the sofa and he sat at the end, next to one of the study tables that had been shoved against the wall. Soon Sergeant Hawes came in with another officer.

"Is Miss Ryan here?" he asked.

"Not yet," said Ellen. "She said about nine o'clock."

"Right, we've still got a few minutes." Sergeant Hawes opened his notebook. "Has anyone heard from Paul Rigo?"

People shook their heads uneasily. The police were still asking questions. And Paul had been expecting a bad grade from the adored Lisette. And Paul had disappeared.

"Have you asked Cheyenne about him?" asked Ellen.

"Just saw him in the hall. He hasn't heard either," said Sergeant Hawes.

Rob, in sweatshirt and jeans, came bouncing in, looking around hopefully. When he saw the policemen his eyes narrowed slightly, but he did not slow down.

"Sergeant Hawes!" he exclaimed, all friendliness. Ellen was disgusted. The philandering Dane, unaffected by all the misery he had caused.

"Hello, Mr. Jenner," said the sergeant.

"Haven't these people offered you a seat?"

"Well, thank you. We hoped we wouldn't have to stay long. We're just waiting for Miss Ryan. Have you seen her?"

"No, I was wondering where she was myself." Some of

the crew members exchanged surprised glances. "Anyway, have a seat." He waved grandly at the battered furniture, then turned to look at Nick inquiringly. Nick knew what had happened, thought Ellen; he'd been the one who had called last night. But he returned Rob's gaze neutrally now. Rob, after the briefest hesitation, strode over and hopped up to sit on the table at Nick's end of the sofa, swinging his legs over the edge. Ellen was pleased to see, now that he was closer, that he was tense. He waited for the conversations to pick up again, then spoke quietly to Nick. "She call you too?"

"Yeah."

"Hell," said Rob, subdued. "I'd hoped it was just me. Looks bad."

When Maggie arrived a minute later, she looked strained and exhausted, and the sling showed white against her blue shirt. "Poor kid," murmured Jim, shocked. But she walked firmly over to face the policemen.

"Hello, I'm Maggie Ryan. My roommate says you want to talk to me."

"Yes, thank you, Miss Ryan." Sergeant Hawes and the officer stood up politely. "I'm Sergeant Hawes."

"Sorry it's taken so long. I've had a hell of a couple of days here."

"Yes, we heard about your elbow, and the car trouble."

"That's not all, Sergeant Hawes. That's not all."

"Do you want to go somewhere a little more private?"

"Sure. If you want," she said, and suddenly, terrifyingly, looked full at Rob. Ellen felt a chill.

The policemen started for the stairs. Ellen was one of the few close enough to tell that Rob, sitting in a relaxed posture, swinging his legs over the edge of the table, was actually taut in every muscle. He blurted suddenly, "See me later, Maggie?"

"Don't be ridiculous," she said scornfully. But she slowed and looked at him again. Rob's eyes dropped before hers.

"You'll tell them about Joe's?" he asked contritely. He wants to hear, Ellen realized, no matter how bad it is.

"Joe's? My God," said Maggie. She stalked over to face him, her good arm cocked indignantly on her hip. And Ellen realized that she wanted him to hear too, and that, whatever their problem, these two were still attuned, still flying in deadly formation just beyond the reach of the rest of them. Except maybe Nick; no longer dull-eyed, he seemed to be following their hidden line.

"Miss Ryan?" The officer took a couple of steps toward her. She turned to him, indignant.

"Did he tell you I was at Joe's?"

"Yes," said Rob quickly.

"Yes, he did," admitted Sergeant Hawes, bowing to reality.

"My God," said Maggie.

"Miss Ryan, let's—"

But she continued as though the sergeant had not spoken. "I can't believe it. You would actually lie like that in a police investigation?"

"Think, Maggie," Rob said urgently. God, he could look handsome. "It's true. And it's best for everybody that it is."

"Miss Ryan—"

"Don't worry, Sergeant. He's not telling me what to say. He's lying. I should know better than anyone what a liar he is."

"Maggie. Think what you're saying. Think!"

"Think yourself, Rob! This is not a game. Not a play. It might be murder." Ellen felt Nick flinch beside her, and caught the flash of regret and compassion in Maggie's eyes before she continued. "Sergeant Hawes, I'm sorry. But this makes me mad! Mr. Jenner, as you have probably heard, has been flirting with me all term. Sunday, closing night, I learned that he was not serious."

It was Monday, thought Ellen, and was aware of Nick's sudden stillness beside her too.

"Miss Ryan, don't you want to tell us more privately?"

She said harshly, "Thanks, but don't worry about me. Everyone will know eventually. It might as well be now. And I want him to know that it's about time he told the truth."

"Mr. Jenner?" Sergeant Hawes turned to Rob. "Didn't you tell the truth?"

Rob said in a low voice, "Not quite the whole truth." His gaze followed Maggie, hope draining from his face. She was crossing the room toward David Wagner's chair.

"David," she said gently, "I know why you said what you did. But it's time to tell them now."

"Oh, God, Maggie, no!" David buried his face in his hands. Her good hand hovered an instant over his hair, protectively, before she turned back to the policemen. Beside Ellen, Nick's head shook infinitesimally, sorrowfully.

"Sergeant Hawes, the problem is that David is Dean Wagner's son," Maggie continued earnestly. "I'm sure you understand that none of us want to hurt the dean's family in any way."

"Of course." Hawes had given up trying to get her away.

Rob said desperately, "Maggie, don't drag other people into something that concerns just us. Really, just us."

She ignored him. "The problem is, if you're the dean's son, you have to be extra careful with your reputation. With what people think of your morals."

"Maggie, shut up!" Rob, blue eyes icy, furious, slid off the table to start toward her, but suddenly found his arm imprisoned by Nick's big hand.

"Stay there, Mr. Jenner," said Sergeant Hawes, and the officer stepped a little closer and took Rob's other arm. "Now, please, Miss Ryan, just tell us what you did Sunday night."

"I am telling you. I just wanted to explain first why David said he was alone when he really wasn't. And Rob knew he would say that, and took advantage of it to force me to lie and say I was with him. Well, I wasn't with him. I was nowhere near him. I was not at Joe's."

David, trembling, raised anguished eyes to Rob; but Rob would not meet his gaze. The handsome body still held itself proudly from habit, but Ellen could see that he was defeated, all hope gone. Nick, rather than restraining him, almost seemed to be supporting him now.

Sergeant Hawes was becoming impatient. "All right, Miss Ryan. You say that Mr. Jenner and Mr. Wagner did not tell the truth. You've told us where you weren't. So where were you?"

"Okay. First, I already told you I had kind of a scene with Mr. Jenner."

"And after that?"

Maggie turned a little, compassionately, toward David, her hand resting on his bowed head again. "After that," she said matter-of-factly, "I was with David, driving around the lake."

Rob stood very still.

A shadow of relief and admiration pulsed through his body and was gone. But that couldn't be, thought Ellen; Maggie had just destroyed his alibi and accused him of lying. Then Nick unaccountably released his arm and leaned back in the sofa, hands clasped behind his head, gaze still on Maggie.

"Mr. Wagner, is that true?"

"Look, I know it sounds bad," said Maggie, heading off David's reply. "But that's what I'm trying to explain. David is a good friend, and when he saw what a mess I was in, after what Rob did, he was very sympathetic. But he was just comforting me, nothing else. It wasn't what it sounds like. It was just friendship."

"How long were you driving around?"

"Oh, hours. I don't remember exactly, I was pretty worked up. I do remember we stopped once to walk along the shore, up near Tomaqua where they have those little cliffs. And I stupidly fell off. That's how I did this." She motioned to the sling. "And poor David tried to help me, and he slipped and got pretty banged up too. Look." She jerked up the front of David's shirt. There were ugly weals across his ribs. "And see my hands?" she added. She held out her right palm, still raw and red, and even Ellen, who had witnessed the frenzied gymnastics, almost believed her for a moment. David, frowning, pulled down his shirt.

"Mr. Wagner? Is that accurate?"

With an odd glance of defiance at Rob, David said, "Yes, sir."

"Please don't worry, Mr. Wagner. I'm sorry Miss Ryan chose to talk in front of so many people, but I'm sure they will be discreet and keep the best interests of the college at heart."

Everyone nodded. David said, "Yes, sir."

"Poor David," whispered Jason. "What a prig he has to be."

Rob pushed himself back up to sit on the table again. Sergeant Hawes glanced at him, then said unexpectedly, "Mr. Anderson?"

"It could be," said Tim. "I told you I really couldn't see them well. I just assumed it was Rob because he and Maggie were usually together. But now that you ask, I think I would have noticed if the guy had been blond. He was just a dark shape to me, because Maggie was driving, and I was on her side of the driveway."

"Oh, did someone see us?" asked Maggie, pleased. "There, you see, David, it would all have come out anyway."

"Mr. Jenner?" said Sergeant Hawes, and a shiver of anticipation ran through the watchers.

Rob was swinging his legs again, just a little, and was regarding the toes of his sneakers mournfully. "Yes, it's true," he said. He raised contrite eyes to the policeman. "Sergeant Hawes, Miss Ryan makes me very ashamed. I'm afraid I misjudged her character and the situation from the very beginning. She's right to insist on honesty." The blue eyes, sorrowful, shifted to Maggie. "If there were any way in the world to go back and start over, I would."

"You're admitting that you did not tell the truth?" asked the sergeant.

"It was very close to true." He still seemed to be speaking to Maggie. "But I only told part of it." She gave a brief nod.

"You support her account, then?" pursued the sergeant.

"Yes, I do. We quarreled. She returned a ring I had given her." He pulled it from his sweatshirt pocket. There was a mild sensation among the crew members. "I hoped she might change her mind later. Right after the show, I saw her and David Wagner together in the parking lot. We all know that David is in a peculiar situation because of his father's position, and later when I heard that neither of them had been seen all evening, I put two and two together."

"You knew Mr. Wagner would claim to be alone?"

"I suspected he would."

"And you thought she would back your story to protect him?"

"I hoped so. I knew she would want to protect David and the college from needless scandal. And I had hoped we would be on good terms again, and that she would support my story." He looked sadly at the ring and replaced it in his pocket. "My action was very wrong, I know. But I was really trying to avoid as much trouble as possible for her, and for David, as well as for myself."

"Great motive," said Maggie, "but you'll avoid even more trouble if you just leave me alone."

He turned to her and said carefully, "Henceforth I vow it shall be so for me." And Maggie's defenses cracked for an instant, and she bit her lip and turned away from him.

Sergeant Hawes said, "Mr. Jenner, now, we still have to ask where you really were. And why you did not tell the truth."

He drew a deep breath. "Sergeant Hawes, would it be possible to take you up on the offer of a more private room? I'd like to save the shreds and patches of my reputation among the students if I can."

"Certainly," said Hawes. "We'll go up to the men's dressing room. Miss Ryan, Mr. Wagner, thank you. We will be discreet with your information, of course."

"Thank you, Sergeant Hawes," said Maggie. She watched as Rob, with a glance of abject penitence, went up the stairs with the policemen. Then she turned back and carefully aimed a friendly, hearty slap at David's swollen shoulder. Tears sprang to his eyes. "There, you see, David?" she said genially. "Nobody here is going to tell on you. It's never smart to withhold information." She ran out the door toward the stage. He gazed after her with hatred and with respect.

Ellen stared too, perplexed. Maggie had lied. About Sunday night. About when she had quarreled with Rob. About her injuries. About being with David. And in the course of those lies, Ellen had seen Rob go from concern to the depths of angry despair, and then suddenly almost back to normal, even though his alibi had been annihilated in front of policemen and friends. And Rob had supported her lies, and so had David, honest square David, and so had Tim.

Ellen noticed suddenly that Nick was regarding her with friendly eyes.

"Nick," she said, and stopped.

"Don't ask, Ellen. We heard better than truth."

"But—"

"Do you know *The Taming of the Shrew?*"

"A little."

Nick quoted, "Forward, I pray, since we have come so far,/ And be it moon, or sun, or what you please,/An if you please to call it a rush-candle,/Henceforth I vow it shall be so for me."

"Oh," said Ellen.

"Stick with her, Ellen. You'll never have a more worthwhile friend."

"Yes. That I knew already."

But she saw that Nick was losing interest in the conversation already, his friendly concern fading to leadenness again.

Cheyenne stuck his head in the door and said, "Got to clean up here this morning, soon as the cops leave. Everybody out."

They got up, except for Nick, and milled toward the door. Ellen glanced down at him, but something about his dark eyes told her she could not help. Then she saw that Maggie had edged back into the room and was talking to Jason in the corner. He was patting her good shoulder in clumsy sympathy. I'll ask her now, Ellen decided.

But as she drew near, she froze at Maggie's soft words. "Jase, you once offered me your peerless soul and body. Is the offer still open? One-time basis?"

Jason stared at her for a startled instant, then managed to say lightly, "Of course. A gentleman would never retract such an offer."

"Well, you can keep your old peerless soul anyway. But I want to get laid, Jase. Right now."

Ellen had turned away in confusion, and as they started for the stairs Jim came back in from where he'd been waiting for her. "Coming?"

"Not yet," Ellen said, taking her decision. Clearly she would have to make do without Maggie's advice. "I want to ask Sergeant Hawes something when he's finished with Rob. I'll meet you in the library, okay? Shouldn't be too long."

"Okay," said Jim. "Main reading room." He went out too.

With a last look back at Nick, Ellen went slowly upstairs. There was a low murmur of voices from the men's dressing room. She sat down on the bench by the prop room to read the notes for her history exam while she waited. After a few moments there was a step behind her in the hall.

"Waiting to see the police?"

"Yeah," said Ellen, glancing back, and then did the most stupid thing she had ever done. She asked, "Listen, did you tell them about your sister?"

"Why? Ancient history."

"Yeah, I know. Just wondered." And then she did the second most stupid thing she'd ever done. She turned back to her history notes.

There was a shock of pain on the back of her head. The world flared white an instant before the wave of blackness sucked her down.

XVIII

It smells to heaven.

Nick leaned back in the corner of the sofa, his eyes closed, his arm flopped on the table where Rob had been, and dreaded the future. He had been distracted briefly by the concerns of these people he cared about, and had concentrated on them almost gratefully while he could. But now those problems had reached a resolution of sorts. Maggie, hurt but not destroyed, had made her choice. She had saved David and the department's good name, and had tossed Rob to the policemen to squirm for a while; but he would doubtless invent something just scandalous enough to explain his lie and wriggle out. It was no longer a murder investigation anyway. Nick was not really worried about him. And, as the last people drifted out of the greenroom, he realized that he could not put off his own terrible task much longer.

Lisette was dead.

He had to face that. He thought he could, eventually. He had faced the possibility many times before.

She had committed suicide.

He knew the strength of the inner horror that she fought constantly, and he had known that she might lose someday. Now, with her fingerprints on the hypodermic, and her own incontrovertible note, there was no denying it.

But she had killed herself without asking him to help. In fact, she had been assuring him for weeks, in word and action, that things were better for her.

She had lied.

She had not given him a chance to help her this time.

Maggie's calm words throbbed in his memory. "You're angry at her, because she left you and didn't give you a chance to try." Giving him that chance had always been the agreement, unspoken perhaps, but part of the foundation of their life. She would let him know somehow when it was bad. She always had.

Now she had betrayed him.

And he was angry with a rank helpless rage that blocked all decent emotions. Except shame. A sweeping shame that he was so selfish, that he felt only the insult to himself, that he did not feel grief or sorrow or regret, but only this obscene, unspeakable fury at her final betrayal.

Once again his mind teetered to the edge of this truth and then drew back. He could not come to terms with it. Everything he had believed about himself, about her, about their life, had been a lie.

How could she have done it to him?

And how could he, big ox, sit here furious at the frail tortured soul he had loved so long?

He must find something to do. Close up the old emotional shop for a while longer. O, my offense is rank, it smells to heaven. So, stow it. Forget it. Lock it away. Find something to do.

But the nagging thought circled back. One person could settle his doubt.

If he didn't check, wasn't that as bad as what she had done to him?

If he was right, he would lose twice over. If he was wrong—well, he had to give Lisette this last chance. He stood up resolutely and began to search.

Ellen was floating in a void, in peace and silence and dim light. A thought came to her. She'd been hit on the head. Was this death? The undiscovered country. She blinked, and things came a little clearer. For one thing, her head ached. For another, there was tightness around her mouth. A cloth. And there were Lekos a few feet away. And the edge of a catwalk behind them. A harness tight around her shoulders. Odd country, death.

She blinked again. The pain localized a little, head and bound mouth. She managed to raise her sore head a little to look up. The gridiron. The ropes attached to the flying harness disappeared up there into its pulleys.

So she was floating. Someone had granted her wish.

Someone had pulled her hastily, like Laura's dummy, from the dressing room hall onto the catwalk. Now she was dangling high in the flies above the stage floor. Not dead after all. But when she looked down again toward the faraway floor and saw who was standing down by the pin rail, fraying the rope, she realized that she soon would be. When the rope gave way, she'd fall, like the sandbag that had almost hit Lisette. And today there was no help. The police were on the other side of that soundproofed door, the others gone. She would fall, her gag would be removed, and there would remain only the dead heap of silly Ellen, who had stupidly tried out the harness alone, using a frayed rope.

Could she swing to safety, like Tarzan? Or climb up the rope to the safety of the gridiron? But her hands were tied together. And, with this rag in her mouth, her teeth were useless. The only thing she had that was even a little sharp was her belt buckle. Desperately, she began to rub her wrists against it.

The worst thing was thinking of how sad Jim would be.

"Maggie."

It had been a long search. He had called her room; no answer. Then he had walked over to the library and looked through it thoroughly. Finally, back in the theatre parking lot, he had met Jason. "Seen Maggie?" Nick had asked.

There was a flicker of pleased embarrassment in his eyes. "She was in the woods behind the gym a few minutes ago."

The hazy sunlight drifted through young leaves and lit her blue shirt as she leaned disconsolately against a trunk. "Hello," she said dully. Damn Rob, she really had been hurt. And now it was his turn to hurt her.

Unless he was wrong.

She said, "Thanks for getting our tragic hero under control back there. I was afraid he was going to panic too soon."

"Would've served him right."

"Yeah."

"Wish I could be as decent to my enemies," he added.

That made her think a minute. She pulled off a leaf and twirled it in her fingers. Finally she said, "Nick, you're being too kind to me. What I did will hurt Rob a lot." Nick remembered the look of wounded defiance that David had given his groveling, impotent hero, and decided she was right. She frowned thoughtfully. "And you're being too hard on yourself. She really gave you no hint at all?"

"None," he said shortly. There were some tiny white flowers in the young grass. He ground his toe into a patch of them, carefully, and when he glanced up, she was still studying him. "Look," he said, "I blew it about Rob and you, I know, but that's because Rob lied to me, not because I wasn't tuned in. If I'd listened to my guts instead of to him, I could have saved you a lot of trouble. I'm not an insensitive clod."

"God, no."

"And with Lisette I'd had years of hard practice. If she'd wanted to—" He broke off. All right, the hell with it. Do what you came to do, cruel and ridiculous though it is. Nick the brute. He said, "I've got to ask you something, Maggie."

"Sure."

"Back there you said it might be murder."

"Nick, I'm sorry. I was kicking myself as soon as I said it."

"You didn't really think it was?"

"No." She was puzzled. "There's evidence, Nick."

"I know." What a stupid project this was, done for the sake of a hateful memory.

"Do you really want to talk about it?" she asked.

"No. I don't want to. But I have to."

"I see. Okay." She leaned back against the tree, one knee bent, foot braced against the trunk behind her, and considered. "We'll leave aside the note and the hypodermic for a while, then. Who could've done it?"

Why not? He leaned against a neighboring tree and crossed his arms. "Okay. Not Laura. And no one in the greenroom. That clears everybody except you and David and Rob and Paul."

"What about Grace and Judy and Cheyenne?"

"Possible. Maybe. They left about fifteen minutes before Ellen went to get her."

"And Ellen?"

"No. Not enough time."

"Brian? Dean Wagner?"

"Christ, this is stupid! There were a million people who weren't in the greenroom, who could have done it. But nobody would! Even Laura was just playing nasty jokes."

"Those barbiturates at the restaurant were more than just nasty," said Maggie thoughtfully. "She never even admitted she'd done that."

"She wouldn't have admitted anything if you hadn't caught her at it. Anyway, we've always said she just miscalculated. The photos were unpleasant, but never dangerous."

"Right. And as Ellen says, the timing is crazy. Why wait till closing night if you want someone out of the show? The only way this could make sense as murder is if the person wanted her to stay in it."

"Yeah." It didn't make sense as murder, she was right. The only thing that made sense was betrayal.

"Anyway, Laura was in her dorm. Who else is there?"

Nick returned to the game. "Well, there's Paul, who has so conveniently disappeared. We all knew he was in trouble. But Lisette wasn't the only one giving him a low grade."

"Maybe she was supposed to be more understanding because she was in the show too."

"Maybe. But I can't really believe that either, can you? A kid like Paul? Mr. Peacenik himself?"

"You're right. He didn't do it." She was sure. Too sure?

He went on. "And there's Rob. If he really thought David was threatened, he might do something desperate. I mean, he did do something desperate."

"But he would have planned a better alibi. He's too bright. Besides, Nick"—she drew a shaky breath—"he really is a gentle and loving person. Damn him. He really is."

"Yeah. I know that too." She was right, poor kid.

"Okay. Go on. Who else?" she said brusquely. Wanting to move on. But he hesitated.

"Really, this is stupid, Maggie. I don't want to accuse people at random."

"So far your accusations haven't been random. I can think of two more, easily."

"Two?"

"Well, for example, Grace has had the hots for you since the first week of rehearsals."

Startled, Nick asked, "How did you know? Did Rob tell?"

"Oh, did he know too? No, we never talked about it. But I'm very observant. At least I am about everyone's business but my own." A bitter voice.

Same here, Nick thought. He said, "You were up against a master, Maggie. Talented, and practiced, and very much in love."

"Yeah." She made an effort, rallied. "Well, anyway, I haven't told anyone about Grace, if that worries you."

"Good. That happens to people sometimes, Maggie," he explained earnestly. "They can be happily married and still be attracted briefly to other people. It's not serious, usually."

"Yes, sir, Uncle Nick, sir. I'll remember."

"*O'Connor's Pompous Advice to Youth,* Chapter Seventeen."

She smiled a little. "It's just that you're being so chivalrous. Here's someone who fits all the qualifications. She'd want Lisette around until the end of the show, and then she'd want her out of the way. Perfect motive. Flattering to you. So why not be suspicious of her?"

"Damn it, Maggie, I'm not suspicious of anyone, really! But . . ." But what? I want someone else to take the blame? He stopped. He couldn't go through with this after all.

"You're still being chivalrous, Nick. Who else did you think of?"

He glanced at her uncertainly. Challenging eyes, bluer than the May sky, sympathetic. She knew, had probably known since he arrived, what he was leading up to. How could he do this to her? He liked her, and trusted her. He, who was such a rotten judge of people. Nick the bungler. He'd trusted Rob. Wrong. He'd trusted Lisette. Wrong, wrong, wrong.

The challenge in her eyes was fading slowly to hurt, and he knew suddenly, against all reason, that he must go on, for her sake as well as Lisette's. Nick abandoned thought and went with his guts.

"You," he said. "I thought you could have done it."

"Dear Nick!" Relief in the young voice. "I shall grapple you to my soul with hoops of steel!"

It was the right reaction, but not the one he had come to

hear. Hell. He said, trying not to despair, "I'll accuse you of something horrible every day, if it makes you so happy."

"It's just that at the moment I seem to value honesty above all other human virtues."

His bitterness broke through. "No matter what it costs your friends?"

A little breeze fluttered the leaves and her black curls as she moved across to him, her good hand gentle on his barricading crossed arms. She said, "Nick, you pay me an incredible compliment. And I know it hurts to face it. But that's what you came to find out, isn't it? Because your problem is with the note, not with the fingerprints."

"Yes. Easy enough to wipe the hypodermic, press her hand on it. But the note is different."

She was compassionate, gentle, implacable, making him face it. Well, that was what he wanted from her, wasn't it? She said, "Maybe Lisette wrote that note on the mirror herself. Or maybe someone else wrote it."

He nodded. Spell it out. "And if it was someone else, it had to be someone who knew about Jennifer Brown. Which means you or me."

Her hand dropped, and she stared at him. "What did you say?"

"Well . . ." He frowned. It was obvious, wasn't it? "You were the only one here who knew about her. Even Rob didn't know. I still don't know quite why I told you."

"My God." She was shaken. She had turned away and was rubbing her forehead with the palm of her good hand. There was a stirring of unease in Nick's tired mind, a new tickle of suspicion. Had he miscalculated again?

"Look, Maggie. Did you tell anyone else?"

"No, no, of course not." She brushed off the question. What was wrong with her? He explained carefully, "Well, if you didn't do it, and you didn't tell anyone, then it has to be suicide." With all that that implied.

But she was thinking, no longer listening to him. Finally she dropped her hand and, suddenly decisive, started for the stage door. "Come on!" Then, noticing his hesitation, she added, "Look, Uncle Nick, don't be afraid. If I turn out to be a murderer, at least it clears her, doesn't it? Also, I only have one arm." Which was such an exact transcription of his own thoughts that he had to smile.

"Where are we going?"

"To see if Ellen was right about the timing." She was moving fast. She glanced up the stairs as they entered, then ran down and through the empty greenroom. He followed, puzzled. She opened the door to the stage and went into the cavernous twilight. "Hey, Cheyenne!" she called. "Got a question for you."

"Yeah?" He was adjusting something by the fly rigging, removing a sandbag wired to one of the ropes as a counterweight. "What do you want?" He took a few steps toward them, eyes flat in the dusky light.

"The night Lisette died." She stepped past the stage-left wagon and stopped in the center of the stage. "Tell us about it."

"I've told everybody. I'm tired of talking about it."

"You said you went with Grace and Judy to get the account books, and then came back to the greenroom to look for Paul. You got there just before Ellen went up to get Lisette."

"Right, that's what happened. He'll tell you. He was there."

"That's right," said Nick slowly. But he was thinking, Ellen left fifteen minutes after Judy. Getting that book couldn't have taken that long. And as the implications smashed into his battered emotions, he grasped the lofty ramparts wagon beside him in disbelief.

Maggie said, "There's a little more to it, isn't there, Cheyenne? Something you left out." She crossed toward him.

"Like what?" He was edging back toward the rigging lines.

"Like the fact that Jennifer Brown was your sister."

The shifting pattern jelled. Nick launched himself across the width of the stage. But Maggie cried, "Nick, stop!" and at the note of terror in her voice he checked.

There was a gleam of steel now in Cheyenne's hand. Just a knife, thought Nick, I can cope with a knife. But the knife was not wielded as a weapon. Instead, Cheyenne had laid it gently across the support rope that had held the sandbag. Nick followed Maggie's uplifted gaze and saw the problem.

High above them, gagged and tied and dangling from the grid, was Ellen.

Very high above them. And without the sandbag counterweight, slicing through that already frayed rope would send her plummeting to the wooden floor.

If she fell, she would die. If she fell, Cheyenne would escape, they'd have to get help for her. Futile help.

Maggie was moving around behind Cheyenne, who turned to watch her. She said, "*Vieille taupe! Travailles-tu sous terre si vite?*"

Nick backed away, trying to make his overloaded mind work. Old something, work under the earth—canst work in the earth so fast? Old mole! Suddenly he understood. The enormous rampart that Jason hated so much soared up to fill most of the height of the proscenium arch. If he could move it under Ellen somehow, she might still break an arm falling—but she wouldn't die.

He bounded behind it, lifted the locks off, began to push. For the show, four stagehands had moved it, and he had to turn it a little too, angle it upstage, to get the top platform under her. And he had to move fast, faster than that knife. Maggie was talking to Cheyenne, distracting him. But as Nick laid his shoulder into the huge wagon, got it started at an excruciatingly slow pace, he saw Cheyenne glance back and, in startled comprehension, jump toward the rope again. Nick, straining, was aware of Maggie hurling herself at Cheyenne. But she was lighter, sore, her elbow sprained. Heaving desperately at the wagon, Nick inched toward Ellen. Cheyenne got a leg behind Maggie's, flipped her off balance, and began to saw at the rope again. Maggie bit him in the calf. He swore, turned back to her, and she swarmed over him again, grasping for the knife. He grunted, peeled the fingers of her good hand from the knife, shoved her away sprawling, and sliced through the rope.

Too late. Nick was hauling on the brakes, steadying the wagon. Ellen thudded onto the platform far above him.

"Hey, Winfield, you all right?" called Maggie.

Three measured thumps. She was alive.

But Nick's sense of triumph evaporated as Cheyenne, taking advantage of Maggie's moment of distraction, tucked his knife in his belt, seized her sprained arm, and tugged it free of the sling. Slowly, he screwed it around behind her. Her face was white with pain.

"Don't move, Nick," said Cheyenne. "Let's not hurt her."

Again, Nick checked himself, and Cheyenne obligingly eased a fraction of the pressure on her arm. Maggie, with an exasperated glance at Nick, clenched her jaw against the pain and drove back with her healthy hand to grab Cheyenne in the crotch. Before she could tighten her grip he jumped back, swearing, still holding her hurt arm and pulling his knife from his belt again. But she had won space to whirl toward him, reducing the pressure on her hurt arm.

Then Nick was upon them. He hardly felt the cut on his arm as he reached for the knife, twisted it from Cheyenne's hand, and pried Cheyenne's fingers from Maggie's arm. She dodged away from them. Cheyenne, writhing expertly, almost escaped him then; but Nick was quick too, and trained and heavy, and when he hit Cheyenne something switched off in his brain. Everything focused in on the bright clarity of the present instant. The world seemed murky except for this thing in front of him, this object of stringy meat and gristle and bone that had to be broken. He couldn't quite remember why, it had something to do with Lisette. The objective Nick would remember later. Right now the thing had to be broken. It was not murky like the rest of the world. It was very clear, like a cartoon outlined in ink; it had a frightened face on it, and he could pick it up easily and slam it into the brick stagehouse wall. It fell but then started to twist around again, so he picked it up again. Through the haze he thought he heard its voice. He had to mash the thing against the wall again, until it stopped moving. He wondered how long it would take. He had never had to kill this sort of thing before.

Kill.

The word stabbed through him, and part of the murk cleared away. He seemed to be holding Cheyenne by the belt and the collar. The head was flopped over and there was blood running down the face. He was still moving. Thank God. The head straightened a little and then flopped down again.

"I think he'll come round," said Maggie in a strained voice. "Nick, are you okay?"

His own voice sounded a bit funny too. "Yeah. Now I am." The murk was fading away.

"Get one of those ropes and tie him. You'll have to do it. I've only got one hand." She held Cheyenne's limp head by the hair with her good hand while Nick bound his arms behind him, and then his legs. His eyes opened a little. Nick straightened and stepped back. His own arm was bleeding, he saw with surprise, a long knife cut angling from biceps to wrist. Not deep. He found his handkerchief and dabbed at it. Maggie had whisked up the rampart wagon and was fumbling at Ellen's bonds with one hand.

The backstage door opened. "Ellen? Are you in here?" It was Jim, squinting in the dim light.

"Jim! Go get Sergeant Hawes. He may still be upstairs with Rob," called Maggie, tugging at the gag.

"What's going on? Is Ellen here?"

"Damn it, Jim!" shrieked Ellen the unflustered. "Get the goddamn police!"

Jim went.

The adrenaline was still surging through Nick's system, and he clenched his hands by his sides to keep from moving. Cheyenne, bound on the floor by his feet, was watching him, alert again, and a bit of the old sardonic look crept into his smashed face.

"You must have loved her, you poor bastard," he said suddenly. "But I saw through her. I knew what she'd done to my sister."

Nick's mouth tightened. He held himself still.

Cheyenne went on. "I was building a show. I couldn't even go to her funeral. You know how I found out? I went later that summer. I talked to one of her friends. And she said that she'd admitted it to her. She admitted it, and the stupid police couldn't catch her!"

"Lisette blamed herself. But the amount she gave your sister didn't kill her, you know." Nick managed to sound almost normal.

"Bullshit."

Maggie was down again, her cautioning hand on Nick's arm. He changed the subject. "Were you the one who called our agent? Asking if she'd work upstate?"

"Yeah. I never dreamed she'd go on acting. I couldn't believe it when I saw her listed in the Equity book. I was ready to quit here, go find her in New York. But then Brian started talking about a centennial here, and I figured it would be easier."

"So you dropped that sandbag," said Maggie. "And drugged her at the restaurant. It wasn't Laura after all."

"I still don't know why that didn't work," said Cheyenne. "I saw her drink the coffee. Maybe she was adapted to it. That's how I knew I'd better go to the needle. Get it right into the bloodstream."

"But why did you wait so long?" asked Maggie. "Why didn't you try again right after the restaurant?"

He turned bruised, surprised eyes to her. "The show needed her," he said, as though the logic were obvious. "At first I figured Judy or Laura would be okay. But that next rehearsal, right after the restaurant, she must still have been hung over from the dose I gave her. But when she did the nunnery scene, I saw. Brian was right. Damn bitch could act. Terrific scene. So I had to wait."

"Because she could act?"

"Because of the show. A professional thinks of the show."

Maggie shook her head in wonder. "Goddamn it, Ellen, you were right!"

The backstage door opened. Sergeant Hawes and the officer came in, followed by Jim, and stopped when they saw Cheyenne, battered and tied.

"What the hell is going on here?" asked Sergeant Hawes, forgetting to be polite for once. Jim, troubled, moved to Ellen's side. Cheyenne frowned up from his seat on the floor, then the bruised scowl shifted to Ellen.

She said, "Cheyenne was just explaining. He believed Mrs. O'Connor killed his sister five years ago."

"But she didn't," said Nick.

"Bullshit," said Cheyenne.

"It'll be better if you tell them, Cheyenne," said Maggie. "For you, for Brian."

"Okay. I killed her. I want a lawyer," said Cheyenne.

"Certainly." Sergeant Hawes, surprised, pulled out his book. "Would the rest of you wait outside? But don't go too far, we'll be coming right back for your statements."

As they went out, Maggie turned to Ellen and asked acidly, "What the hell were you doing up there, blithe spirit?"

"Well," said Ellen apologetically, "I heard the police mention Jennifer Brown, and I thought maybe they should hear about his sister. And, well, I asked him if he'd told them."

"Jesus!" exclaimed Maggie. "Dumb! Why didn't you tell me?"

"I tried! You kept disappearing!"

"Or the police, then?"

"That's exactly what I was waiting to do when he coshed me!" said Ellen indignantly.

"Coshed?" Jim was alarmed.

"I'm okay," Ellen reassured him. "But Maggie's right. It's no fun being the ingenue."

"Come let me look," he said, worried, drawing her into the greenroom.

Maggie and Nick drifted out to the parking lot again to wait. The hazy morning smelled of warm asphalt and of things growing. She turned to him, touched his cut arm. "Are you okay?"

Nick said wonderingly, "I almost killed him." Another illusion about himself shattered. Nick the loathsome.

She said, "God knows you had reason. But you didn't."

"It was so damn close."

"Yeah. I wondered there for a minute. But I figured good old Uncle Nick would control himself. And you did."

Yes. There was that. He said, "Thank God." They had paused a few steps from the door. His mind jumped to a new detail. "I didn't know he'd lost a sister. I never made the connection."

"Wasn't hard, once you told me her last name." She shrugged, and winced.

"How is your elbow?" he asked, suddenly concerned.

"It'll do," she said. "Lost a few more hunks of ligament, I guess. The doctor who strapped me up this morning won't be pleased." She smiled at his distress. "Hey, it's okay. Look, the fingers still work."

"Do you want to go right to the doctor now?"

"No, no. It can wait a little. I'd like to be sure they take him. Wouldn't you?"

They sat on the little wall that divided sidewalk from parking lot and waited. Nick's mind was still struggling to assimilate this new fact, this new pattern. Could he believe in it, after all? In her? Had she resisted? Or had she seen Cheyenne as a deliverer?

Soon the policemen brought him out, Cheyenne's dark eyes opaque in his bruised, noncommittal face, the police walking one on each side. Cheyenne saw them on the wall and gave an unsmiling, ironic nod.

Maggie asked suddenly, as though reading Nick's mind, "Cheyenne, did she say anything?"

"Nothing special."

"Did she fight?"

He stopped, but the policemen pulled him on so that he spoke over his shoulder as he climbed into the patrol car.

"Sure," he said, grimly triumphant. "Like a tiger. Just what you'd expect. Kept saying, 'Not now.' Wouldn't even write a note, so I had to write it on the mirror." He snorted. "Oh, and she said, 'Tell Nicky I don't want to die.' That's all. Nothing special. Just what you'd expect."

He disappeared into the car. Doors slammed and the engine rumbled and the acrid scent of exhaust filled Nick's nostrils. And suddenly belief came, and tears, and harsh ridiculous masculine sobs that shook him, helpless, with their urgency. She pulled his head onto her lap and held him with strong scarred hands, crooning, her young body arching over him like the sky.

The morning faded.

Forty thousand brothers could not, with all their quantity of love, make up my sum.

Oh, Lisette, Lisette.

XIX

Ellen pushed in the catches of her suitcase and looked around the room. No posters, no books, only naked institutional furniture, and her boxes and suitcases, and Maggie's. An incredible term, over at last, leaving her a legacy of a trial to attend, a tender skull, and Jim. Final exams had never seemed so irrelevant.

Everything would be different next year. Living with Jim. Working in the theatre without Cheyenne. Also without Jason, and David, and the others who were graduating, and without big sad Uncle Nick, who had thanked her and Maggie warmly for coming to the funeral, and then had driven away to the city and out of their lives.

Maggie came in and lighted gratefully on her bare mattress. "It's getting hot out there," she said. She was shiny with sweat.

"Good ol' summertime," said Ellen.

"You ready to go?"

"Yeah." On her way home to Pennsylvania, Ellen was going to drop Maggie at the Binghamton station, where she could catch the bus for Cincinnati. "What did he say?"

"My advisor?"

"Yeah."

"He said fine. Twenty-one hours is a lot but it's mostly math, so I told him there wouldn't be any problem."

"And there also won't be time for theatre."

"Right. One of the chief charms of this plan."

"Are you sure you ought to drop your English major, Maggie? Only two courses to go."

"Ellen, right now I don't even want to think about Shakespeare or poetry or mythology or goddamn violin music."

"Yeah. The realm of pure form for you." Ellen decided not to point out that being an English major didn't actually involve any goddamn violin music.

"Pure form and early graduation," said Maggie. "And graduate school somewhere far from here."

"Where?"

"Haven't decided. Preferably some nunnery."

Better change the subject, thought Ellen. She said, "I brought up your mail. It's on your desk."

Maggie stood up and looked at the two envelopes. One, from a magazine, she dropped into the wastebasket; the other she opened with interest, and skimmed over, and smiled.

"Who's it from?" asked Ellen, remembering the stamp and postmark.

"Paul Rigo," said Maggie in a pleased voice. "He's okay. He's met a guy in Toronto who can help him get a job doing sets. Community theatre."

"Toronto!" said Ellen.

"Right."

"My cylinder head gasket!"

"Right."

"The man Tim saw in the car with you was Paul!"

"Right again." Maggie smiled at her.

"Idiot," said Ellen affectionately. "So that's where you were!"

"Right. Shall we go?"

"Um—this little package came for you too." Ellen pushed it across the desk diffidently. It was from one R. J., now of New York City.

Maggie looked at the box a long time, and then hurriedly ripped it open, glanced at the contents, and threw it in the wastebasket. Wordlessly, she hoisted one of her suitcases and started out to the car.

Ellen picked up one of her boxes to follow, but before she left she peeked in the wastebasket.

It held a bunch of flowers. Kind of cute, he had said, a weedy little plant with little yellow flowers, four petals.

Not daisies, this time.

Rue.